Texas Shorts Volume I

An Anthology of Short Stories
Written by Texas Authors

Presented by the
Dallas Area Writers Group

Anthology copyright © 2018
by the individual authors

No part of this book may be reproduced or utilized in any form
or by any means: electronic, mechanical or otherwise,
including photocopying, recording or by any informational storage and
retrieval system without permission in writing from the publisher.

This anthology is a work of fiction and non-fiction. Names, characters,
places and events in the fiction works are either the product of the authors'
imaginations or are used fictitiously, and any resemblance to actual persons,
living or dead, events, circumstances or locales is entirely coincidental.

Table of Contents

Introduction 1
Acknowledgments 2
Was ich Leide, What I Suffer
    by Zoie Montoya 3
Big Women
    by LK Simonds 13
A Touch of Rogue
    by Tayla Lindsey 22
The Crash
    by Jared Abraham 32
When He Shows Up Again
    by Eva Camilla Allyn 41
The Brown Backpack
    by Connie Childress 49
Three Gifts
    by Gary Christenson 58
Annual Affair
    by Teri Daniels 65
Stuck
    by Anrica Easley 76
Raccoon Eyes
    by Dawn Richards Elliott 85
Adelaide
    by Laura-Ann Elliott 94

The Darkness Behind the Light
    by Dave Hare 104
The Turnspit Dog
    by H. J. Hill 115
Marshmallow Dragon
    by Dana L. Horton 125
In Search of the Big Trees
    by Eldon Irving 135
The Grand Tour
    by Eldon Irving 140
Rain Check
    by Eldon Irving 145
Stained Glass Pews
    by Angela Jones 150
Dada, Do Dat 'Gin
    by André King 162
God's Glimpses for the Future
    by Pamela Flynt Knight 168
We Break From Inside Out
    by Lisa Moak 177
The Mysterious Gift
    by Ray Reed 186
Christmas Lights in July
    by B. K. Shaddick 193

What the Heck Am I Doing Up Here?
  by Stella Kittles Sikes 201
I Am Nothing
  by Mary Ann Taylor 207
The Eleventh Commandment: Three Candidates
  by Mary Ann Taylor 215
The House
  by Mary Sue Tiffin.. 225
The Top Hat and the Feather Boa
  by Catherine Tucker.. 236
Amy Calling
  by Judith K. Werner.. 248
Vanilla Mama
  By Catie Riley Wright... 256

Introduction

The Dallas Area Writers Group (DAWG) began as a study group in the Duncanville home of Alan C. Elliott in 2004 to meet a need—there were no writer groups in the Best Southwest area of Dallas County at that time. Since April 2006, monthly DAWG meetings are held at the Zula B. Wylie Library in Cedar Hill on the second Tuesday of each month.

As a 501(c)(3) non-profit organization, the Dallas Area Writers Group is eligible to apply for grants. The DeSoto Arts Commission has awarded grants to the DAWG for four years and these funds have been used to help present the "Write to Publish: Climbing Toward Success!" writing workshops.

DAWG held its first short story contest in 2017. It was an overwhelming success, receiving forty-four entries. Authors of the top three stories were announced at the 3rd annual "Write to Publish: Climbing Toward Success!" writing workshop presented by the DAWG. These winners were awarded cash prizes and the DAWG board of directors voted to publish the top thirty stories in an anthology—thus the genesis of *Texas Shorts, Volume I.*

Texas Shorts, Volume I contains a rich tapestry of tales—both nonfiction and fiction—skillfully told by talented Texas authors from every walk of life. The range and depth of their stories offer complex insight into the lives of unique and interesting characters, exploring many of life's major themes, using vividly described settings, strong voice, and engaging dialogue. We hope you enjoy reading these wonderful stories as much as we've enjoyed bringing them to you.

Acknowledgments

Texas Shorts, Volume I exists because of our extraordinary authors. We are extremely grateful to each and every one of you for sharing your amazing stories with the Dallas Area Writers Group (DAWG) in our 2017 short story contest.

To DAWG's Literary Contest Director, Tamara Warner, a heartfelt thanks for your tireless efforts in coordinating and marketing DAWG's first short story contest which yielded the stories comprising *Texas Shorts, Volume I*. To Patsy Summey, DAWG's Secretary/Treasurer, thank you for skillfully editing the stories with a keen eye for detail. To DAWG's Vice-President, Catie Riley Wright, thank you for superbly organizing the stories, bios, and photographs for publication.

To artist Christian Brooks (www.christianbrooks.com), thank you for beautifully conceptualizing an original idea for the cover art of *Texas Shorts, Volume I*. Thank you, Cindy Rodella-Purdy (www.CreativeCatMedia.net), for your creative enhancements to the cover design.

We gratefully acknowledge author-speaker-publisher, Mitchel Whitington (www.whitington.com), for your publishing assistance in making *Texas Shorts, Volume I* possible. Your work is exceptional.

And finally, special thanks to DAWG's founder, Alan C. Elliott (www.alanelliott.com), who conceived the idea for the artist's rendering for the *Texas Shorts, Volume I* cover. Thank you also for providing the perfect title. And to the other contributing members of the DAWG Board of Directors—Eldon Irving, Andi King, Mary Sue Tiffin, and Lily Welborne—for the various planning and developmental tasks you completed toward making *Texas Shorts, Volume I* a reality—thank you.

— Catherine Tucker, DAWG President

Was ich Leide, What I Suffer
by Zoie Montoya

The loud noise squalling from the city of New York could hardly be heard from the inside of the Symphonic Orchestra House. A man sat within the building on a small wooden stool, torn between twisting his hands in anxiety and darting them to the cello beside his seat. Any moment now, a page would be sent from the judge's room to fetch him.

In all honesty, traveling from a little fishing village, Hafnir, off the west coast of Iceland to the bustling American city was quite the experience. It still took him time to adjust to how everything moved oh-so-fast paced. After all, the customs officers had only allowed him passage into the country yesterday. It had taken weeks sitting in a dull little waiting room with makeshift cots built into the wall before he had been granted clearance. Then it was just him and his cello, large and yet insignificant compared to the growing city, on their own. Walls and walls of buildings rose above him, some half-built, others already completed. He could not fathom the number of people here in just one place, it seemed as if all his own home country could fit into one building, whereas the citizenry here burst at the seams.

"Sir," a voice piped up.

The blond stuttered nervously before nodding, grabbed his instrument case by the handle, and yanked it up with a small grunt. He calmed himself as he sighed softly, telling himself that all would be well, so long as he did not lose his nerve. He had not spent half a lifetime practicing his craft simply to lose control in front of a set of foreign orchestra directors.

"This way," the younger man uttered, turning around mechanically and leading the way.

He followed with as much grace as he could manage, reciting the notes over and over in his mind. The customs men

Was ich Leide, What I Suffer

at the port had not allowed him to bring his pack, telling him he was only allowed to bring one carrier with him. Naturally, he chose his cello—the thing his parents spent their livelihoods trying to purchase for him. While he knew some of the traveling rules for the United States, at that horrible moment, he realized he was not fully prepared for some of the stipulations. He was only thankful he had been able to sneak some clothes into his cello case—otherwise he would have walked into a new country and his audition with nothing but the clothes on his back, and the instrument he played.

Three men in finely pressed pinstripe suits sat among the orchestra pit at the front of the atrium's stage. They turned slowly in their seats when they heard the loud bang of closing doors, and the Icelandic man stepping into the auditorium. Two of the three suits stood up and greeted the blond with polite shakes of the hand.

The third man stayed seated, facing the stage.

"Ah, Isleifur Bragisson, yes?" The first man asked, leading the musician towards the dais.

"Aye," he nodded eagerly, following the two directors.

"Well, do attempt your best," the second suited man sniffed, eyeing the cellist up and down with skepticism.

"I will," he nodded again, making his way up the stairs to the seat that awaited him at the center of the platform.

The two men joined their waiting companion, sitting down before each picked up a thick black journal. In tandem, the three of them opened to a specific page, removing a small crimson ribbon that had nestled in the crease between pages.

Nodding, the first looked to Isleifur, pressing his fountain pen to the page as he asked his question. "What instrument do you play, Mr. Bragisson?"

"The caello, sir."

"As we can see," the third judge drawled rudely, ignoring the look shot at him by the first. "What piece will you play?"

The Icelandic man grinned, "I play Frédéric Chopin, *Prelude in E Minor, Opus eight, number four.*"

"Chopin?" The second admired, with a wistful glint in his eyes. "Quite ambitious considering it is not a piece designed for your instrument. I remember when I first heard that piece several years ago at a concert."

The silent *"don't ruin it"* hung limp in the air between the professionals.

Isleifur nodded with a slight grin—confident in his abilities—before tightening his necktie. Satisfied, he leaned over and picked up his bow from the case on the floor and reached out for his cello. As he sat, the judges found that the great instrument seemed dwarfed compared to the great man's size—as though the body of a bull had been placed in a classy suit and told to play an instrument of elegance. The first judge snorted and laid his head against his hand, eyes curious; the second judge folded his hands neatly and smiled reassuringly to the man on the stage; the third judge scoffed and leaned back in the velvet-cushioned chair, a loud *'c-c-cureeek'* echoing through the empty theatre as he did so.

"You may proceed," the third judge yawned.

Leyfa mér að gera vel, Guð—*allow me to do well, God.* The cellist tilted his head to the side and closed his eyes.

The strings seemed to welcome him as his fingers met them. Running his bow over the empty space between the neck and the bridge, he made a test draw to see that everything was well. The third judge sneered. Isleifur, ignoring the crass man, began his piece.

Drifting mournfully across the room, the music fluttered and flitted from the cello. Lilting in such fragile ways, the song floated through the room as the cello cried in gloom when Isleifur played his tune. The strings ached in the wake of the bow. Flowing, the music vibrated in pain while the melody began to wane. His eyes pressed together, minding his fingers to not make a mess. Deepness reached out, each note wandering. The music lightened a bit, a brightened plea—begging for any way, to make whatever wrongs fade. Dipping, the song tripped over itself, realizing the mistake made of such a vain cry. Strings shivering so swiftly side by side, they wept—completely hopeless.

Eyes squeezed tighter, tears pricking the corners as he remembered: his father, his mother, and everything they did to ensure he reached this point.

Here he would prove a worthy investment to his parents.

As his bow came to the final draw, he gave a shaky sigh, reopening his eyes.

The first judge sat forward in his chair, eyes still closed and a wistful smile stretching across his jaw. The second judge clapped softly, humming the eerie tune as the last of the echoes died away in the auditorium. The third judge leaned back, mouth open and speechless.

Isleifur stood. "Erm…did I do waell?"

"I believe," the first judge said opening his eyes, "you did incredibly well, Mr. Bragisson."

"Really?"

His chair squealing in loud protest again, the third judge stood straight up and left the auditorium in a flurry of frustration.

The second judge smiled pitifully, closing his book, and placing his fountain pen in the pocket of his waistcoat.

Continuing, the first went on. "You did extremely well."

A collective nod exchanged between the two.

Isleifur smiled widely. "*Takk fyrir.*"

"Isleifur, a telegram shall be sent to you if you have been chosen for a cellist role with the New York Symphony Orchestra."

Barely concealing his excitement, the cellist placed his belongings into the instrument case, zipped it up, and walked off the stage. To each of the judges, he bestowed a handshake and the biggest grin he could muster.

"Takk, takk vaery, vaery much."

Leaving the auditorium, he jumped up in the air, kicking his heels together. The cello in his other hand thudded harsh against his side. Taking that as a reminder, Isleifur composed himself, although his silly grin remained. He had tried his hardest—he had played his best—and he felt as though his mother and father had something to be proud of.

A paper boy, perhaps fifteen years old waited just inside the doors that led to the courtyard outside. Cap and vest full of holes, his feet were bare and muddy. He looked up, bright blue eyes hopeful, as he saw the well-dressed man from Iceland.

"Aye, mista!" the boy greeted, "New York's an' only New York's besht an' worsht—toppa the 'ighlights Octoba third, 1875. Penny-a-pape!"

Pausing, Isleifur thought about it. "A paenny?"

"Sure thang!" the newsie winked. "But, if ya feel like tippin' a good-ol' boy like me, a nickel'll be 'preciated."

"Why not?" the man grinned. "A nickael, you say?"

He knew that money proclaimed itself scarce, and what rested heavy in his pocket was also his lunch money—but this boy had nothing. He hardly had shoes on his feet, if that's what the lad could call them. Fishing through his jacket pocket, among a few pennies he found a nickel and handed it to the lad.

"Take it. A gift. No paeper."

"A gift?" the newsie echoed.

The brawny man nodded.

"Good day ta ya, mista!" Taking off his hat, the boy gave a dramatic bow.

Isleifur laughed and walked out the doors.

His feet pattered down the steps and he found himself facing the opening courtyard to the orchestra house. From the dark gates that hung a few paces ahead, he could see several houses and buildings, as well as the wharf on the horizon. However, the blond frowned as his eyes landed on the sight of a man being forcefully pulled away from the gates and off to the side. Knowing the tell-tale signs of a scuffle anywhere, he pursued after the victim.

His eyes met the sight of three heavy-set dockworkers who surrounded a black-haired man. They laughed and jeered at him, pushing him from one worker to another—as if playing some cruel child's game as grown men. The target of the taunts, a tall pale man with dark blazing eyes, clutched a long black case closely to his chest, eyes glaring as he tried to catch his balance.

Noting the long black hair tied back with a simple red ribbon, and the long sagging brown shirt and flaring cotton pants with a strange topknot at the waist, Isleifur knew this man to be a foreigner like himself. With a decisive nod, not willing to leave the man in a precarious situation, the cellist intervened.

"Good day, fraends," he greeted, eyes cautious as he approached—footsteps landing heavy on the cobblestone. "Would you bae so kind as to—"

"Keep movin'," the first of the brutes, one with a wool cap, bit in a harsh snarl. "This don't involve ya."

Taken aback, Isleifur looked at the abused. Compared to himself, the stranger was very thin, although it seemed his frame was thickened by the baggy cotton clothes he wore. Taking in the man's peculiar clothing, the long, pony-tailed black hair, and the narrowed angry eyes, the Icelandic man could immediately identify the nationality of the other.

An Asian, he realized with a wry sort of amusement. No wonder. The Americans' dislike of the Eastlanders is not unknown, especially since they took the majority of the jobs on the American railroads in the west…at least those are the rumors he'd heard.

Sighing, he set his cello case down and rolled up the sleeves of his jacket—the material crumpled and bulged at the crease of his elbows. At once, the American men took in his stout, tall build. At over six feet, and weighing two hundred and twenty pounds, he was no small man to be trifled with.

A dockworker in a pale blue shirt looked between the two foreign men and lifted his brow. His lip curled in distaste and he spat at the feet of the blond. Fists balling, he could hardly contain his anger. People like these, he hated them. Every one of them. Money and jobs came by hard enough—they didn't need some wanderer from some other country stealing jobs.

Another worker with a black coat stiffened, and grabbed the shoulder of his pale-shirted companion. He shook his head as if to say it wasn't worth it. With his free hand, he began to usher the hatted man away.

As the three of them walked away, the man in the blue shirt turned his head and barked out, "Betta watch yerself, foreigners! Ya won't get 'way with much 'ere."

And they left without any more quarrel or word.

The Asian man turned and glared at Isleifur, unhappy. Frowning, the Icelandic man felt as though he slipped an unknown boundary. Without a second glance to him, the black-haired man turned away, ebony case still clutched to his chest.

"*Arigato*," the Asian said. "However, I did not need your help."

"I not like those maen, *faviti*—idiots. Sorry," Isleifur apologized, "but I would not laeve you to thaem."

The other looked at him from the corner of his eyes before nodding, accepting the sincerity of a stranger.

Looking at the object placed so sacredly close to his chest, the Icelandic man realized the man's container as an instrument case.

"Um…'scuse mae, but is that not violin case?"

The raven head turned around and raised a brow. "What of it?"

"Did you audition?" The stout man could barely contain his excitement. *A fellow musician!*

"No," the Asian drawled, his tone dark and furious. "I wasn't allowed to."

"Oh."

Brushing down his suit, Isleifur sat down against the wall that surrounded the orchestra house. He smiled expectantly at the other foreigner. The black-haired man seemed surprised at this action and cocked his head to the side. The blond made a quick gesture with his hand.

"Play for mae?"

The Asian blinked, looked around anxiously at the crowd milling around, and joined the Icelandic man at the curbside.

"Why should I?" he asked in a brusque voice, shaking his head and taking a seat.

"I am not as ignorant as I saem," Shaking his head, the blue-eyed man shrugged. "I know thaey will not pick mae for this orchaestra. I talk strange. My name is strange. I am a strangaer to thaem."

Fushiyuma looked mildly apologetic, and curious.

Isleifur sighed, "My mam, she bakes bread for a living, and saews nice clothes for import to Britain during night. My pabi, he works at sea, and only comes home twice a month. Thaey put all thaey had, so I could have this caello. And then even more for mae to come here. I wondaer if you are same. So play for your parents, if nothing else. That way thaey will know you're thankful."

The black-haired man unhooked his suitcase and opened it after a mournful hum. He took out a dull and beaten looking violin and placed it on his shoulder before pulling out the bow.

He dipped his head gracefully, his long ponytail slipping over his unoccupied shoulder. "I am Fushiyuma Hijikata."

"Isleifur Bragisson." The northerner smiled. "What would you play?"

The eastern man thought for a moment before giving a decisive nod. *None but the Lonely Heart* by Pyotr Ilyich

Tchaikovsky. I saw a performance when I passed through Germany and admired his music."

"Aye, Fushiyuma! I know thaet song waell. I, too, enjoy this naew Tchaikovsky faellow!"

The Asian sat back a little more interested. "Such a strange song, yes? A piece based on a poem written by Goethe, about a pained lover."

"Aye, poor girl in my opinion."

With a bit of a smirk, the raven-haired man shook his head. "Well, then, let me remember how to play our 'poor girl's' sobs on my instrument, yes?"

Isleifur proffering his cello case slightly. "Two playaers are baetter than one, yeh?"

Pursing his lips for a moment before picking up his bow, Fushiyuma nodded. "You may start, if you know the opening."

Taking the opportunity, the Iceland-born opened his own suitcase and pulled out his cello. Nodding his head to his new acquaintance's count, Isleifur placed his bow upon the strings and drew when the melody deepened slightly for his instrument's part.

The song opened softly, like a bird flying away from a mountain home—faint and regretful. Suddenly, Fushiyuma's violin cried gently next to the cello, like a child seeking comfort. They played together, sitting on the curb outside the Orchestra House. New York's sun rose heavy and slow to the sounds of the sad bird and the crying child.

Fushiyuma smiled without mirth, as did Isleifur.

And the music fluttered above the sounds of the city.

Was ich Leide, What I Suffer

Zoie Montoya

Zoie Montoya currently lives in Texas, attending Stephen F. Austin State University for a bachelor's degree in Creative Writing. She has written the novel *Dragon's Battles* as part of the *Dragonbrave Trilogy*. Zoie has also won awards for short stories: "With Daring Hope," "When Day Embraces Night," and "The Miraculous Return of Benjamin Buckles."

Big Women
by LK Simonds

There was a time when she was considered willowy, with lithe flanks. A lizard body, she'd heard somewhere. That was in her twenties and thirties, even into her forties a little bit, if she remembered right. "You ought to be a model," said one of the ground instructors. Not hers, thank God. He cornered her in the break room during the first week of classes. He smiled. That smile didn't know rejection. There wasn't any doubt in it. "Where've you been all my life?" he said.

"For about half of it, I wasn't born." That was the first time she saw who she was, what she would do when confronted. Even though she was a bundle of nerves, fearful they wouldn't let her pass the course, she faced the challenge. She stepped into it and faced it down. Beat it back. She was twenty-three.

That was forty years and forty pounds ago. She'd aged during all those afternoons and late nights and early mornings bellied up to hotel bars and other bars, decompressing after flying back and forth across the country. Decompressing had compressed her, stacking her like bricks. Not like, "That dame is stacked," but in a different, not pretty, way.

The crew went to a dive near DFW Airport called the Euless Yacht Club. The incongruously named Yacht Club was a watering hole for air traffic controllers. There weren't many pilots there, but they went anyway. She drank good scotch all afternoon and listened to a local band. Her glass reflected the tiny white Christmas lights strung around the ceiling. A guy, a controller at the tower, tried to pick her up, not knowing she didn't mix business with pleasure. Not knowing that, if she were so inclined, she would've mixed it with her first officer, who'd tried so hard to impress her. The first officer had smiled apologetically every time he made a mistake, not knowing she was all gooey inside over his green eyes.

It was summertime, and she wore a sleeveless, yellow blouse. She liked that blouse, but she didn't recall what became of it. "Those are some guns you've got there," the controller said, pointing to her arms.

"Excuse me, what?" She was listening to the music. She only wanted to think about the music and the warm scotch and the twinkling glass.

He leaned against the bar, facing her. "You're a tall drink of water, aren't you?"

"Do you have any more clichés?" she said. She didn't bother to look him in the eye when she said it, even though she didn't mind confrontation. She waded into conflict like a prize fighter.

Nowadays—now that she was a stiff old broad—she wished she'd learned to be demure, at least to behave demurely, when the situation called for it. Nowadays, she doubted many things she'd said and done. Not the causes she'd fought for—never those—but the way she'd gone about it.

* * * * *

He liked delivering pizza. It got him out and about. Here and there. To and fro. He could've lived off his inheritance—he was a man of simple needs—but he liked driving around the neighborhoods, meeting new people all the time. Their faces always brightened when they opened the door and found him standing there, holding—as if it were a silver tray of cocktails—the vinyl pouch that kept the pizza warm. Even though the women—sometimes men, but mostly women—even though they hadn't placed an order, and confusion swept across their faces, even then they always smiled. "I'm sorry, there must be a mistake," they said, almost to a person.

Sometimes, the young ones tried to put one over on him. He probably seemed befuddled and middle-aged slow to them. "Oh, thanks," they said, reaching.

He'd swivel, sliding the pouch out of reach. "That'll be forty-six fifty."

Their eyes would widen and they'd say, "There must be a mistake."

"Yes. I made a mistake," he'd say. And he would walk away.

The young ones who were quick thinkers said, "I paid online."

"What'd you order?" he would ask. Then he'd peer into the pouch and wait. They never knew, of course, so he'd walk away, down the sidewalk, to his car.

It was all very amusing.

He changed his delivery territory every few weeks. That kept things fresh. Just when he got to know a neighborhood like the back of his hand, he moved on to someplace new.

* * * * *

She was on a diet, now that retirement was upon her. She couldn't turn back the clock, but she would dial back the scale. She'd be thin again, as she was before she was a captain, and a check airman, and a chief pilot. She would practice restraint along with gentleness, as she'd practiced approaches while working on her instrument ticket. They would become part of her in the way navigation and airmanship were. She wouldn't even have to think about them.

She liked to eat. She battled her palate every day. It lusted for red wine and chocolate, beer and chips with salsa, and thick, juicy New York strips charred Pittsburg rare. She loved salad greens, as long as they were covered with blue cheese crumbles and French dressing. She desired baked potatoes, served all the way, and lobster dripping with butter. She liked

Crème Brulee and Baked Alaska and Mississippi Mud Cake. She could almost taste the Carne Adovada at that place on Second Street in Albuquerque—the one that used to be in a bowling alley. She missed the Steak Diane and cheesy scalloped potatoes from that supper club in Milwaukee. She often thought about fried chicken and collard greens and jalapeño cornbread served in the little joint on Beale Street that stayed open all night. Especially lately. Lately, it seemed all she thought about was food, good food, the best food to be had at every layover. That was part of it, enjoying the best of everything. The thought that she might not go on enjoying the best of everything made her irritable—in a vague, unacknowledged way.

* * * * *

It was surprising, really, how lackadaisical people were about home security. Take the front door, for example. There was no end to the houses whose front doors opened right onto the porch, with no screen door or storm door or iron gate to protect its occupants from whoever had decided to call. Maybe he was only the pizza delivery guy, or maybe he was a fiend dressed as the pizza delivery guy. There was no way for them to know the difference. That was the whole point.

He drove around his new neighborhood, shaking his head, and making tsk-tsk sounds at all the unprotected entrances. It was hard to feel sorry for people who were so lackadaisical all the time. So smug. People whose lives were wrapped in good things. The best things, they thought. Everybody thought their stuff was the best. They thought *they* were the best. *My* place. *My* stuff. *My* wonderful life. Me. Me. Me. Selfish, selfie me. He never felt sorry for them. Not for a minute.

He drove past the hunter green door on one house again and again, not knowing or caring what drew him to it. There were scads of hunter green doors. That's how it was a lot of times—most of the time—he just knew. Something in his chest pointed, strained, yearned, and he followed it. He followed it like the old diviners followed their wishbones, until they swung to a specific spot out of all the possible spots and said, "This is the place. Strike here."

* * * * *

She ignored the doorbell when it rang because she wasn't expecting anyone. Why would she respond to every solicitor, vagrant, and Jehovah Witness? That would be like responding to spam email. No one in their right mind would do anything but dismiss it. Delete it. You couldn't stop it; that was for sure.

The doorbell was followed by an insistent knock. Three quick raps. She thought maybe it was someone she knew, someone dropping by unexpectedly. She thought this, despite the fact that almost everyone she knew—certainly those who knew her well enough to drop by unannounced—lived elsewhere. She took her phone from the pocket of her uniform slacks. She wouldn't miss her uniform, the navy slacks and jacket. Even the captain's epaulets she would not miss. They were mannish and couldn't be softened, even with the most expensive blouses. Not even with the best blouses. There were no incoming texts on her phone.

She went to the door. She saw a blue cap—on which was printed Mr. Joe's—bobbing in the high, beveled window. Without thinking about much more than that, she opened the door. The man standing there wore a blue, short-sleeved shirt that matched his cap. He was a tall, thin man with a big Adam's apple and lean, sinewed arms. A flat vinyl pouch rode on one upraised hand like a tray of cocktails. Behind him, parked at the bottom of her driveway, was a white Honda with a delivery topper.

He smiled and said, "Pizza?"

"Sorry, there must be a mistake," she said.

He unzipped the pouch and peered inside. He said her address, as if it were written there, inside the vinyl pouch.

"Right, but I didn't order a pizza." She thought about the pizza they used to get in the terminal at Raleigh-Durham. Pizza and wings to die for.

"Can I use your phone?" the pizza guy said.

She pulled her cell phone from her pocket. "What's the number?" She pressed the numbers as he spoke them. She was very good with numbers of all sorts: Weight and balance numbers, numbers of passengers, aircraft performance numbers, headings and speeds and altitudes and altimeters and runway assignments. "What's your name?" she asked while the phone rang.

"Mike," he said.

"There's no answer, Mike."

"Hmm. Well, I hate to go all the way back to the shop, if it's right here. Close by, I mean." He held the unzipped pouch at waist level, and she could see the cardboard pizza box inside.

"Isn't that getting cold?" she said. "You don't carry a cell phone?"

"I do, normally. I dropped it the other day. I was walking my dog, and he lunged unexpectedly. At a squirrel, I think. He's a golden retriever, my dog. I named him Ralph. You know, after Ralph Kramden on the *Honeymooners*." He laughed. "Did you ever see it?"

"Sure," she said.

"To the moon, Alice," he said. "Bang! Zoom!" He laughed again.

"So, what are we doing?"

He glanced around behind him, as if he might divine the house that wanted pizza. "Do you have a computer? If it was an online order, I could log in and check the address myself."

"Yeah. I don't think so."

"No? Oh, I understand. I guess. It's just that I don't want to lose my job."

"Why would you lose your job?"

"I'm supposed to have a cell phone."

"Do you want me to call them again?"

"No, I guess not." He looked crestfallen.

"What? You couldn't buy a twenty dollar prepaid phone? It isn't that hard."

"I know, I know. It's stupid. It's just that my wife's been sick, and I'm working two jobs. I feel like I'm meeting myself coming and going."

She glanced at his left hand, at the gold band. "Look, Mike, sorry for your troubles, but you need to go figure this out. Somewhere else. Sorry."

"Oh," he said. "Oh. I wish I could just get a peek at that online order."

"I can try to pull it up on my phone."

"Well, that's the thing. The mobile site doesn't work. I need a laptop."

She glanced at her laptop on the kitchen counter, thinking, I could get it, just to get rid of him. "Wait here," she said. As she turned to go into the kitchen, she sensed him come forward, following. She stopped abruptly, before he had a chance to get through the door. She planted her feet and faced him. "What did I just say?" she barked.

He took a step back. "Sorry. I thought—"

"What did I tell you?"

"Okay. Okay."

She slammed the door in his face. Tomorrow, she thought. I'll be demure tomorrow.

*****

He drove to the corner and parked. He leaned across the seat and reached into the vinyl pouch, into the empty cardboard pizza box. Inside the box, swaddled in a chamois so it wouldn't rattle around, was his beautiful Bowie knife. She was pure and unchanging, and she alone was worthy of desire.

He gripped the bone handle, which he had selected for its perfect mating to the contours of his palm. He visualized its creamy ivory, and he ran his thumb across the irregular black ridges that variegated it. The knuckle of his forefinger rested comfortably against the brass holster, against the little smudge of tarnish from the oil in his skin. He knew every inch of her blade by heart—all ten of them. With his mind's eye, he saw the curve from her spine to her point, loving it the way some men love the curve of a woman's throat. He loved her tip. He thought about it opening soft, white dough. Smearing it red.

He held the knife until he felt like himself again. Composed. Confident. Certain.

"Shake it off," his mother used to say. "Don't be a titty-baby." Secretly, that had frustrated him. She had maddened him. Come to think of it, he had never liked big women.

LK Simonds

LK Simonds is a Fort Worth local. She has worked as a waitress, KFC hostess, telephone marketer, assembly line worker, nanny, hospital lab technician, and air traffic controller. The initials LK pay homage to her air traffic control operating initials. She's an instrument-rated pilot and an alumnus of Christ for the Nations Institute in Dallas. LK loves stories because they let us live a thousand lives in one. Her website is www.lksimonds.com

A Touch of Rogue
by Tayla Lindsey

Click.

A slight breeze wafted across the grounds and students. It carried the scent of summer on its back, throwing sand and sunsets into their olfactory lobes. It hurled itself across the students trickling down the school steps; it played among the leaves of the big oak trees; it began to smell of chill rain and autumn storms. *Click.* She lowered her camera.

He turned around, probably looking for the source of the flash of light. He didn't see the girl, but the girl saw him. Tapping her fingers along the rim of the camera, her eyes tracing his outline absently as she watched him. The school faded from her vision.

Then she saw through the lens of her camera, for she had raised it back to her eye to observe him. His head thrown back in laughter, the people around him making the scene into a tableau of high school perfection. Sweet dreams, sweet summer fading into a crisp fall.

Across from her inspiration, a girl in a vintage dress was being charmed by the boy sitting next to her, in a neatly pressed and tucked-in shirt. When she bent to examine the picture, displeasure swept over her and she raised her camera, once again attempting to save the moment between the boy and the girl forever. She took another picture, this time of her original subject. He had turned his face slightly toward her, an idyllic serenity masking his features.

A great point of frustration for her emanated from the halcyon of the moment, which refused with an almost arrogance to register in her photographs. At last, she gave up and turned on her heel to walk away. She dropped her face to look at the pavement below her shoes. He, the person she'd been photographing, was an admirable photographer himself. More than admirable. *Incredible.*

His mind had touched hers one day in the hall. She had been walking down the hall when she brushed into him, and his notebook dropped from his hands. Pictures went everywhere, and as she was scrambling to pick them up from underneath the feet of her peers, apologizing profusely, she stumbled upon perhaps the most amazing picture she'd ever seen.

It was of a young brunette couple, both wearing glasses, both smartly dressed. Candlelight flickered over their faces and the female raised a glass of wine to the male, who had his arm casually slung over the back of the chair. The slight arc of his eyebrow and the depth of the female's withdrawn posture fascinated her. There was a story behind the picture, she could feel it.

But that wasn't the point. The point was that *he* had taken the picture. The astounding picture that had swept her off her feet, reminding her of her own failures in photography, and presenting the obvious. He could *teach* her so much, if he were inclined to do so. She had complimented him on the photograph, but he had only given her a strange smile in response and walked away without a word.

Click.

She knew this area well. It was one she walked past to reach school, and one that she'd seen him heading to school from, too. The setting sun bronzed the tops of the pine trees and warped the color of the pavement underneath her feet. The houses, two stories with ominously long windows, peered out at her from underneath the shade of the evergreens. Long, circled driveways wound down from the slope of the road to the doors of the houses, and she hovered in front of one. *Click.*

The shadows of the trees threw distorted silhouettes onto the road, obscuring the tar and dissipating the cracks into a blended background. She turned her attention to the road rather than the houses, for it lead to a beautiful mock-Victorian

Painted Lady, with not one but *two* turrets spiraling into the sky.

She followed the tar until she stood across the street from the Painted Lady. This house was the one he walked to school from every morning. A shutter in the second story window hung slightly ajar, one of the hinges rusted through. *Click.*

A moment passed before she felt compelled to look down at the porch, where he stood. His hand on the doorknob, his eyes on her. She allowed her eyes to wander back to him, at how he stood on the faded welcome mat, at the chipped and despondent gnome statue sitting underneath the windowsill.

He was walking. Walking across the street. Toward her. Why? When he stood, perfectly masked, just under the twin evergreens on either side of the path up to the door, she took another picture. His hands in the pockets of his dark jeans, the last shreds of sunlight flashing off his violent scarlet hair and turning it a bright gold. However, when she raised the camera again, he remained unperturbed, and instead waited just in front of her.

"I have an incredible idea for a shoot." While his hands moved constantly through his speech, illustrating his growing excitement, his eyes did not leave hers. *He must be trying to seem professional.* Abruptly, she realized he was talking about the assignment they had due the next morning for photo lab.

A moment of silence as she attempted to locate words. Before she could, he reached out, grasping her hand and dragging her back across the road. As they traced his footsteps down the path toward the front door, she couldn't help but take in the stained glass mural rose on the front door. *How beautiful.*

Inside the foyer of the house, she stopped for a minute to take in the living room. Unexpectedly enough, the living room made use of the first turret by placing a fireplace around the curve of it, and windows in the rest. The plush, worn-down couch had a blanket thrown over it to cover up the damaged sections.

They passed by the kitchen on their way down the hall, but she hardly caught more than a glimpse of cutesy tile before he jerked her through a doorway. Inside, it was simply a bathroom, with a tactful curtain concealing the shower and lavatory facilities. Instead of a sink, there was a wooden table, furnished in opened and half-used makeups.

Foundation dusted the table top, the shattered compact sparkling amidst the lip rouges and eye liners. She glanced up from the table and at the mirror, at the contrast of his red hair to her fading platinum, at his blue eyes to her brown. At his pale complexion to her tan skin.

Then she turned to him, an image fixated in her mind. "Let me make you up. I think...You need a touch of rouge." And she smiled, and lifted the rouge from the table, and made his face over in the vivid hues and tones. Then, her fingers, methodically parting his hair. A vise grip on his arm as she hung on it, turning to the mirror, angling it just so the image would be perfect. His glasses, crooked on his face, glinted in the fake lighting. *Click.*

Minutes, or perhaps hours, along with an entire roll of film, passed by. From the experience, she gathered that he truly did have a gift. For example, she watched him choose to take a picture of the mantle, with the family photographs on it. She would've taken a left-to-right angle, exposing the many photographs and just hinting at the embers below.

But he didn't. He focused in on one picture, from right-to-left, with the others ever so slightly faded. Why did he do that? That one picture, in comparison to the montage of others, seemed unprofessional. Two teenage girls, the flash of the camera causing a shine to their faces, their smiles a touch too wide and sappy. Mawkish. *Schmaltzy.*

She cocked her head, and raised her camera, hoping to find the intrigue he found underneath the lens. But as she adjusted the focus, she tilted the camera back slightly, and a beam of sunlight hit the dust motes floating through the air beside the fireplace. *Click.* She examined the picture, and stared down at it in surprise. It was so…different. So *alive,* in comparison to her other photographs.

However, she pushed this discovery to the back of her mind for the time being. "I'm Phoebe." She offered her hand, as well as her name, and while she meant it as a handshake, when he grasped it, he didn't let go.

"That's a beautiful name. I'm Will." He slid his fingers through hers, and she squeezed his hand gently, trying to signal her release. Then, with his free hand, he raised his camera and *click.* She tore her hand away, flabbergasted, and took the camera from him to inspect the picture.

Their fingers, loosely intertwined, at awkward angles. Her chipped fingernail paint, and the tan line on her finger from where she used to wear a ring. What? Why would he take such a picture? Mechanically, it had no elements of interest, no depiction of style or metaphor. Unless she was too basic, too low-level, to grasp it?

Now Will spoke again, stretching her imagination with his hand motions as he described his next idea. He was smiling almost too widely, and his voice had an undertone of shakiness. *He must be excited about this.* Phoebe nodded in response to his question, and when he turned his back to prepare the mantle above the fireplace, she stared at him.

From a distance, Will was placid. Insouciant. That, that very trait, was the reason Phoebe studied him. The reason he became her subject. And now, here she was, shifting her camera to copy the angles he created, to take an in-depth look at the process allowing him such beautiful pictures.

After all, as she watched him tenderly move the photographs from the mantle, he was so very interested in doing this project with her. This…Photography workshop.

Without warning, she felt the world fall out from underneath her feet. For a split second, as she was lifted into the air, the unexpected movement incited a rush of adrenaline. But she composed herself when Will sat her on the mantle, her bare feet dangling over the embers. He smiled at her, and she merely acknowledged his smile with a grim nod.

Click. After the flash died and the stars erupting in her eyes faded to brief sparks, she examined Will's posture and facial expression and slowly put together why he hadn't taken another picture. Was something off about the photo? Phoebe shifted slightly, eager to sort out the issue and continue taking pictures.

"I can't do this." He ran his fingers through his hair, and looked up at her unsteadily.

"Why not?" Phoebe's inspection of him intensified, because her subject seemed to be losing his cool. He shook his head, a bit jerkily, and pulled her off the mantle, setting her back on the ground unevenly. She staggered, catching her footing, and brushed into his shoulder as she walked by. He jolted back, as if an electric shock had traveled between them, and Phoebe froze.

He shook his head again, and then nodded, as if he had cleared his thoughts. Now he closed his eyes, falling back on the couch and covering his face with his hands. Eerily, as if he had no control over it. All the color drained from his flesh until he was no more than an apparition, white as snow. She, too, had no control over herself, because she raised the camera. *Click.*

Then Will jumped up from the couch, walking very quickly to the staircase to her left. Phoebe stared after him, slowly lowering her camera as he disappeared up the stairs. What had just happened? She had thought they were taking photographs, and then he'd just up and *left* like that. As she let herself out the door, she looked back at her camera, at the new pictures. Though she hadn't had much success copying him, the one picture of the dust motes had turned out truly spectacular.

Maybe I don't need to be just like him.

Click.

She couldn't understand it. *Click.* Phoebe tapped her pencil against her notebook, staring at Will. *Click.* He was taking picture after picture after picture. *Click.* Now he looked her way, and started to walk toward her. *Click, click, click* crunch. The tip of her pencil broke on the lined paper, and she watched Will make his way toward her.

He neatly dodged the potted plant sitting in front of the two-person desk, and looked at her as he sat down. His chair shifted slightly, the legs squeaking on the wood floor, and he leaned into her peripheral. Phoebe turned to look at him. *Click.* She jumped, startled by the flash soaking up the room.

Will swallowed, and she looked into his eyes as his pupils dilated. Why was he so excited? Did the photography project turn out that well for him, too? She smiled at him, and looked back at the desk, at the worn swirls in the wood, and the scratched initials from over the years.

Idly, she traced one of the swirls with her finger, gazing up at her camera. A little squeak of the chair moving again, and then he was ever so much closer. Phoebe turned her head to look at him, and he leaned on the desk.

"The pictures are amazing, Phoebe. *You're* amazing. This, this changed everything." Phoebe nodded, still staring at him. She felt disembodied by her inability to understand him, an unusual and unwelcome emotion.

"Thank you, Will. I really enjoyed your mentoring." Now a blithe smile took over her face, because this *was* something to be happy about. *This* was something natural and understandable, something easy. Something unlike Will.

He swallowed again, and cleared his throat. When she looked back at him, expecting a speech, he thrummed his fingers on the desk, the steady beat resounding in her ears. She waited patiently for him to speak, to reciprocate the sentiments. "Phoebe, do you love me?"

What?

"No..." Phoebe couldn't rip her eyes away. The quiet of the classroom seemed to fade away, and the tunnel vision gave her a piercing migraine. "I saw yesterday how to take dynamic pictures rather than flat ones. I discovered the importance of subject matter. I've learned a lot, just from being near you."

But he didn't hear anything except the first word. "I mean nothing to you." He sat back in his chair, staring at the desk, at his own camera. "I...Guess I thought we had something. Didn't we?" Then he stood up in a flurry of motion, knocking his chair to the ground. Phoebe snatched her camera off the desk moments before he turned it over. "I thought we had something."

Papers, textbooks, pen, notebook, camera, photographs. Thrown in the air, moving in slow motion, as if time didn't exist outside this moment. The camera, hitting the ground and smashing, a thousand pieces exploding into shrapnel. The desk, scraping the floor, splitting down the middle from the force of his throw.

"I don't *understand* you." Will shook out his hand, and Phoebe clutched her camera to her chest, swamped in a sudden relief. "I don't *get* you. I don't think I ever will." The entire classroom fell silent, the few other students staring at Phoebe and Will. The teacher, sitting at her desk, jolted up.

I'm never going to understand him. The realization came hours later as she replayed the memory, but for right now, Phoebe merely watched it unfold. *I don't understand him. But I don't need to.* "What a relief, Will. I don't understand you, either." Her voice, flat and alien to her own ears, and Will's, heavy and passionate.

"I'm not crazy."

"You are crazy." Relief gave her energy, and she spoke with it, cradling her camera in her arms. "You have the strangest, most intangible process. What *are* you? Tell me, please, because I *don't get it...*"

Will turned away and walked to the door. Almost out in the hallway, he glanced over his shoulder. "Not crazy. Never crazy. Just...obsessed."

In response to this, Phoebe raised her camera. The swirl of papers fluttering from the ceiling fan, the frightened students, the irked teacher. Will, fury, and wild emotion, in the doorway.

Click.

As she lowered the camera, she saw the title. *A Touch of Rogue.* A touch of makeup, to cover up, a touch of incomprehension, a touch of uncontrolled, rogue obsession.

Tayla Lindsey

Tayla Lindsey spent a portion of her childhood in Asia, and moved back to the United States at around nine years old. She is the second youngest of five children, and practices the martial art of Brazilian Jiu-jitsu with her sister. She participates every year in National Novel Writing Month (NaNoWriMo), and has been writing novels since she was six years old.

The Crash
by Jared Abraham

Safiya stared at the red and blue flashing lights, while in her arms, Amira cried. "You're just tired," she soothed in Arabic, patting the baby's back. "Go to sleep, little princess." When Amira continued to cry, Safiya turned her eyes back to watching the flashing lights. Red then blue. Red then blue. The blinding flashes hurt her eyes, but staring at the lights made it easier to listen to her daughter cry.

"Ma'am," the police officer called, as he came back to her.

She tore her eyes away from the lights, to look up at the young man. Her difficulty understanding English had kept them from communicating. When words had failed, he'd pointed to a spot on the curb and pantomimed sitting down. She'd obeyed and hadn't moved since.

"Let's try this again. Can I see your license?"

Safiya forced a smile, as she rubbed Amira's back. *What else can I do?* She couldn't help but stare at the gun on his belt, only a few inches from his hand.

"Your license," he said louder. Safiya cringed at his angry eyes, remembering what happened when officers back home had that look. When she kept the smile plastered on her face, he made a rectangle with the thumb and index finger of each hand, and said, "liiiiiceeeeense," drawing out the word.

Safiya nodded her head and reached for her purse. Amira's cry had begun to slow down, and she snuggled her head into Safiya's neck, beginning the long ritual required to stop crying. Safiya used her free hand to dig through the purse, doing her best to not jostle the baby.

"Finally," the officer said.

In the bottom of the purse, Safiya found her wallet, and fumbled it open with one hand. From the wallet, she took out her largest bill and held it out to the officer. "License," she said with a smile.

"No, I can't take that," he yelled, holding his palms out and taking several steps back. Safiya jumped in fright, and the next moment, Amira arched her back, and let out a loud wail again. "I'm sorry," the officer said over the noise, rubbing his forehead.

It must not be enough, Safiya thought. *When will this night end?* She started to pull the rest of her money out of the wallet, but instead the police officer knelt in front of her and stopped her hands. "Let me," he said. Taking the wallet, he turned it over and looked for her driver's license himself. It wasn't slid into the clear, plastic pocket designed to hold driver's licenses, so he looked in several other pockets without success. He had stayed away from the pocket with the money, but he finally looked in there when all the other options failed. Behind the small bills, he pulled out a folded piece of paper.

"Driver's Permit," he read. Closing his eyes, he breathed in, held the breath, then exhaled slowly. Safiya shuddered more at his eyes closed in frustration than at his earlier angry eyes.

When he opened his eyes, the paper still said, "Driver's Permit."

"This isn't a driver's license," the officer whispered, not caring that Safiya didn't understand. "Do you not have a license?"

"License?" Safiya pointed at the piece of paper. She took her hand away from Amira's back and made a thumbs-up sign, hoping that it was right. With Amira still crying, though, she wasn't able to keep the smile on her face any longer.

"No, this isn't a license," he said in a tired voice, shaking his head. "This is a permit. For practicing. You need someone else in the car with you to drive with this."

The lady from the car Safiya had hit came over. She was middle-aged, with bleach-blond hair falling over her shoulders. She didn't look as tired as Safiya, but it was a close race. "Did

The Crash

you say that she doesn't have a license?" Her eyes darted toward the smashed rear-end of her Honda, surrounded by shards of red glass. "I bet she doesn't have insurance either," she sighed.

"Probably not," the officer replied. "I've asked about an interpreter, but there aren't any available."

"I wonder where she comes from," the lady said, not hiding her glare at Safiya.

"Somewhere conservative with how her head's covered. Maybe refugee?"

"I've heard that women aren't even allowed to drive in some of those...those Muslim countries." She scowled and nodded to herself. "I bet she's never driven before. That's probably why she ran into me."

That wasn't why Safiya had run into her.

She grimaced, while staring at Safiya's failed attempts to soothe Amira again. "Damn immigrants," she growled. "If they're not gonna learn our language, they shouldn't come here."

Safiya didn't understand the lady's words, but over Amira's continued crying, she heard the anger in her voice. She knew whom it was directed at also. She wracked her brain for words to use as an apology, but she couldn't think through Amira's wails. So she looked at the lady over Amira's shoulder, and she forced her tired, stressed out lips to smile. Smiled to say, "I'm sorry about your car." Smiled to say, "I'm not scary." Her smile was met with a sneer.

"I wonder if she can call anyone to help her out," the officer said. "Her car looks drivable, but I can't let her drive it home without a license." Pulling out his phone, he pointed to it and asked Safiya, "Can you call someone? Someone who speaks English?" He held the phone to her ear and repeated, "Call?"

In response, Safiya again searched through her purse, until she pulled out a notebook. On the first page, she pointed to a name, Abdul, written next to a phone number. "Does he speak English? English?" the officer asked.

Safiya nodded her head, pointing at the name. "English," she said while nodding her head.

The officer took a deep breath and dialed the number. After a few moments, he said, "Hello. Is this Abdul?" A silence followed as he listened, then he glanced at the driver's permit and asked, "Do you know a Safiya Kader?" The officer smiled as he listened again. "This is Officer Peters, with the Fort Worth Police Department. Your wife was in a car accident tonight—she's ok. So is the baby, but we're having a hard time communicating. Could you come help us out?" After a pause, he continued, "Great. We're at Hulen and Oakmont, in the Walmart parking lot. Do you know the place? Good, please come as soon as you can." Officer Peters walked back over to Safiya and gave her a thumbs-up. She returned the gesture with a smile, then forced herself to try again to soothe Amira to sleep.

* * * * *

Over twenty minutes later, Abdul arrived. Despite the cold, he was covered in sweat. Running to Officer Peters, he gasped, "I am sorry I took so long. That is our only car, and I do not exercise."

"That's ok. Thank you for coming as soon as you could," Officer Peters replied. "Why don't you check on your wife, then we can talk."

"Thank you. Thank you, sir." Abdul knelt in front of Safiya and placed his hand on Amira's now sleeping back. "Are you hurt? Is Amira injured?" he asked in Arabic.

"No, we're ok," Safiya answered. "She's finally asleep." She sighed. "It's been hard."

"What happened?"

The Crash

Safiya closed her eyes and shook her head back and forth. "I'll tell you later. Let's just go home."

Abdul understood what she wasn't saying. He remembered the soldiers that he'd worked with back in Iraq acting in similar ways to hold back the tears that were the only natural reaction to what they'd seen. To what some had done. He didn't push the conversation though. There would be time for that later, at home, with Amira asleep in her crib.

He rose and went back to where Officer Peters stood, talking to the other driver. "What happened, officer?"

"She needs to learn to drive," the lady shouted.

"It appears that she rear-ended Ms. O'Neal here at the light, Mr. Mahmud," Officer Peters cut in. "The damage isn't too bad. Both cars look drivable, but it also appears that your wife was driving without a driver's license and possibly without insurance."

"And now, who's going to fix my car?" Ms. O'Neal shouted.

"I am sorry for this," Abdul said with a nod to Ms. O'Neal. She didn't return it. "I hope you are not injured," he said to her. Turning to Officer Peters, he said, "She has a driver's permit, yes?"

"Yes, but a permit is not the same as a license," Officer Peters answered. "A permit means she must be driving with another licensed driver. A permit is for learning to drive."

"Oh!" Abdul placed a hand on his forehead. "We did not know this. We thought permit meant…"

"Still, it's the law, sir. Your wife can't drive by herself legally without a license. What about insurance? Do you have liability insurance for the car?"

"I am sorry, but we must not. What is this insurance?" Abdul asked.

"It's also required to drive. The insurance pays for repairing the car of someone if you are at fault in an accident."

"I will pay," Abdul reassured Ms. O'Neal.

"I bet you will." Her voice dripped with sarcasm.

"Let me get your information, then I'll give you both a copy of the police report. You can work out the details between yourselves." The officer asked Abdul a series of questions, and he filled in the blanks. When Ms. O'Neal wandered out of earshot to make another call, Officer Peters added, "I should give your wife a ticket for the accident, driving without a license, and driving without insurance. I have to write the ticket for the accident, but I'll only give her a warning for the license and insurance. It seems y'all have enough to worry about."

"Thank you for your kindness," Abdul said, placing his hand on the officer's shoulder. "You remind me of someone I once knew, back in Iraq."

"I've never been to Iraq," the officer said. "But I did serve in Afghanistan." He, too, closed his eyes, just for a moment, and shook his head back and forth.

"Were you in the army? I worked as an interpreter with your soldiers in Iraq."

"Nope, Marines. But we had Afghani interpreters with us, also. Got us out of some tough spots." Officer Peters paused, looking Abdul in the eye. "I'm glad you made it here. Mine didn't."

"I'm sorry. What happened to him?" Abdul asked.

"Same old story. Promises made, promises broken."

"I'm sorry," Abdul said again.

"Here's your copy of the citation," the officer said as he tore off a pink sheet of paper, keeping the white original for himself. He stared at Abdul for a moment, then reaching into his pocket, Officer Peters said, "And, here's my card. Call me if you need anything." He paused and his face clenched in pain for just a moment before he looked Abdul in the eye. "I've still got promises to keep. Even if I've tried to forget." He squeezed Abdul's hand, then moved off to speak to Ms. O'Neal. Abdul Mahmud thanked Allah, then followed to figure out how he'd pay to fix Ms. O'Neal's smashed-up car.

The Crash

* * * * *

The drive home didn't take long. Safiya had been afraid that putting Amira in the car seat would wake her, so she held her in her lap. Officer Peters had pretended to not see, and he never asked to see Abdul's non-existent license. "How will we pay this ticket," Abdul whispered in Arabic. "And the repairs for her car."

"I'm sorry," Safiya whispered.

"That's not..." Abdul began in a loud voice. And then remembering sleeping Amira, he whispered, "That's not what I mean. I'm not mad at you. It's just...a lot of money."

"Perhaps the agency can help," Safiya said, her exhaustion evident in her voice.

"Perhaps. Perhaps they will return my call."

At the apartment complex, Abdul parked on the street. After climbing the steps and unlocking the front door, Safiya carried Amira to her crib, holding her breath as she pulled the door closed. *Please stay asleep. I'm so tired, too.* When Amira didn't make any noise, she tip-toed into the bathroom to get ready for bed.

Abdul joined her, but he still didn't ask. Instead, they brushed their teeth together. In silence, they changed into pajamas, finished in the bathroom, and climbed into bed. It was only in the darkness that Abdul finally asked, "What happened tonight?"

Safiya was silent for so long, that he thought she must be asleep. "Amira was crying in the car," she finally said. "Her crying was so loud. And she just wouldn't stop. I talked to her. I sang to her. I screamed at her. None of it worked. The more she cried, all I could think about..." A sob rose from Safiya's side of the bed. Abdul moved closer but when he placed a hand on Safiya's back, she jumped, and he removed it.

"All I could think about was that night," she continued, the sound of tears in her voice. "About how the children cried on the street. How they died there. I was driving then, too." Her voice grew faster as the memory spilled out. "Except, the street exploded right in front of me, and I crashed that time, too. I woke up and there were bodies everywhere. I couldn't tell who was who. I got caught up in the memory. It seemed so real. I only realized what was happening when I hit the car in front of me."

Abdul took Safiya in his arms, and she curled into his embrace. Silence descended on Safiya and Abdul, as they lay in the darkness. They both had made promises, to themselves and to others. Tomorrow would be soon enough to get back to keeping them.

The Crash

Jared Abraham

Jared Abraham, who lives with his wife and three young boys in North Texas, teaches English at a small community college, and volunteers with a refugee resettlement program. When a spare moment is (rarely) found, he does his best to get lost in the Colorado Rockies. Jared's work has been published by *Short Fiction Break* and *Dodging the Rain* literary magazines. You can find him on Facebook and Twitter, as well as at jaredmabraham@wordpress.com.

When He Shows Up Again
by Eva Camilla Allyn

Isabella caught a whiff of Carlos' cigarette behind her. The same kind of crap Mexican tobacco he'd always smoked. She stood like a statue—her scrawny hands grasping the grocery cart handle, and stopped breathing. Her mind said run, but Carlos clenched her arm before she could react.

He jerked her around and breathed nicotine in her face. "I'm back."

Isabella pulled against him, but his grip held her tight. "Get away from me."

Carlos grabbed Isabella's purse with his other hand. He knew exactly where she kept her cash. He snatched a wad of twenties and stuffed them into his jeans pocket.

"You're hurting me." Isabella jerked away. "I'll scream." Her eyes darted up and down the aisle looking for help. She saw no one.

"No, you won't. You won't do anything. You're a stinking mouse."

He was right. She didn't know why. She didn't want to hurt Carlos. Maybe she still felt something for him. No. She hated him. She thought about the gun in her purse, hidden in the side pocket, and was glad he didn't find it. "That's my money. I earned it."

"I know how you earn money."

"It's for the twins' groceries. Give it back."

"For the twins. For the twins. That's all you ever said. I told you to get rid of them. They ruined you."

Isabella hustled to the other side of the grocery cart, her back pressed up against cans of soup. "I've turned things around. I got a real job. I could have you arrested for talking to me. The judge told me so."

When He Shows Up Again

Carlos smiled through yellowed teeth. He pushed against the basket, trapping Isabella between it and the shelves. "Call the cops. What I know'll put your ass behind bars. You won't like it there. And then what about your precious twins?"

"Our twins."

"They ain't mine, I tell you."

"They could be."

"From day one, I told you, get rid of them."

Isabella jerked her arm loose.

Carlos pressed harder on the basket.

The shelves behind her cut into her skinny spine. She glanced right and left. She saw no one.

Carlos put a hand on his pocket and whispered, "Careful, now. I got my little gun right here that you know I ain't afraid to use. This is your chance. You and me. We'll go to Chicago. We'll be a team again."

She knew his gun. She'd seen him use it. Maybe he was right. If she went with him, someone would take care of the twins. They'd be placed in a home that could afford toys and clothes and piano lessons. She always wanted her twins to have piano lessons. They'd never get them if they stayed with her.

A large tattooed man turned the corner and pushed a cart down the aisle. Carlos flinched. Isabella squeezed from behind the basket. She stepped next to the man and followed him around the corner.

She hurried to the service counter. A buxom middle-aged woman with big hair and red lipstick wrinkled her brow at Isabella. "What's a matter, girl?"

Isabella hugged the counter as if she'd crawl over it any second. "I need help, Ruby. Carlos is back."

Ruby glanced at four video screens showing different parts of the store. She scratched under her armpit and straightened a bra strap under her too small Save-a-Bunch Grocery Store tee-shirt. "Dirty scumbag. Don't see him now. When'd he get out?"

"A week ago. He wants me to go with him."

"You're not doing it, are you, child?"

"I ain't crazy. I paid every red cent I had to get the divorce legal and everything. And now I've got sixteen credit hours at Ridgemont. Earned every one of them. It's the best thing, besides the twins, I've ever done. I ain't giving that up."

"As I see it, girl, you got three choices. Hide yourself where he can't find you. Get him thrown back in the slammer. Or, get rid of him permanently. You know what I mean."

Isabella grabbed a wad of her hair and stuffed it in her mouth. She sucked on it and her body shook.

"Get that hair out your mouth, girl," Ruby said. "Listen to Ruby. You got a gun?"

Isabella spit the hair out of her mouth. "Yeah, but I never shot anyone." Ever since she saw what Carlos could do with a gun, she hated them. But, she kept the one he gave her anyway.

Ruby leaned in toward Isabella. "Keep it close, girl. Nobody's gonna say he didn't deserve it. But right now, it ain't safe here. I'll walk you to your car. He knows better than to fool with me. He fool with me and I'll sit on him and flatten him like a turd."

Ruby came around the counter, put her ample arm around Isabella's waist and led her out of the store. Isabella's eyes darted back and forth. She didn't see Carlos, but she knew he was watching. She slid into her rattletrap Kia Rio, locked the doors, and sped out of the parking lot.

Less than a mile away she saw Carlos in her rear view mirror. She thought about running into a telephone pole. Then people would come and help her. No, that's no good. She turned down one street, and then another. He followed.

At an intersection, she pulled behind a cop car. She kept close to the cop as he entered the freeway. Carlos tailed for a while then pulled away. When she was sure he was gone, she exited and drove to the edge of town. At the Trailblazer Motel, she talked the owner into letting her have a night free. She'd brought him a lot of business in the past, and promised him more in the future. She didn't mean it. That part of her life was gone. Or, was it? She still looked pretty good.

Isabella climbed the stairs; pushed open the door, locked both locks, and sat on the couch for two hours, thinking. She couldn't go back to her apartment. He'd find her for sure. She'd leave California and take the twins to Phoenix. She figured there was enough gas in the tank to make it. Ruby would clean out her apartment and send her the stuff she needed. Carlos would never think to find her there, she hoped. She'd get a job, and start again. They'd leave tomorrow morning. Maybe she'd have to turn a few tricks to get some cash. It turned her stomach.

At 2:20, she went back to her car, and drove to the day care. No Carlos. It didn't make her feel any safer. The twins wondered why they weren't going home, but were excited when she told them they were on vacation.

Using loose change from the bottom of her purse, she bought a dollar burger and a strawberry drink for the kids to split. *Sesame Street* and *Blue's Clues* on the motel TV occupied them until bedtime.

She gave the twins a bath, ran her fingers through their brown curly hair, and tucked them into bed. They were so beautiful, just like angels. Perfect ears, perfect eyes, perfect mouth. How did she make anything so perfect? She said a silent prayer. She didn't expect anyone was listening.

After closing the door to the bedroom, she pushed the stained green curtain back a little. Yellow lights on telephone poles lit the parking lot as several girls milled around the motel office. Before she'd met Carlos, she'd have been down there with them. It looked safe, even inviting. What was so bad about that life? Mack looked after her. Yeah, he beat her sometimes and took most of her money, but she knew who she was and what was expected of her. It was a simpler life.

She wedged a chair under the front door knob, sat on the couch, opened her purse, pulled out a leather holster, and set it on the coffee table. She unsnapped the holster, and slipped out the Glock. It felt heavy and demonic. When she put it on the coffee table, its metal handle clanked against the glass. She hated it. But, she knew Carlos too well. He didn't want to take her to Chicago. He wanted revenge. The prosecutors promised he'd get twenty to life if she testified. Now, less than four years later, he was out there, somewhere, looking for her, and he wouldn't give up.

She clicked on the TV. A lady newscaster, standing in the front yard of a house was reporting a murder-suicide. Flashing lights from ambulances and police cars lit up the landscape. People in uniforms, just doing their jobs, walked back and forth across the lawn. All the members of a family were dead—three children, a man, and his estranged wife. A video showed paramedics loading body bags into a coroner's van. Isabella clicked off the TV, and put her hand on the gun.

The image of the body bags made her brain feel like scrambled eggs. The reporter asked how a mother or father could kill their own children. Isabella knew exactly why they did it. One quick violent moment and all worries and fears would be gone forever. She closed her eyes and imagined picking up the gun. She'd walk into the twins' room. They'd be asleep. She'd tiptoe to the bed and point the barrel at Jessie's head. Once she pulled the trigger there was no turning back. She'd do the same to Jamie. Then she'd point the gun at her own head and finish the job. It would only take seconds. Very simple. Very easy. Very final.

Isabella opened her eyes. Tears gushed down her cheek. She felt like vomiting. Her body shook. How could she imagine such a thing?

Or, had she already done it? She jumped up to check the twins, but froze. Soft footsteps padded up the stairs outside her room. Isabella stuffed a wad of hair into her mouth.

The steps stopped near her door. Isabella reached for the gun. Her trembling hand hit it and it slid off the table. She scrambled for it, falling to her knees. Her fingers grasped the revolver's handle. She held it with both hands, and stood, shaking. Her finger slid toward the trigger. Carlos taught her years ago. "Don't jerk the gun. Squeeze the trigger firmly." She pointed the gun at the door.

The knob turned.

Isabella's heart felt as if it would break through her chest. Sweat dotted her upper lip. She knew how Carlos worked. She'd seen him break through doors before. Like at the vacationing couple's hotel room. A quick smash. Rush in. Catch the victims off guard. Do what you came to do. She never knew why he had to kill them.

She waited, steadying the revolver with both hands. She bit her hair.

Something smashed into the door. The wood casing splintered, but the chair kept the door from opening.

Isabella stood stiff, her legs slightly apart. A drop of salty sweat fell into the crease of her right eye. Her vision blurred.

A second crash threw the door to the side.

She saw a hazy image of Carlos standing in the opening. Her voice quivered. "Go away."

Carlos staggered into the room. He held a gun in his hand. "I'm gonna kill you. I'm gonna kill you all." He raised his right arm. "I'm gonna kill you. And then the twins."

Isabella's gun weighed a thousand pounds. Squeeze. Pull the trigger. Her hand wouldn't obey.

Carlos stepped closer, the barrel of his gun staring at her.

Isabella froze. This was the end. She'd tried so hard to make a life for the twins. But, life didn't deal her a good break. People like her never got a break. It didn't matter how hard she tried. All the work, the tears, the college courses, it had all been garbage. She prayed one last prayer for her kids. She didn't expect anyone was listening. She spit out her hair.

A clap of gunshots echoed through the motel parking lot.

Doors from neighboring rooms flew open and lights turned on. Then men and women in tee-shirts and night shorts rushed to the broken-down door. Someone screamed.

Flashing lights from ambulances and police cars lit up the parking lot. People in uniforms, just doing their jobs, walked in and out of the room. One of the cops pushed a button on his walkie-talkie. "Two adult victims. One male, one female. Both deceased from gunshot wounds. We located two children, both unharmed. Send a CPS worker."

A paramedic knelt beside Isabella, and put two fingers on the side of her neck. "Wait a minute. This woman has a pulse."

Eva Camilla Allyn

Eva Camilla Allyn was born on the wrong side of the tracks in Dallas. After struggling through high school, Eva discovered her writing voice as a student at Mountain View College. Now married with two children, her goal is to use her writing to tell stories that entertain and enlighten. "When He Shows Up Again" is her first short story to be published.

The Brown Backpack
by Connie Childress

About 30 years ago, my late mother and I ventured out on a journey to Springfield, Missouri, where our whole family was born. She'd come from a big farm family that lived near the Niangua River in Celt, Missouri, so we always had many relatives to visit in and around Springfield. Often her little sister, Aunt Rita, would fly in from California where she was a fourth-grade school teacher. If Rita was in Missouri, that made the trip even sweeter.

My family bought a small farm in Forney, Texas, after all of us children went off to college. Both Mom and I were teachers, so we had a lot in common. My daddy and brother, David, owned the Ace Hardware Store in Wills Point, just east of Forney while our sister, Elizabeth, lived in Tyler, Texas.

Mom and I planned our trip to go through Tahlequah, Oklahoma, where we'd stop and visit with some friends. It was a cool Tuesday morning about 7:00 a.m., June 17, 1987, when we were ready to leave Forney for Oklahoma. My parents' 1986 gray Cadillac was carefully packed.

"Don't forget the ice chest, Becky," Mom said.

"Yes, I've got the ice chest in the back seat already. Let's go tell Daddy goodbye."

Daddy was in his recliner reading the paper with the television on.

He said, "Becky, now you all be careful driving and call me if you need anything."

I reached over his shoulder and gave him a hug on the neck and said, "We will, Daddy. Love you! We'll call you when we get to Tahlequa this afternoon. We should be there by one or two. Depends on how many antique stores we decide to stop and visit."

The Brown Backpack

Mom said, "Bye, Victor, we'll see you when we get back. Be sure and call David or Elizabeth if you need anything. We'll tell everybody in Missouri you said hello. There's meatloaf and potato salad in the refrigerator. I left you a piece of German chocolate cake, too."

As we merged on to Central Expressway, traffic patterns were heavy as usual and then it thinned out. About 11:30 a.m., we stopped at a roadside park in Oklahoma and had our lunch.

We'd brought half of the German Chocolate cake to share with Janet's family in Tahlequah where we would spend the night. Janet was a long-time Texas friend. We'd met when I took guitar lessons from her husband.

At Tahlequah, our conversation went from how their little six-year-old grandson and my nephew, Justin, were growing up to what all we planned to do in Missouri. We also talked about the plight of education and all the changes in programs, teachers' salaries, and all the wasted money spent in education, but we had a rule: We could talk about education for five minutes and then it was a closed subject. Hey, we were on vacation, right? In fact, when Mom's sister, Aunt Rita, was around, we really applied the rule because it was just too much to take away from our precious vacation time.

After having such a nice visit with Janet and her parents in Tahlequah over a home-cooked meal, we retired early. Wednesday, June 18, we said our goodbyes, gave out hugs and hit the road. We planned to meet some of our relatives about 1:00 p.m. in Branson at a restaurant.

We got away from Tahlequah about 9 a.m. and the next part of the trip was the 152 miles to Branson, Missouri, about four hours. Of course, that time frame would include at least one stop at an antique store or a junk shop. It was a good highway and the traffic was light.

When we stopped, we looked at old books, depression glass, farm equipment, kitchen accessories, and just whatever they had on display. So many times, Mom would see something and say she had grown up with that and didn't want it in her house. Seems like different generations either go for the antiques or leave them behind. I think they make such great accent pieces and they can be mixed with almost any kind of furniture.

I had been collecting green depression glass for years and spoons from different places I had visited. I was fascinated to learn that the depression glass would appear as a gift in an oatmeal box one week and a detergent box the next. Some Saturday matinee tickets or an oil change at a gas station would include a piece of depression glass, too. And now, people collected them like valuable antiques.

As a general rule, I entered an antique store and never told them that I was looking for fans, spoons, green glass or political buttons from days gone by. Seems like the price went up whenever I announced that.

We entered Arkansas and decided to look at some antique stores in Harrison, then get more ice for the ice chest. Harrison was a town of 12,000 with a motto of "Adventure Awaits You." Well, you can say that again, because we didn't know we had the adventure of a lifetime awaiting us right there in Harrison, Boone County, Arkansas.

As we approached the town, we knew there would be some antique stores. Of course, this was long before the internet or any way to Google "antique stores in Harrison, Arkansas." We came through the town square and saw a few antique stores, but decided to go on through town. Antique stores on the square were often a bit pricey.

Just as we left the square off Johnson Street, we saw a schoolyard and past it was an empty field with a house on the right. A sign said, "Walter's Antiques." So I pulled over and parked the car in the shade and got out. Mom decided to stay in the car.

The Brown Backpack

The shop's door was open and I yelled, "Hello, is anybody home? Hello, is your store open?" I turned towards the car and said, "It doesn't look like anybody's in there."

Mom replied, "I don't see anybody either, but here comes a lady out of her house. Maybe she's the owner."

Just as I turned back towards the house, I saw a teen-aged boy on a bicycle come past the house peddling very fast. He was headed towards town and was wearing a brown backpack.

Then the lady came walking to our car and with a friendly smile, said, "Hello and how are y'all doing today?"

Mom said, "Just fine. We just took a little break from the highway."

The lady asked, "Are you looking for anything special?"

I told her, "We're just taking a rest break, but I might look around, if that's okay?"

She offered for me to go inside her store and look around.

I said, "Well, we don't have a lot of time, but I would like to see what you have."

I followed her in the store and she had several sets of dishes, some antique furniture, lots of items in boxes but you couldn't tell what they were. She also had some old military uniforms, clothing and some shoes.

I looked around for about ten minutes, then told her, "Thank you very much, but we need to get on the road."

As I got back in the car, she and Mom visited some more.

She told us, "Y'all be careful and have a safe trip."

As we approached the Arkansas/Missouri state line around 1:00 p.m., we ran upon a roadblock set up by the Arkansas Highway Patrol and a sheriff's car. The summer sun was high above us and the temperature was rising. As we slowed down and stopped, the uniformed officer said, "Good afternoon, ladies. My name is Sheriff Jones with the Boone County Sheriff's Department. May I please see your driver's license and your proof of insurance. And who owns the car?"

I handed him my Texas driver's license and insurance card and Mom's license and insurance.

Mom said, "I own the car."

He then asked where we were going and we explained we were going to meet our relatives in Branson and planned to spend a week in Missouri visiting family near Springfield.

Now, this is where the adventure of a lifetime really begins! The sheriff said, "We're investigating a robbery of a lady's money bag at Walter's Antiques—back in Harrison, Arkansas." He went on. "Do you ladies know anything about that and did you stop at Walter's Antiques back in Harrison?"

I looked at Mom and answered the sheriff, "Yes, sir, we did stop at Walter's Antiques and I got out of the car and Mom stayed in the car. I walked up to the store and yelled out, 'Hello, is anybody here? Anybody home?'"

I explained that a lady came out and greeted us very friendly-like, and she took me into her shop and showed me around for about ten minutes, and then we said our goodbyes and left.

Sheriff Jones sternly said, "Ma'am, the owner of Walter's Antiques gave us your Texas license plate number, the exact description of your car and the two occupants in the car. She described you both. She says that she had left her money bag on a dresser in her shop near where you were standing when she took you in to show you her merchandise."

"At first, she thought she'd left it inside her house but as y'all drove off, she discovered it was missing from the shop. It had about $2,800 in it."

The sheriff continued, "The state of Arkansas has probable cause to search your car, since they have a positive ID from the store owner and you fit the description."

I looked at Mom again and could tell she was getting nervous, but we both tried to stay cool and calm. The most I had ever been stopped for was a speeding ticket and I was just trying to think straight and say the right thing. I had taught

The Brown Backpack

government before and usually carry a small copy of the U.S. Constitution in my purse.

I explained to Mom, "Under the Fourth Amendment of the U.S. Constitution, we the citizens are protected from illegal search and seizure of our properties, unless the government has probable cause to search our property. In this case, they *do* have probable cause."

"Please get out of the car." So we stood on the shoulder of the road while they began their search.

The officers looked throughout the glove compartment, front and back seat, and our purses. Then they proceeded to look in the trunk. They took out our suitcases and went through them. They even removed the spare tire, some tools and other odds and ends from the trunk.

Mom and I were in shock and, of course, I knew what she was going to say, "What will Daddy say about this?"

I told Mom, "We know we're innocent, so we don't have anything to worry about. Of course, you know we have a great family lawyer, and so we just need to relax, pray about it and see what happens."

The officers still couldn't find the missing money bag, so they repeated the procedure to make sure they hadn't missed anything.

The next thing we knew, we were escorted to the highway patrol car and told, "We're going back to Harrison, Arkansas, for further investigation."

They put Mom and me in the back seat. I guess they towed our Cadillac back to the jail.

We arrived at the town's square about dinner time. By this time, the local news stations from Fayetteville, Arkansas, and Springfield, Missouri, greeted us with flashing lights, cameras and notepads. It was like they had captured Bonnie and Clyde all over again.

As Mom and I were let out of the car, we held hands. She was in tears and I was trying to be strong and think. We had to talk to Daddy back in Texas *ASAP*. We were not booked at that point, but I knew we needed to talk to him, my brother David, and my sister Elizabeth. Daddy and David would be at the hardware store in Wills Point so that would be the first phone call. The second call would be to Elizabeth in Tyler.

Robert Mars was the lead detective and showed us the restroom and offered Mom a cup of coffee and gave me a glass of water. He and Sheriff Jones were in the interrogation room waiting for us.

Before we began, I asked, "Officers, may I make a couple of phone calls to Texas?"

I called the Ace Hardware Store and my brother answered the phone. Mom was standing by my side. I tried to remain calm as I explained what had happened to us. David said he would get in touch with our family attorney, Philip Watson, in Richardson. David said he thought Mr. Watson and Daddy would be on the next plane to Fayetteville, Arkansas. I knew my brother could handle it with calm and ease…not so sure about Daddy's response. Then I called my sister.

"Elizabeth, you're not going to believe where Mom and I are!"

The detectives began recording our conversation.

I told them, "Victor Stanford is my daddy, and he and our family attorney will be flying to Fayetteville this evening."

We were read our Miranda rights and booked into the Boone County Jail in Harrison, Arkansas, at 6:34 p.m. This was not where we had expected to spend the night.

"Daddy is going to have a fit! And everybody in Buffalo, Missouri, will hear about this! Oh, dear!"

Mom and I held up the best we could. We were given some chicken soup, an apple, and some milk for our dinner. Mom tried to enjoy her second cup of coffee.

Daddy and Mr. Watson flew to Fayetteville and arrived at the jail in Harrison in a rental car about 9:30 p.m. Our bond was posted and we were released. They gave us a court date for

The Brown Backpack

us to appear before a judge about this missing money bag. Then we were free to go.

Mr. Watson took the rental car back to Fayetteville, then spent the night, and flew back to Dallas the next morning. Daddy decided he'd drive the Cadillac back to Texas with Mom and me. We spent the night in a hotel and left for Dallas the next morning. We stopped for lunch in Oklahoma at Bakers, a favorite family restaurant and had hamburgers and the best onion rings in the state.

We survived the adventure with lots of prayer, research, a good lawyer, and support from family and friends. Elizabeth is a news hound. A week before we were to appear in court back in Harrison, she came across a newspaper article about a young man who was killed in an auto/bicycle accident on the edge of town in Harrison, Arkansas.

A young man by the name of Robert Wilson was riding his bicycle and came barreling down the street, not wearing a helmet and slammed into an SUV that was waiting to cross the intersection. Wilson was dead at the scene just a few blocks from Walter's Antiques. Inside his brown backpack was found his billfold and a zippered money bag with the name Walter's Antiques and $2,800 in cash.

Our unbelievable adventure came to a quiet close. I don't recall ever going back to Harrison, Arkansas. I know I don't want to find out what other "Adventure Awaits You" might be lurking there.

Connie L. Childress

A native of Missouri and a Baylor graduate, Connie Childress is retired from teaching, but continues her love of teaching as a substitute teacher. She has written educational curricula and a grant on Character Education. She enjoys writing short stories and studied Screenwriting and Video Production at the Art Institute of Dallas. Connie enjoys traveling, swimming, tennis, and is a student of Tai Chi.

Three Gifts
by Gary Christenson

"Cassandra, chop, chop. We leave in ten minutes. Let's stick to the schedule." Naomi Connor marched through the living room carrying suitcases, snacks, water, maps, cell phone, and her purse. "I have everything organized and prepared."

"Mom, relax. It's a visit to Granny, not a diplomatic mission to a distant star." Cassandra saved the latest iteration of her doctoral dissertation in theoretical physics, and yelled back at her mother, "Ready in five!" *Mom, your military experience and your accountant training make you rigid, conventional, and closed.*

They left their Nebraska home for a summer vacation to visit Cassandra's grandmother in Illinois. Naomi drove three miles per hour over the speed limit and calculated their arrival that evening between 7:45 and 8:05. She asked her daughter, "Do you have a real job lined up after you defend your dissertation? Positive intentions, good looks, and intelligence won't pay your student loans."

Cassandra sighed and thought, *Mom believes I should think conventionally, and I'm tired of it.* Instead of indulging in a shouting match, she turned away and studied wheat waving in the sunshine.

"Well? I want an answer." Naomi insisted.

"Mom, chill! I have a post-doc offer at Princeton. If I take it, the post-doc delays the student loan repayment three years."

Naomi dropped the subject. At 7:58 p.m., they arrived at the home of Cassandra's grandmother in rural Illinois. After greetings, hugs and kisses, they carried bags inside, opened wine, and chatted. Granny asked, "What's new with both of you? How are your careers progressing?" They talked for several hours discussing their accomplishments with Granny.

Cassandra woke the next morning when she heard a loud crackling noise. She peeked out the bedroom window. "Einstein's bones! A crop circle is forming in Granny's field." After pulling on clothes, she grabbed her phone, tip-toed out the front door, and ran toward the circle.

An undulating tube of light stretched from the clouds to the ground, flattening wheat as it created a design in the field. Cassandra watched, took pictures, smelled ozone, and walked into the circle after the tube disappeared. *I'm scared! This is so weird. What's the physical mechanism that created the tube of light, and how did it flatten the wheat stalks so precisely? Is this safe?*

A long time later, she had no answers but felt at peace, which seldom occurred, except when she was deep into mathematics. The spell broke when a drone helicopter buzzed around the crop circle. It landed on a nearby gravel road next to a pickup. A man retrieved the drone, saw Cassandra, and waved to her.

"Hi, I'm Jim. I photographed this crop circle. Are you a friend of Mrs. Connor?"

"I'm her granddaughter. You see these things often?"

"Nope. They rarely happen around here. You interested in crop circles?"

Cassandra said, "I'm professionally intrigued. Can you email me your drone pictures?"

"Sure. Give me your address and I'll send them to you."

"Thanks! I want an aerial perspective." Cassandra wrote in his log book and said, "I have to be going. Thanks, again."

The pictures arrived that afternoon. She examined the intricate design of the circle and realized it might contain a coded message.

At dinner, her mother noticed the distracted look on her daughter's face. "Where are you? You've been distant all night."

Three Gifts

Cassandra answered by asking, "Did you see the crop circle that formed this morning in the field behind the house?"

Naomi answered, "Yes. So what?"

Granny's eyes twinkled. "I did. What do you think?"

"It's the most amazing thing I've ever seen. A guy named Jim took pictures with his drone helicopter. I think the circle is a message. Aren't you interested?"

Her mother looked exasperated and announced, "Not even slightly. Let's be practical instead of living in the stars."

Granny stated, "I'm interested." Naomi glared at her.

Cassandra smiled and said, "I'll work on it. Mom, you might be surprised."

* * * * *

By two a.m., she had broken the code. The circle pictures showed concentric rows of flattened wheat interspersed with standing tufts which reminded Cassandra of binary code. She searched the Internet and discovered an astute individual decoded the message from the 2002 Crabwood circle when he realized the tufts of wheat in combination with blank spaces were representations of the binary ASCII code used by computers. Cassandra converted the ASCII code and produced this translation:

cassandra lat 41,36,00 n lng 96,46,14 w noon june 21

She opened Google Earth and discovered those coordinates designated a location 40 miles from their home in Nebraska. The date was a week away. Cassandra slept little that night.

"I decoded the circle." Cassandra dropped the bomb at the breakfast table.

Her mother choked on her coffee and Granny asked. "Tell us. What was the message?"

Naomi frowned and drummed her fingers on the table. Cassandra said, "It was ASCII code, mentioned my name, and defined a location in Nebraska at noon on June 21. I want to go there."

Her mother slammed her coffee cup on the table and shouted, "I don't think so!"

"Mom, this is important. We have to go."

* * * * *

On June 21, Cassandra and her mother drove toward the designated spot. An angry Naomi said, "I hope you're happy with this wild-goose chase. Nothing good will come from it." She fumed and drove eight miles per hour over the speed limit.

Cassandra smiled as she said, "I'm doing it for science."

"Crap! You're doing it because you're stubborn, impractical, and to spite me."

"Mom, I think you'll be surprised."

They finished the trip in silence, left their car on the gravel road, and walked into the field. Cassandra turned around and saw neither houses nor vehicles.

Naomi complained, "I hope this is over soon. Annoying grasshoppers are flying everywhere." She checked her watch and stated, "It's 11:50. We leave this nonsense at 12:15."

Cassandra ignored her. She knew something special would occur.

At noon, a high-pitched sound assaulted their ears. They looked up and saw a shiny round object descend toward them. The ship that landed was as large as a naval destroyer. Naomi sputtered and exclaimed, "Wow." She stumbled, as she ran back to her car.

Cassandra watched, feeling amazed, shocked, and overwhelmed. A moment later, her stomach tightened in fear. She backed away, stared in awe and mumbled, "OMG! This flying saucer is not a secret Air Force project."

A deep voice boomed from the saucer. It sounded gentle but mechanical. "Do not fear. We will not harm Cassandra or

Three Gifts

Naomi. We want your help and shall exit our craft to speak with you."

A hole opened, and a stairway emerged. Three alien beings descended and walked toward Cassandra. They wore white garments and had large foreheads and humanoid features. Two stood over seven feet tall and the third was a foot shorter. Their eyes were luminous, and they appeared to glide over the Nebraska farmland. The tallest held out his six-fingered hand toward Cassandra.

Naomi shrieked, "Don't touch my daughter."

"Be not afraid!" The sounds emerged from a box on the chest of the alien.

Cassandra touched his extended hand, enjoyed a warm tingle, and relaxed. She asked, "How do you know our names?"

"We have studied you, your academic work, genetic code and your mother. We use resources and information beyond the technology of your race."

Cassandra asked, "What do you want?"

"We want you, Cassandra, to become a liaison with our race, the Kargosh. Your people need guidance and will receive many benefits. You can accept or reject this offer. Do not choose today. Let your intuition guide you. If you accept, return to this location in eleven days."

She stared into his eyes. His non-hostile alien presence reassured her. Naomi screamed, "Cassandra, come here right now! We're leaving."

Cassandra smiled and said, "Thank you. I will leave now and choose later." She wandered toward the car. *Amazing! Wow! Did I imagine this? Do I want to become involved with aliens?*

Naomi gripped the steering wheel, tapped her foot, and glared at the aliens while waiting.

* * * * *

Eleven days later, Naomi and Cassandra returned to the field. "You know I disapprove?" Naomi was insistent and hostile.

Cassandra replied. "I must do what is right for me."

They reached the spot a few minutes before noon. Cassandra walked into the field leaving her anxious mother waiting in the car. At noon, the alien craft landed. A metallic stairway descended, and a voice thundered out, "Enter! Do not fear. You will be safe."

Cassandra climbed the stairs and disappeared inside the vessel.

Naomi worried. *I don't trust aliens. They might abduct my daughter, damage or kill her. I should have stopped her.*

* * * * *

Over an hour later, Cassandra emerged, smiling radiantly. She floated down the steps carrying a golden bag which contained two other-worldly spheres. The stairs retracted, and the alien craft ascended.

Naomi examined her transformed daughter and demanded, "Tell me."

"Soon. When the changes are complete." Minutes later she said, "Mom, I've never felt this alive!"

They drove home in silence. *What happened to my daughter? What did those alien creatures do to her?*

As they rested in their living room, Cassandra announced, "The aliens didn't harm me. They showed me fantastic technology and visions of our future."

Naomi asked, "What else?"

"They gave me three wonderful gifts that will transform our world. The two spheres will improve physical life on earth when the human race is ready. I alone can activate the spheres."

Naomi asked, "And the third gift?"
"I'm pregnant."

Gary Christenson

Gary Christenson writes fiction and articles as The **Deviant Investor**: www.deviantinvestor.com He is the author of several books, including *Buy Gold Save Gold! The $10K Logic,* and *Gold Value and Gold Prices 1971–2021.* He is a retired accountant and business manager with over 30 years of experience studying markets, investing, and trading. Many years ago he did graduate work in physics *(all but dissertation).*

Annual Affair
by Teri Daniels

Denise knew that affairs were wrong. However, the attraction was so strong, she couldn't help herself. She had a great husband, wonderful children, and a successful career. Yet, something was missing. Instead of seeking counseling, she started having an affair.

She downplayed her actions by telling herself, it barely counted as an affair. The rendezvous occurred only once a year. While the affair was limited to one week, it was the best week of her life—year after year.

It started innocently. She had left her family to attend her annual college homecoming festivities. She was looking forward to seeing old friends, catching up, and renewing relationships.

Excitement filled the air, as she and her college roommate, Linda, walked toward the stadium for the football game. Nothing compared to their homecoming experience. They could smell roasted corn, bar-b-que, and turkey legs coming from the various tailgaters. Fraternities and sororities had booths set up, and old-school R&B could be heard above the laughter, conversations, and football game commentator.

Denise's daughter had set up her Facebook page with her maiden name, so her high school and college friends could find her. The plan worked. Linda connected with Denise on Facebook and talked her into returning to Pine Bluff for their college homecoming game. She didn't have to do much convincing. Denise worked as a social worker with Child Protective Services. Her job was taxing and she was looking forward to de-stressing and having fun.

"I can't believe we're actually here," remarked Linda, excitedly.

"Yeah, it's been 23 years since we graduated. A lot has changed."

"Yes, but I still feel like I did when we were 19. Hoping to see friends, visiting the vendors, and sampling the food from the tailgaters."

"And the best thing," exclaimed Linda. "We still look good!"

"Of course, we do."

As the two laughed, they heard the football announcer say, "Touchdown!" The band started playing and the crowd went wild. "Just like old times, we're late again," said Denise. "But unlike old times, we can now afford reserved seats. Let's hurry up." They laughed again and began to make their way to the stadium. Denise and Linda were weaving their way past the crowds when she ran into a man.

"I'm sorry, I didn't see you," she said as her eyes met his.

"Denise! What are you doing here?"

"Oh, my gosh! Anthony?"

"In the flesh." He hugged her and whispered something in her ear. Linda wondered what it was. Anthony and Linda exchanged pleasantries, but it was clear it was strained. Linda wondered if his being here would ruin their "girls' weekend." He told Denise how great she looked and that he hoped to see her again, before she headed back to Tennessee. He then whispered in Denise's ear again and slid her something in her hand. Linda noticed, but decided to wait and see if Denise would mention it. How rude, thought Linda. Whispering and talking secretly in her presence.

Denise had dated and fallen in love with Anthony when they were juniors in college. They had a big argument right before graduation and went their separate ways. He moved to Chicago and she began her career in social work.

"Wow! Can you believe we just ran into him?"

"Don't forget, you're now married."

"I know, but he still looks good." He hadn't shaved and had razor stubble around his chin. Rather than think he was unkempt, she thought it was attractive. He obviously took good care of his body. He was still lean with muscles in his arms. He smelt good also. Why was she noticing all of these things? Denise hadn't thought about him, like this, since college.

"Stop it," said Linda, interrupting her thoughts.

"What?"

"You're still thinking about him."

Linda and Denise had run into other college friends, who had invited them to come to a party that night. Linda accepted the invitation for them both. She had heard that one of her ex-boyfriends would be there, and she wanted to see him. Linda had been divorced for 10 years, and she was very interested in seeing if the two of them still had sparks.

When it was time to get ready for the party, Denise feigned a migraine. She wasn't a very good liar, and Linda didn't believe her.

"Was it a business card or a hotel card key?" asked Linda.

"What are you talking about?"

"I saw Anthony slide something in your hand."

Busted, thought Denise. "It doesn't matter. I have no intentions of using it."

"Yeah, right" said Linda, dismissively. "Look Denise, I don't know your husband, and I'm just now getting to know you again, but I don't think an affair is the answer."

"Thanks for the advice, now go have fun, Linda."

"Oh, I will. Don't wait up for me—if you're here, that is." Linda gave her an 'I know what you're planning' kind of look, as she left the hotel room.

Denise showered, changed, and paced the room for an hour—before she finally decided to leave.

"I wondered if you would come," mused Anthony, as she entered his hotel room with the card key he had given her earlier.

"I started not to."

"I'm glad you did," said Anthony as he handed her a glass of wine.

"I've never done anything like this before," said Denise, nervously.

"I'm not asking for much—just tonight."

"I'm married."

"So am I."

"What's up with your wife?"

"Probably like your husband, she is not willing to do much out of the ordinary. We both have demanding jobs and our life has become routine. As the years have passed, I've stopped asking her to do things."

She nodded, as if she understood, and sipped her wine. She looked out the hotel window. They were at the Hampton Inn. It wasn't a five-star hotel, but it was the best hotel in the city.

Homecoming was probably the biggest revenue generator for the city. Alumni from all over the world returned to pay homage to their alma mater. It was a fun and exciting time for most colleges, but especially for the graduates of UAPB. The alumni came by the thousands, donated money, and got caught up on the latest advancements and changes taking place at their alma mater.

Anthony put some music on. Not just any music, but good old-school music. Before she knew it, she was swaying to the sounds of Marvin Gaye's "Let's Get It On." How appropriate, she thought.

He took the wine glass from her hand and kissed the back of her neck. He then proceeded to undress her and guide her to the bed. She knew she should stop him, but honestly, she didn't want to.

As the morning sun peeked through the curtains, Denise realized that she should try to get back to her hotel before Linda discovered she didn't come in last night. She slid out of the bed, made her way to the bathroom, freshened up, and got dressed.

"Why are you dressed? Going somewhere?"

"I didn't mean to wake you."

"You didn't. Answer the question."

"I'm leaving. Linda will be up soon, and I don't want to have to explain my whereabouts."

"You do realize that you are grown and owe no one an explanation—don't you?" As he said this, he came toward her.

"Anthony, don't."

"Don't what? Make you squeal? Caress the small of your back?"

As he reached for her, she stepped back. "I need to go."

Denise noticed several things about Anthony. He was more confident and self-assured than she remembered him being when they dated in college. He was also very assertive and more experienced than she remembered. She didn't know why, but all of this made her even more attracted to him.

He took her hand, turned it over and started kissing it. He seemed oblivious to the fact that he was undressed.

"Anthony, I'm leaving."

He sighed. "Okay, if you're leaving, when will I see you again?"

She looked at him in disbelief. How could he suggest that they see each other again? He had told her that he traveled a lot for his job, as a salesman of hospital equipment. Tennessee was where his parent company was located. This meant that he was in Tennessee quite often.

"You won't see me again."

"Wrong answer." He started nibbling at her neck and attempting to unzip her dress. He knew that she was too weak to resist him.

"Anthony, please stop."

"If you want me to stop, you need to answer my question." He said this, just as he had successfully unzipped the dress.

"Okay, okay" she sighed and collected her thoughts. "How about in a year?"

"What?" He looked at her like she had spoken a foreign language. As she continued, he seemed intrigued.

"Look, we are both married, with grown children and spouses that aren't interested in adventure. This 'thing' we have can be our annual get-away. The truth is, Anthony, if you reach for me again, I can't resist you. I want you, and you know that. However, I think we should walk away and make plans to hook up sometime next year. If it goes well, it can become an annual event. What do you think?"

She could tell that he was contemplating what she had said when he asked, "How do I know you will show up?"

"After last night, it will be the highlight of my year."

He believed her. Last night had been better than anything he had experienced in many years. She had given him more than physical pleasure. They had connected on an emotional level that he thought was lost forever. "Okay. However, I get you for more than one night. Can you get away for a week?"

"Wow, that's a tall order—but, yes, I'm sure I can do that."

He then pulled her into his arms and kissed her. He kissed her with such desire, she was left wanting more, when he finally pulled away. "You'd better leave now, or I won't be waiting until next year."

She quickly gathered her belongings and headed towards the door. "How will I know when and where to meet you?"

"I will make all the arrangements. You'll get a text from me with the details in January. We will meet in September. Don't stand me up."

"I won't," she said, as she took one last glance at him before leaving.

Anthony stood there wondering why his marriage lacked the passion he had experienced last night. If he and his wife could make love like that, he would never have felt the need to sneak away to his college homecoming, without informing his wife. If anything, he would have brought her with him. He smiled, as he thought, she never would have said yes—and now, he was glad that he hadn't asked her.

That was the beginning. Anthony and Denise continued their annual affair for the next five years. He booked them in great locations and always at five-star hotels. Once a year, Denise felt truly alive. Having this secret affair wasn't planned, it just happened. But like all great affairs, it took an interesting turn.

They were at The Loren at Pink Beach resort in Bermuda. It had been a wonderful week. They lounged on the beach, danced all night, drank too much, and made love over and over again. She wished she felt this passion all the time, but she would take what she got, and make it last until her next annual 'visit.'

While in the hotel lobby, awaiting their ride to dinner, a gentleman recognized Anthony. "Anthony Ollie?" Anthony turned.

"David Spencer, good to see you. You know I've been trying to get on your calendar."

"How about that. We come halfway around the world and run into each other. Who is this lovely lady?" inquired David, while motioning his head towards Denise.

"Forgive me. David, this is Denise. Denise, David." Denise and David Spencer shook hands. They both noticed that Anthony didn't offer any further explanation than their names. Denise was glad, but wondered what Mr. Spencer was thinking. Anthony and David chatted for another minute or two, then made plans to play golf the next morning. From their brief encounter, Denise gathered that David was a client, or at least a prospect.

Their ride came and they departed.

When they were seated at the restaurant and had placed their orders—Denise brought up the chance meeting.

"Anthony, who is David Spencer?"

"He is the CEO of three hospitals. I've been trying to get a meeting with him for the last three months. I'm trying to get him to allow me to test our products in his hospitals. The fact that he invited me to his tee time is a good sign. I'm making the sale tomorrow." He was confident, and she liked seeing him this way. "But, I think you are concerned about him seeing the two of us together, correct?"

"Yes."

"Do you know David Spencer?"

She looked at him puzzled. He knew she didn't know him. "Of course not."

"Then chances are, he doesn't know anyone you know either. Don't be concerned. This is our time together, and we are not going to let an unplanned encounter, with someone I barely know, ruin it." With that, he squeezed her hand and smiled.

The next morning, while Anthony went to play golf, Denise decided to catch up on her walking. She hadn't kept up with her regular routine, although with all her activity with Anthony, she was certain she was burning a significant amount of calories. She walked along the ocean front, then decided to do a full pace jog. She jogged until she was out of breath. When she slowed down, she started coughing, panting, and gasping for air. Her head started spinning and she passed out.

When she came to, she was lying in a hospital bed. What happened and how did I get here, she thought. She noticed the monitor on her left. It appeared to be monitoring both her heart rate and blood pressure. She tried to sit up, but her head felt a little light so she laid back down. A nurse walked in and asked her how she was doing. She asked the nurse what had happened and was surprised to find out that she had an activity-induced asthma attack and had passed out. This had happened once before, and Denise had been advised to limit her activity when the weather was humid and hot. However, she neglected to follow the doctor's advice. Another jogger on the beach saw what was happening and called for help.

Denise was grateful, but she was also thinking about Anthony. "What time is it?"

"It's 2:45 pm."

Oh, no, she thought. Assuming he had completed his golf game, went out for lunch, and was back at the hotel—she knew he would be wondering where she had gotten off to.

Just as she was about to ask for her phone, Anthony walked in. He looked worried, and that touched her heart. "Denise, baby, are you all right?" The nurse told her she would be back later and departed. "I've called you a dozen times. The hotel clerk told me someone had been taken to the hospital, so I took a chance and came here. You had me worried sick."

"I'm fine. I had an activity-induced asthma attack. While gasping for air, I fainted. Luckily, someone saw me and called for help. I think my ego is more bruised than I am."

Anthony leaned over her and kissed her cheek. He looked at her with such intensity, that she wondered what he was thinking. She didn't have to wonder long. "I love you. I don't want to lose you, and I don't want what we have to end."

"Anthony, what are you saying?"

"I'm saying that once a year is no longer enough for me. I want what we experience during our annual affair, to be a daily thing."

"I don't think that's possible."

"Anything is possible, Denise. We just have to be willing to do what is necessary to make it happen."

"Let's talk about this later, Anthony."

Reluctantly, he agreed. "Okay. They're keeping you overnight for observation. I'm staying here with you."

"We depart tomorrow. Are you sure you want to spend your last night in a hospital?"

"I'm sure I want to spend my night with you." He was both decisive and self-assured. She didn't know why they hadn't discovered this magic years ago. Despite the difficulty and changes that would be required to make a lifetime of fun and excitement with Anthony, the prospect interested her.

The next morning, the doctor released her. Anthony had changed his flight arrangements, so he could accompany her to Dallas/Ft. Worth International Airport. She was scheduled to catch a connecting flight to Memphis, Tennessee. He had originally planned to go straight to New Mexico, but decided to ride to D/FW with Denise and then take a flight to New Mexico. He had two days before his meeting, and he wanted to ensure that she was okay.

They were seated in first class. Anthony had the aisle seat. Once the plane took off, the flight attendant gave the safety instructions. Denise rested her head on Anthony's shoulder. "Are you okay?"

"Yes."

"Let's listen to the announcements."

"I'd rather sleep. We've heard these announcements before."

"Listen anyway."

The flight attendant made an additional announcement to the entire plane: "Ladies and gentlemen, we have a couple on the plane that is celebrating their 25th wedding anniversary. Let's give them a hand."

Everyone clapped, and a couple of people gave the man a fist bump. The lady sitting across the aisle, leaned over to the man and inquired, "What's the secret to a long, happy marriage?"

Anthony looked at his wife, smiled and answered, "Role play."

Teri Daniels

Teri Daniels lives in Dallas and enjoys everything romantic. She loves romantic suspense stories and Sandra Brown is one of her favorite authors. When not reading or watching romance movies, Teri enjoys her work in education.

She is currently working on several romantic suspense stories that she hopes to have published within the next year. Teri's pillars are faith, family, friends, and fun.

Stuck
by Anrica Easley

I wake up on a beautiful crisp, fall day. The trees are making their turn from green to a bright gold with undertones of red and orange. All the colors stand out boldly against the light blue sky as the sun makes its morning debut, giving a hint of how gorgeous this Friday will be. I'm on my morning walk, the eve of my 40th birthday, deep in thought.

Times are changing, and they are changing fast. Gender roles are getting more blurred with each dropping of the New Year's ball. It's not uncommon for a man to stay home and care for the children and keep the house tidy, while the wife is out working—bringing home the money to finance their busy lives. That's if there is a man in the home or picture at all, or children for that matter. Women are getting educations, working demanding careers, heading corporations, running for president, and making other powerful political moves while putting marriage and children further down on their to-do lists, if at all. Gone are the "damsel in distress" tales of dainty women not wanting to break a nail by taking care of repairs at home. Today, a woman could be burned at the stake in the minds of strong feminists who believe that to house any desire or dream other than the one to take over and control the world makes you a stereotypical, one dimensional female from the early 1900s. To house a desire for a traditional relationship leading to, God forbid, marriage is "so cliché," they say.

Well, here I am—well educated—with an MBA from Spellman College, where I graduated at the top of my class. I head one of the fastest growing financial services companies in the United States. I own my home, have investment properties in the city where I live and in two other nearby cities, and a beautiful beachfront property in Abacos, Bahamas. I've taken my piece of this world and am running it like a boss! Any desires I've had for family and companionship, I've kept safely locked away in the secret places of my heart, waiting to be unlocked when...when...When?

No man at home. No children. Just me, my accomplishments, and my stuff. Sure, I have the Sunday brunch with my equally successful friends, the quarterly book club meetings, the various committees and boards I serve on, Yoga class on Thursday, spin class on Saturday. A full and busy schedule keeps me more distracted than it does fulfilled. Something about it all becomes more and more cliché to me with each passing year. "I might as well start my cat collection now," I say to myself as I come in and start 15 minutes of Yoga stretches to loosen the fatigue that has built up in my muscles from the 8-mile walk.

My thoughts follow me to the shower, and as the hot water cascades down my face and body, I can't wash away the thoughts that have been lingering all morning. I've spent all my adult life trying so hard not to be what people expected me to be, that somewhere along the journey, I forgot to be me. I ignored my vulnerabilities, refusing to let them surface. I've managed to stay soft on the outside because there is still something that may never change about the power of soft, feminine energy—but feel tough and calloused at my core. When the natural desire for motherhood rose, I pushed it back down, and locked it away for after I had single-handedly conquered the world. With no help from a man, partner, or companion. "I am woman, hear me roar," I say in the mirror, putting the finishing touches on my make-up, and give my best super-hero pose before bursting out in laughter at myself, to hold back tears.

Forty never looked better, though. I think as I give myself the final once-over before grabbing my purse and heading out the door to fight rush-hour traffic.

On the drive to the office, I listen to yet another relationship "expert," a thrice-divorced man, tell women how

Stuck

to get and keep a man. I roll my eyes and almost break a nail trying to switch the radio off. Today is not the day for another "expert" talking about a matter they have yet to master.

As I walked into the building, I run in to Charles. Charles was tall and slender with smooth mahogany skin. His jet-black hair was cut low and neat and gave way to a close-cut beard that framed his face. A very handsome man that I've given a second look or so every now and then.

"Good morning, Rachel. How are you?" he said, as he held the door open.

"I'm well. How are you?" I replied.

Charles is a managing partner for a legal firm on the floor above where I work. We've only spoken in passing and briefly at the building Christmas social last year. I've thought about fully embracing this "new millennium woman" role that I am told exists and asking him out, but there is still something about a man taking a traditional role and being the pursuer that I will always prefer over being Superwoman.

"Not bad. Busy as usual, but it's finally a weekend I'm not working—so, I won't complain," he said with a smile.

Wow! He has a great smile. I smile in return and begin to feel a little warm as we start up in the elevator to our respective floors. I'm not old enough for hot flashes, so I call my episodes "Warm Fronts" that seem to come on when I'm nervous or flustered. But, of course, I keep the look of a person who is as cool as a cucumber, as I hear an old commercial jingle echo in my head, "Never let 'em see you sweat." When I get off the elevator, I wish Charles a happy Friday.

My day was like any other day, chock-full with meetings and calls and planning and projecting. During some short down time, the thoughts from earlier resurface. What do I even want at this point in my life? I have all that I need and more than I want. Except the obvious. But what's next and how do I get to it?

The day drudged by, but finally came to an end. As usual, I'm leaving the office well after dark, heading to the elevators. I am tired and just want to get home, bathe, and catch up on my recorded TV. I was not in the mood for all the socializing and schmoozing my friends and colleagues so graciously planned for me, a rooftop party at the Soda Bar, Downtown. "Talk about cliché," I say to myself, and laugh out loud as the elevators open.

"Finally, Friday," Charles says with an energetic smile.

"Finally!" I say with an over-dramatic sigh of relief.

You should ask him to your party, my inner-self suggested. But I dismissed the thought.

Why would I do that? I reasoned back. I don't even know him and besides, men like him do not go for…before I could even finish my thought, there was a huge rumble, and the elevator shook with such force that I stumbled in my stiletto heels into Charles, throwing us against the elevator wall.

"Whoa!" Charles yelled. "Are you okay?"

"Oh, my God!" I said, as I tried to regain my footing.

"I think we are stuck," he said, as he started pushing each button on the panel, none of them lighting up.

"What?!?!? Oh, my God!"

"Yep," Charles said keeping his cool.

Great! I thought.

"Are you okay?" Charles asked again.

"I'm okay," I said, "You? I fell into you pretty hard."

"I'm fine."

We could hear the ringing of the elevator alarms on the lower level indicating to building security there was a problem. The emergency lights glowed softly, and I side-eyed Charles from feet to head. He was tall. I could tell he had a nice physique under his perfectly tailored suit. His hair owned a soft wave pattern on his face and his lips were full and… "Hello? Is anyone in there?" a loud voice came from the speaker.

Stuck

Charles stepped up to it and said, "Yes, and we are okay. It's two of us in here, Charles Tyler and Ms. Rachel…"

"Oh, Long. Rachel Long." I said, still giving him the once over, or I should say, the fourth over.

"Ms. Rachel Long," Charles continued. "Neither of us is hurt. But the lights are out. Do you know how long it will take to get this fixed?"

"No, sir, Mr. Tyler. We have called technicians out and hope to have you going soon. We are sorry for the inconvenience, but we are on it. We'll check on you intermittently, while we wait for help," said the guard.

"Thank you." The call ended with a beep and Charles turned to me and said, "What a way to start the weekend, huh?"

"Yeah," I said and reached down to take off my shoes. "Might as well get comfortable."

"May as well," Charles said and took off his suit jacket and loosened his tie.

It must have been the lighting and the thinning oxygen level, but my eyes were transfixed on his broad shoulders and how his biceps slightly bulged through his shirt. I became painfully aware of how long it had been since I had been on a date or *with* a man, in general. In my thirties, men just became a waste of time. Not long ago, it dawned on me that finding a partner is a little harder when you've done the work to get on a level playing field with them. Men in my demographic fit in one of two extremes: the macho man who wanted to control everything including me, my money and my career path to assert his machismo; or the man whose ambitions rival that of a turtle living in the World Aquarium. I've entertained both and what seemed everything in between, and all I have to show for it was a wall full of affirmations and calloused insides. So, for the last four years, I've done me. I've traveled. I've invested. I've poured myself into my work so feverishly that I did not notice my climb up the ladder into the corner office or the time and energy it took for me to get there. Now, here I am on a broken elevator, pondering my next move, and wondering if there is room for my internal desires.

As the minutes begin to pass, Charles and I have a chance to talk. He said, "I would have never guessed how nice and down to earth you are—and you are funny."

"Why does that surprise you?"

"Whenever I see you, you seem focused. Stern." He did an impression of my "stern" face.

"I do not look like that!" I said laughing.

"You do," he laughed. "You walk with purpose and determination that one may think you don't have time for friendly chit chat."

"The proverbial Ice Queen," I say.

"Well..."

"No need to explain. I get it. We have a label for everything and everyone, and I just so happen to fall in the category of most career women. I've heard worse." I say with a shrug.

We continue to talk about our jobs, the market and the current state of the union. We asked and answered a dozen questions from one another, sharing ideas, debating and contemplating one another's points of view. Inevitably, we hit the subject of relationships. He told me a little about the relationship he had just ended. He said, "It was like trying to fit a square peg into a round hole. I wanted it to work. I tried to make it work, but at the end of the day you can't make something be what it was never meant to be. You know?"

"Oh, my God, yes!" I agreed. I told him about my last relationship that came to a dramatic end. "He wanted a woman who was accomplished but dependent on him. Someone who was attractive, but not more attractive than him. He wanted a virgin but with enough experience to keep him fulfilled—if you know what I mean." I said. "Trying to be everything to one person was too much. Or, kind of like you said, I was trying to fit in a mold that I was not made for."

Charles sat beside me. "What kind of mold do you fit in, Ms. Rachel?"

"That's a question I've been thinking about all day," I said. "I've worked so hard to not conform or fit in anyone's prepared mold until I feel as though I'm stuck tightly in one I created myself, still based on societal perceptions, and I am slowly outgrowing it. I'm feeling like I am ready for a change. Like, I want something different."

"What do you want?" Charles asked.

"I don't know. I want to want what I want without having to sacrifice who I am. Without being labeled one thing or another." I said. "I want it all, unapologetically and without limitation. I want Prince Charming to ride up on his horse to take me to places I've never been, and, yet, be comfortable with me owning the stable where he rents space for his horse, as well as my ability to show him things he's never seen. I want to be made to feel soft again. To feel safe, to be vulnerable without judgement. I want to exist in one dimension at a time without being labeled one-dimensional." I stopped when I noticed I was going on a full-on tangent.

"Don't stop. Keep going." Charles said.

"No. I'm sorry. I've just been deep in thought all day trying to figure it all out. I guess that's what happens on the day before your 40th birthday." I laughed to break up the intense energy building in the elevator along with the heat.

"Forty? Nah, you are not 40!" He said.

"You make 40 sound old." I said with a slight neck roll, one eyebrow up and arms folded.

"Nooooo," he said with his hands up in a 'don't shoot' position while holding in a chuckle, "I didn't mean it that way. Just that... you look good. You look real good."

"Well, thank you," I said with an eye roll, trying not to blush.

It was quiet for a second. "So, Mr. Tyler, what about you? What do you want?"

He looked up and to the right for a second and said, "I want a nice stable to keep my horse."

I just sat there with my breath hitched in my throat, mouth open, and blinking blankly.

"Mr. Tyler, Ms. Long, are you guys still okay in there?" The loud voice came through the speaker.

We both jumped. "Yes, we are fine," Charles said, "Just getting a little warm in here."

"We are very sorry about that. We should have you out in just a minute."

"Take your time," he said.

I felt another warm front start to rise. Charles got up to stretch.

I got up to do the same and to face him. Maybe some traditions are okay to break. "Do you have plans this evening, Mr. Tyler?" I asked.

He smiled and said, "No, no plans."

"I hear they are throwing this birthday party for an old lady on the rooftop of the Soda Bar and I would love for you to be my special guest." I said.

Charles laughed a little and said, "I would be honored."

DING! The lights come back on and the doors of the elevator finally opened.

Anrica Easley

Anrica Easley is a native of Dallas, Texas. She is passionate about literacy and believes that reading is an important foundation to learning and crucial to personal growth. Anrica founded and heads the Ladies and A Gent Book Club and enjoys gathering with them to discuss their latest book selection and current events, and just having good old-fashioned "face-to-face" fellowship. She unwinds by letting her imagination run wild on the pages of her journal.

Raccoon Eyes
by Dawn Richards Elliott

    The hypnotic sounds of ocean life no more than 200 yards away might seem to explain my narrow, focused gaze in the cool, early morning. Come in closer though and you'll observe the blank stare interrupted by the occasional crinkling of dark brown eyes. Your bewilderment amidst the postcard scene—white-foam kissing cream-colored sand each time they meet is fleeting. I imagine you mumbling "ahhaaaa," dragging the "a" sound as I brush aside the salty liquid rolling down each cheek—as if in sync with the waves lumbering under the weight of the Pacific Ocean.

    The morning rays cast an orange glow illuminating, for your eyes and mine, three cracks in the *choicedeck*: a needed distraction. "Best material for the salt, air and sea" the chirpy, sun-tanned blonde had said, convincing me to sign over the next few years of my life to renovation debt.

    "Can't trust a damn soul," I yelled to no one in particular, though grateful for a reason to. "Sorry, Mom, I'm not coming for Christmas." Seven simple words float through my mind. I almost missed them, so softly they were spoken. And, yet, too loud to ignore. Since first spoken late last night, the replay persists—delivering its cutting jab with every word, in each round of replay. Before I realized it, my response slipped through.

    "What's new? You haven't been home for Christmas since you left, what 10 years ago? 10 long years. Think about it; you were only 18, a child really."

    "Love you, Mom. You have a happy day."

    I tell you, for the first time, she sounded tired, too. Perhaps that's why, this time, for what seemed like an eternity, I stared motionless at the black screen in the palm of my hand—immersed in the silence of our unfinished story.

"Aaaagh," bitter coffee, long gone cold, jolts me to a reality I'd sooner avoid. All but the part involving Jade, whose short, stout body barely three inches off the ground, is almost perfectly hidden under the aging patio table. I reach down to rub him, trying my best not to disturb the gentle rise and fall of his round belly covered in gray hair deceptively hidden by cream-colored fur.

The caresses calm me—as it usually does. Except when it brings me back to her and the images of his first weekend from the pound almost fourteen years ago. The yellow, lump-filled vomit and diarrhea the color of dark roasted coffee beans took us on a midnight trip twenty miles away. The ordeal made it difficult for me to form an attachment. Can't keep him, I remember thinking over and over again. More than thinking, yelling to counter her shrill wails.

"Mom, you promised. We have to keep him, and you have to pay to fix him—no matter what the hell it costs!!! I need him."

Thank God I pushed through, although I had no choice. Like *batty and bench* as the old Jamaican proverb describes it, for four years they filled each other's most urgent needs. Until they didn't. And Jade, with little choice, turned to me that summer of 2000, when high school graduation last brought the family together. His four legs shot straight up, making room for more caresses. "Sorry for waking you, boy," I gave him one last rub, hastily laced my bright orange running shoes, and nudged him into the breakfast nook, before stuffing my ID and twenty bucks in my shorts waist.

Bolting down three flights of stairs, and grateful for the quick warm-up, I slammed into my running buddy around the sharp corner. "Ouch, Dang, DANG, DANGGGG! So sorry," I groaned, reaching to touch Shelley's cheek, wishing on a star it might ease her pain, and halt the spread of the emerging half-dollar-sized bruise.

"I'll live, and, YES, I will survive the damn nosy looks at work. But take it easy, PLEASE!" Shelley continues in her lazy, Pat Benatar drawl, "The trail will wait, Island Girl, no need to risk life and limb. Worse case, we miss the darn run, maybe chill for a change." With no interest in the empty *I know, I know* she knew would follow, Shelley took off from my driveway, looking back briefly to display that lopsided, hard-to-resist, know-it-all grin.

My early resistance softens as the tip-tap sound of tennis shoes gives way to the squishy softness of damp sand and, just as quickly, to the mushy quiet of wet leaves from the night's dew. Unseen threats from discarded branches of the towering Redwoods close to the trail sharpen my focus. Momentarily.

Today, not even the twinkling rays bathing the trees nor the peekaboo views of the ocean around each curve can silence the replay, "Sorry, Mom, I can't." My baby girl's voice powers through my mind faster than the sprinter's pace Shelley continues to force on us. My once easy, creative, smiling, beautiful girl with an affinity for using humor to avoid dealing with the blows from a tough day. The metamorphosis that follows years of avoiding the uncomfortable, while living in a body and mind that felt much, seemed to unfold overnight. The transformation into an independent teenager angrily demanding freedoms she knew nothing about collided with me, her mom, who was obliged to teach about its realities. Faster than the Silver Bullet Trains that once brought squeals of delight from the black-stained lips and raccoon eyes providing refuge for her searching, youthful soul, she doggedly pursued her brand of freedom.

"I know, I know." Shelley's constant reminders throughout the years would elicit the useless response from me, especially on those all too frequent days when home felt like a scene from the latest war movie. "It's just makeup," she scolded, pleaded, even begged at times, Shelley who never begs. "Chill out, it could be worse. Them black eyes could signal deadly storms. Storms like neuroblastoma, basilar skull fracture, multiple myeloma, real shit," she'd yell with the desperate anger of one who'd loved and lost.

"Ha, it might as well have been," I would foolishly respond, "at least I'd know what to do with that."

August 6, 1973. Independence Day songs reach out to the crowd enticing them to *drink beer, drink gin, and drink up everything.* It's Freedom Day and, as the winner of the music contest describes it, a day when one needs a *big heel boot and bell foot pants* to celebrate. 1973. Eleven years since the black, green, and gold became the symbol of this independent nation. Xaymaca, "land of wood and water," as the Taino people called it. They stood no chance. What enslavement didn't do, European diseases did, and, within a hundred years, the Tainos were decimated. 1973, same year the American singer Johnny Nash popularized the young local talent's "Stir It Up." The Island Star, who in 1973 was mostly invisible to all outside his Island Paradise, where he was mostly ignored by the local elite as a weed-smoking pariah. But not for long. Soon they'd catch-up to the rest of the world and tonight's celebrators rocking in time to the soulful crooning of his revolutionary ballads, masquerading as slow grooving love songs. But not yet.

If you are the big tree, look out, *we are the small axe, sharpened to cut you down* filled every space of the smoke-stained air capturing the mood. It could easily serve as an informal national anthem cutting deep into the souls of freedom seekers. On narrow streets lined by wannabe chefs mixing blends of cinnamon, nutmeg, and peppers which entice and cautions, they celebrate. Excitement, bubbling like fine champagne, spreads quickly, as only a tropical virus can.

Freedom chants grow louder, sweetened by promises that *better mus come* and the sex-appeal of the young, handsome light-skinned political leader. The "sorta-white" leader from a land where chocolate-colored hues on the skins of women, men, and children is the norm. A norm that homemade bleaching cream would eventually aim to erase. Not yet though. Not in 1973, when many of the seeds from the scourge of European Colonialism still lay dormant. 1973. Only eleven years since paradise had shed its colonial rules, or rather the Colonial rulers had shed this paradise, though no one seemed to care who'd shed whom. Drugged by promises of a better time for all, the people danced oblivious to the cracks threatening the cataclysmic eruption which lurked.

Come with me, back to Paradise. Look carefully and you'll see her—the young girl of that time was to become me. She is the one hurrying home, dodging with every move the sweaty bodies of the celebrating freedom seekers. Pushing against the weight of guilt, and fueled by the burn for success, her movements are deliberate, urgently so. She had no time to waste on foolish promises, no matter how enticing.

Look again, but more carefully, so you might sense in her brisk hustle, a sense of gratitude higher than the famous peak from which the dark brew she would later love grows. Gratitude, cultivated from stories handed down from one generation to the next. Stories that reminded her that not so long ago, a girl like her, my younger self, had no chance in Paradise. A girl like her, my younger self. From a proud people with nothing much, *less than two cents to rub gainst one another* the older generation would preach. Nothing but the spirit to fight for every morsel of life. Earned, not given. Paid for with the blood of many and the exile of others to lands far, far away. Her people—my people.

From high above the mountains, they reigned terror on the pale-faced, self-claimed plantation leaders who ruled with impunity. The pale-faced colonialists fearfully traded in their stolen lands now protected by self-imposed property rights laws and the destructiveness of self-hate for an angry peace. "And for what?" Miss P., the young girl's great-grandmother, repeatedly and vehemently spit the words from her tiny body— mostly on Saturday evenings in the last years of her nine-plus decades on earth—when the burn from the white rum loosened her tongue. Many, many years after the cold and loneliness of foreign lands brought her home to die. And, for a few short years, to sit with me in the back yard of the small house her years abroad had paid for.

Miss P. was hard on that young girl, my younger self. The girl with long dark, wavy hair and hazel-colored eyes nestled deeply above sharp jutting cheekbone. The girl whose cafe-au-lait skin whispered loudly her people's legacy. "Stop you foolishness, gal, whe you expec?" Miss P. would scoff at the raw display of humiliation clinging to the sweaty face earned from her mile run home. Home, where for close to an hour each day she'd go seeking retreat from the merciless wrath of school mates and the wagging tongues of their parents warning of the bastard child. Unconcerned, or so it seemed, Miss P. would rail, "You can't get nutten from a pig but a grunt. Stop worry 'bout belonging, gal. Do you wok, tek care of you business and ignore dem fools."

It took a while, years really, but eventually she understood. Tear-stained tales of sacrifice, sorrow, and unfulfilled dreams will do that to a person. It will teach what no amount of preaching can. And she, this girl, my younger self, she got it. She was, and would forever be, a carrier, protecting the hopes and dreams of Miss. P. and all who came before and since.

Long before Saturday night story-time, or school lunch retreats when she turned away from my sweaty tears, uncomfortable with the pain she could not change, Miss P. left Paradise in search of what it had no intention of providing, and to avoid all it kept taking. Five feet two, skin black like coal, and ninety pounds dripping wet, she stood no chance when he forced himself on her. Nightly, after playing the role of the wealthy landowner with his beautiful family. Life has a way of creating beauty out of pressure. That black diamond took off one night, somewhere around thirty years of age, joining the wave of downtrodden aboard the seas. One dark night, on a one-way ticket on a cargo-ship bound for the Motherland, Miss P. left to carve out life from nothing. She left ten people behind. Hungry, but hopeful, abandoned, but certain of her love, they learned as did their children, as I did, the real price of freedom.

Rounding the last two miles of the morning's 15-mile run, still trailing Shelley, my great-grandmother Miss P. is center place in my thoughts. What if she had stayed, not left her children—my grandmother—behind? Would she, or my mom, or me, be just like the rest? Working from before day till long after the sun had set, cooking, cleaning, and washing for others. Eating, hidden away in plain sight, while listening to the boisterous laughter of people who chose to be unaware. Unaware of one-sided lovefests in the kitchen, bathroom, anywhere, everywhere. Lovefests that lightened Miss. P's dark-brown eyes, and coal black-skin with each new bastard she birthed. Working for People who chose to be unaware of the dark night on streets filled with potholes and garbage, where rats as big as cats run free. Streets only a mile or so down the hill, although it might as well have been 10,000.

"Freedom, Mom. Freedom to be," the cries of my Raccoon-eyed beauty follow me to the end of the trail where Shelley had already arrived. "Freedom to be a rock singer not a doctor, to dress as I like. My freedom, Mom, from you. From your never-satisfied quest for perfection. Got a B, Mom. 'Great, but what, baby, what did you do wrong? Why not an A?' The mocking I never understood, dripped like the rich gravy from the stuffed turkey roasting in the oven's heat.

Until now. Deep down, I think I always knew. Knew why I worked so hard, never satisfied, always chasing somebody's dream of success. Knew why I pushed her so hard, to be the best person she could. To never be like them—the freedom-seeking gyrating fools of 1973 in a land some 5,000 miles away from my home thirty-seven years later. To never be like them—the pale-skinned colonialists and their people claiming, demanding, taking just because they can. Freedom: the call of the fool or those with the power to take it.

I was neither a fool nor a member of the powerful. What choice did I have? I, who on the coattails of Miss P. became an immigrant in a place that proudly displays its schizophrenic attitude to outsiders. On the hopes of Miss P. and all those who came before and since, I had no choice but to board that ironbird and never look back. For that decision, my Raccoon eyes never met her people. Never sat under the glimmering stars in the backyard of Paradise on a Saturday night learning the price of freedom. She could never know why I was so hard, mean as she'd often say. She could never know, riding in the backseat of the latest cars to and from schools where school fees are ten times the income of the average person in Paradise. She could never understand. For her, Miss P. was just my *"bitch,"* some old woman from another life, haunting hers.

Sweat dripped like rain from our tired bodies and while my shaking legs felt heavy, my spirit soared. Finally.

"See you, Girl. Call her, D," Shelly yelled, hustling off unaware of my newly found wisdom. I went to free Jade, pausing to take it all in: the hundreds of seals lazily soaking in the mid-morning sun with no regard for the awe-filled humans gaping behind barb fences. On a great day, humpback whales on their way to the Baja seem to float through my living room, almost as if I could reach out and touch.

How could she ever get me? For the second time this morning, I got it. Really got it. For all my efforts, I had failed to love that girl like she needed, without the rot from my own garbage. The same failure that had sent him running after twenty years of trying. He left the papers on the patio with a stamped envelope still trying to make it easy for me. Then he walked away for good. "Hi, Mom, what's up?" She answered on the first ring.

"If you'll have me, Sweetie, I'd like to come to you for Christmas. Me and Jade?"

Dawn Richards Elliott

Dawn Richards Elliott is an economist who is interested in issues related to poverty, homelessness, and human development. She is published in a variety of academic journals including: *Global Education Review*, *Applied Economics Letters*, *International Review of Economics Education*, *Studies for International Development*, *Forum of Social Economics*, *Review of International Development*, *Journal of Developing Areas*, *International Review of Economics Education*, and *Journal of International Women's Studies*. "Raccoon Eyes" is her first creative fiction.

Adelaide
by Laura-Ann Elliott

"Get out of my room!" Cane Brooks screams the words to his twin sister, Adelaide, almost as frequently as he took a shower. *Daily.* Since they were kids, Adelaide needed Cane desperately. She needed someone…anyone, always, every day. Cane, the obvious choice, her birth-mate, but, he seemed to need space to be himself most of the time. They say God never makes a mistake, but it sure seems like they never met the Brooks' kids. Adelaide never felt like his equal. She was more like a younger sister, one that could be bossed around most of the time. One that followed him around, hanging on to his every word—as if her life depended on it. When he did talk to her, it was mostly to fight.

Occasionally, they got along. On these times, Adi, as he'd call her, walked as if she was on air, reaching to the sky which was illuminated by brilliant shades of blue interrupted by the light fluffy clouds that seemed to beckon to the weary and tired soul: come rest with me. This rarely happened.

Cane spent his days lip-locked with his girlfriend-of-the-second, when he wasn't hanging with his boys, that is. And Adelaide? She spent her days with April, her one and only friend. At home, she spent her time with their parents, and Isa, a first cousin, child of Aunt Veronica, their mom's sister. Cane was never there, and at school, where they often had the same classes, no one would guess they knew each other, much less lived together.

After years of trying to become her brother's best friend, she left him alone. Not that he seemed to care that she didn't knock on his closed bedroom door, begging to be let in. To chat, laugh, just be with him. No more did she ask him to go outside or take a swim. And she no longer asked if he'd come into her room, to chill, or to simply study with her. She gave him what he'd always wanted. And he seemed to like the new Adelaide more.

She often found herself feeling lost and alone. Especially in class. She didn't have many friends, aside from April. And though Cane was in this class, he hardly spoke to her. So…she daydreamed. She focused on something, instead of the feeling of isolation. If she held her palm up to the sunlight, she could see her veins and everything in her body, as if she were a machine. Strange, but intriguing, and—when contrasted with her long, dark, black hair—more so, than she seemed to know. Lost in the show from her pale, transparent skin, she didn't hear the tap on the door.

Didn't hear a thing, until the teacher's tone grew impatient. "Adelaide Brooks? You're needed in the Principal's office." Ms. Blake signaled to the girl who'd stuck her head through the door of the history class to leave, as Adelaide did the same.

Head hung low to avoid the curious gaze from thirty pairs of eyes of all shades—black, brown, blue, and green—she awkwardly slithered out of the class, fidgeting with her hands on the way out. Painfully aware of the wagging tongues waiting to be unleashed, and scared of what awaited her, she slammed the door, but not quick enough to avoid the chorus of "Oooos." You'd think they were children instead of high school sophomores. On her way out, she'd snuck a look at Cane who, for the first time in his life, had his nose buried in the history book.

Dr. Johnson joyously greeted her. His Santa smile and jolly red cheeks were a pleasant surprise, and a treat to see, once she had the courage to do as he'd said in response to her timid knock, "Come in, Ms. Brooks." He motioned for her to sit on the comfy-looking chairs, steps from his majestic desk. As usual, she did as told. Sinking into his chair, Dr. Johnson, grin as bright as the 100 watt bulbs in the science lab, leaned forward. "We need to talk about your grades, Missy." The confusion on her face must have been as transparent as the ghost she felt she was. She was an all A's student.

He continued. "Ms. Stein recently got a report from the College Board. Your PSAT scores were perfect—a 1520! With your parents' permission, we responded to inquiries from several colleges, some of the best in the *nation*. The head of MIT's math department would like to meet with you! They're very interested in your abilities, and the possibility that you might complete high school there at the same time you are working on a college degree."

She knew she had done well. In part because it came easy, but truth is, she worked very hard. Harder than anybody she knew. But, MIT! How amazing. How sweet the words. Finally, she'd done it. *Could this really be happening?* Her racing thoughts continued. *Stop overthinking, it's just a meeting—not a personal invitation for early acceptance.* She sighed deeply, unsure how to respond. "I'm way above cloud 9 here, Dr. J, but do my parents know?"

His smile spread wider than the Mississippi river. "Not yet. They still only know that we sent over your complete academic records. If I were you, I'd tell them once school is over. Run back to class, Adelaide. Who knows, this could be your last day taking history, for good!"

Cane liked the way Kelli's mouth hungered for his. He liked the way she'd text him goodnight, and how, whenever he kissed her, she'd give a little half-laugh and tell him a private joke. He liked everything about Kelli. It had only been two months since they first got together at a party Johnny, one of Cane's football friends, gave. He didn't think much of it after, assuming it was another random party hookup. He didn't know how, or why…but things progressed. Nothing too serious, no love business. No racing heart whenever he's with her, or any of that silly lovey-dovey shit. But, he enjoyed being with her. That was enough for now. He liked her. He was just a teenager. He didn't need to fall in love yet.

Her husky tone brought him back to reality. And her. "I want more than anything to kiss you...and other things," Kelli laughs, "God...I'd love another round, Kell, but duty calls," he flashed her his cell phone, and the angry text from his mom, *where are you? It's 5:00 o clock! GET HOME NOW.*

"Shit. I didn't know it was 5 already." Kelli responds, kissing his cheeks, as he rolled out of the bed. She followed him as he left her room, wearing the same sheets they'd been rolling around in since they skipped 8th period. What—3 hours ago?

He glanced back, one last time before heading out the door. She was stunning, and suddenly, he just hated his entire family for forcing him to leave. "I'll call you tonight." He runs out the door hastily, trying to avoid the grounding he knew was coming.

"I'm home!" Walking in, the first person he sees is Adelaide sitting on the barstool typing at full speed, a giddy look on her face, shiny black hair tucked behind her left ear. As much as she pissed him off, he sometimes liked his sister. He liked how whenever she was excited she'd tuck her hair behind her ear over and over, and she wouldn't realize it. "Hey, what's up?" He asked her, leaning on the kitchen counter. He really wanted to know, prompted perhaps by her smile which seemed rare lately. Did she finally get a boyfriend? Concert tickets, date to prom? "Nothing much," she responded abruptly, closing her computer screen as he walked behind her peering. "I don't want you knowing anything. Not that you'll care, but I want you to find out when everyone else does." Not even bothering to ask what the fuck she was talking about, Cane moved on.

"Where is Mom? Dad?"

"Mom was here when I got home. As 4:30 approached, she got worried because you weren't home and went looking for you with Aunt Veronica."

Adelaide

As if on cue, Isa came bumbling into the kitchen. "Mommy's back?"

"No sweetie, but she will be. As soon as they read my text that Cane is here, I'm sure they'll be home."

Isa plopped onto Adelaide's lap, contented with the answer. Adelaide laughs, putting away her laptop to stroke Isa's hair. Isa and Aunt Veronica had moved in almost three years ago after her breakup with Isa's father. The crowd was too much for Cane most of the time. For Adelaide, though, it was good. Mostly.

She was close to Isa and her aunt, and had developed a tight relationship with them, that most days substituted for Cane's dismissal of her. Little Adelaide and big Adelaide. It drove Cane crazy just thinking about it. He urgently needed to go to his room, to escape into the sweet nothings Kelli provided over the phone. Just before he could, the garage door opened. He braced himself for the outpouring of Mother's wrath in *5, 4, 3, 2, 1...*

"Where the *hell* were you? We spent ages looking for you! We went to Kelli's house, but no one seemed to be there, so we went to Brad's house, and he said he didn't know where you were. We called your coach; he said he hadn't seen you. Do you understand how worried we've been?" As annoying as her outburst was, her concern was touching.

"I was... " he started to say, but Adelaide cut him off. Her eyes bright, she took Aunt Veronica's coat and set it down on the table closest to her.

"Guys, I got called into the Principal's office." Cane knew about that. He'd been there. He wanted to know what had happened with that.

"Why?" Aunt Veronica asked before her mom could, concern dripping like hot coffee, and her brows furrowed together, as if confused at the image of Adelaide in the Principal's office. Perfect Adelaide? Why? How?

"I was worried, too, until I went inside." Adelaide continued, without pausing for a breath. "Dr. Johnson told me the head of MIT's math department has requested an interview with me. My perfect PSAT score prompted the inquiry and now, after reviewing my academic record, they think I might be able to complete high school while working on my undergrad degree in Math!" She paused. "I wanted to tell you ALL together but the suspense was killing me! I had to tell you guys, I couldn't keep it in until Dad gets home."

Without a word Cane left, but not before he felt it. Another pang. The same one, all these years that came from wanting to be like her. But he couldn't. And to hide his frustration, he turned against her. All these years, he'd mastered the art of making her feel invisible even though for him she was ever present.

"I had to tell you guys." Adelaide's voice trailed him as he marched toward his room. "I'm calling April tonight to tell her!" As he slipped behind his bedroom doors—as he had so many times—he felt invisible. With them, and without them, he felt like he was never seen.

The tap on his door was light, barely audible. He knew who it was. Adelaide. Do-gooder, and genius who might attend MIT next school year, at the tender age of sixteen. He'd known Adelaide was brainy, but college? She wouldn't go to her own senior prom. When he was a senior, she'd be a college sophomore or fresh person. Tearing himself from his thoughts, he opened the door and asked, "You going to bed?"

"No, to April's place," Adelaide replied. "She didn't answer, so Mom's taking me to tell her and her parents. I'm sure Mr. and Mrs. Linman would like to know." Mr. and Mrs. L treated Adelaide like another daughter. Then again, so did everyone else. Everyone wanted a kid like Adelaide.

"Have fun," he said, sarcastically, turning, not shrinking under her pained gaze.

Adelaide

"You know what sucks for me? That my own *twin* brother can't even be happy for me. Can't tell me congrats. You think no one saw you sulking in the corner? I did. I wanted you to stay, to give me a hug. But you just headed upstairs to call Kelli, someone who may not even GO to college." She sneered, unable to contain the anger oozing from her lips. He didn't even have to slam the door, Adelaide did it for him.

Re-opening the door, he ran after her. "Yeah, you get too many effing congratulations. I could shove them down your throat. Don't bring Kelli into this, she's a good person."

Adelaide's eyes brimmed with tears, and her voice sounded thickened. "Did I say she wasn't a good person? She's all you care or talk about, aside from football, and your friends like Brad or Lewis. But do you even mention us, me? You don't talk to me at school. It's like I don't exist for you."

"How do you think I feel? Being compared to the amazing Adelaide Brooks?"

"NO ONE COMPARES YOU, CANE! NO ONE!" Cane walked back to his room, slamming the door for the second time that night, drowning out his sister's sobs. "Screw you, Adelaide." He muttered to himself, turning to his phone and Kelli.

The next week, Adelaide walked around in a tear-stained fog. All she'd ever wanted was acceptance from her brother. She wanted him to like her so badly, but he hated her. He always would. The worst part was how lonely she felt. To have a twin, a birth-partner you don't feel connected to? She could feel him humming inside of her, but she can't reach him. That's the part that she thinks hurt the worst: his rejection. Nothing could ease the pain. Not the perfect grades, nor the poised act she put on for the world. Apart from April, she was alone. No one at school seemed to like her. Maybe she was a silly, spoiled girl with absolutely nothing real to complain about. Or maybe, she was just sick and tired of living this way.

She felt as if her heart may explode from the weight of her disappointment and pain. It felt like she carried bricks on her small back. A deep urge to lie down, to rest took over… all at the same time that she desperately needed to talk to April. *One ring, two ring, three rings…"Hey, this is April. You know what to do!"* BEEP. Adelaide sighed deeply, throwing the phone onto the marble countertop. She stared at the face in the oval shaped mirror.

"Beauty and brains, the best combination." Her mom loved to say, stroking her shiny, jet black hair that fell past her back, covering the porcelain skin that caused many people to claim she could be a dead ringer for Snow White. Her eyes, greener than a forest, seemed to be losing their color. Could crying as much as she did wash away the pigment? The silly thought passed briefly through her tortured mind. She closed her eyes, thinking back to when she and Cane were younger…

Once, when they'd both been nine years old, she had wanted to play a game. It was "Princess and the Frog," her favorite game as a child. Her mother always told her she was a princess, and she adored the story of a little frog turning into a handsome prince. She skipped to Cane's room, excited, even in a pink dress with a crown atop her head. She called his name, "CANNNEEEEE!" Over and over again, a large smile on her face. She went into his room, and saw he wasn't there. Confused, but not deterred, she sped downstairs, yelling his name, "CANE! Let's play a game! Maybe I'll let you be princess!" She jokes. She opened the back door, to see Cane outside, with a friend of his, a little black boy named Ty. He was in their class, but was always kind of rude to Adelaide.

"Cane! I've been looking for you," She says, out of breath from excitement, "Can we pleaseeee play 'Princess and the Frog?' I'm already dressed!" She heard a snicker. It came from Ty.

"You still play? We're in fourth grade, we're almost ten." He says, chuckling to himself.

Adelaide

"Dude, you still play with her?" Ty asks Cane, starting to laugh even harder at the idea of Cane still playing. Cane's expression turned stone cold.

"Hell, no! She always asks me to, but I'd never. It's *embarrassing* and *childish*. Go play with yourself, Adelaide. No one wants to play that stupid game anyway." He says, and Ty hoots. Adelaide felt herself shrink with embarrassment, as she watched them go back to chatting as if she wasn't standing there. She was so embarrassed, she didn't want to move. She just wanted to become invisible. She felt a tear drop down her cheek, as she shrank back inside, forgetting entirely about the game.

Adelaide felt sad at the memory. She knew her brother truly did hate her from the start. She reached into the drawer to find the Xanax she knew her mother stored for those days when she found life hard. Adelaide needed something to calm herself down. This stress couldn't be good, especially when her meeting with MIT was so soon. She remembered watching her mom slip two pills and did the same, popping them onto her tongue, swallowing with the piped water filling the bathtub. She sat on the edge of the tub, testing out the waters—waiting for it to be filled—to swallow her in its bubbly warmth. To feel nice and clean again, refreshed. *I'm going to be better than ever.*

She took off the last piece of clothing, her socks she'd forgotten about, and slipped easily into the water, closing her eyes. Within ten minutes or so, she felt relaxed. A sense of drowsiness descended, removing all thoughts of Cane from her mind. She yawned, wondering briefly how these little pills worked so quickly. The feeling was so good, she reached for the bottle, popping just one more into her mouth. The bottle fell, slowly to the ground, her hand tired from reaching so high.

A feeling of calming took over her body. She felt herself slip deeper into the deliciously warm waters, and she closed her eyes…

Laura-Ann Elliott

Laura-Ann Elliott is an author and poet who has been writing short stories, books, and poetry since she was five years old. "Adelaide" is her first published story, but she has had four poems published in the online *Teen Ink* magazine (www.teenink.com). Along with writing, Laura-Ann is a lover of animals, and helping out others as much as she can. Laura-Ann currently resides in Fort Worth, Texas, with her small puppy, Oso.

The Darkness Behind the Light
by Dave Hare

The King sat in an enormous throne, overlooking a dark and misty forest. He slowly came into realization that he was looking out over his own kingdom. But, he couldn't remember how long he had been there. His throne sat in the middle of a huge tower with waist-high battlements all around. As he stood and turned to survey the scenery, his broad cape trailed behind him. He breathed in the cool air and let it out in a stream in front of his face. His breath glistened in the pale moonlight and drifted out off the tower, beckoning him to follow.

With the mere thought, he found himself leaping over the battlements, and falling to the ground with incredible speed. He hit the dusty earth, but did not slow down, even for a second. He bolted forward towards the surrounding forest, not sure if he was running or flying. The trees rushed by his face, not that he was avoiding them. In fact, they seemed to be avoiding him.

He dashed up a mountain, far above the trees. The momentum flung him into the air over the summit. Just as his body should have begun to descend, he remained, hovering above the stone blade by several feet. His cape, nearly touching the ground, rustled in the wind. He took a deep pine-scented breath and surveyed the surrounding forest. And he felt two things: great power and great solitude. He was alone and he alone was the master.

He closed his eyes and breathed in his own power. He knew that he could do anything. Nothing could stand in his way. And before him the sun began to rise, cresting the distant horizon. He could feel the warmth through his eyelids and its light radiated red through the blood in his veins. Had he caused it to rise? Was even the sun in his power?

As he opened his eyes, he was temporarily blinded. The white light around him began to take the form of sharp edges where an eggshell ceiling met eggshell walls. The sensations of power and solitude leached from his heart as he sat up in his bed, ears ringing with the noises of the street below his apartment. There was a new fist-sized hole in the wall next to his head, and sheetrock crumbs on his bed. He looked through the hole and realized he was gazing into the eyes of his eight-year-old neighbor.

"Hey, Chris."

Chris did not respond.

Furman let out a deep sigh, kicking his bare legs out of bed. He was mildly amused at the thought of Chris watching him walk to the bathroom in red polka dot boxers and an ill-fitting T-shirt. The mirror in the bathroom revealed a man substantially different from the King in his dreams. But the eyes were the same, though harder to see through thick cheap plastic lenses, and hidden under his heavy eyebrows. He went through the motions of everyday: showered, shaved, dressed. His slacks were nice last decade. He wore a not-so-recently-ironed dress shirt, and suspenders. People make fun of suspenders, but they are more comfortable than a belt. *And more professional*, Furman told himself.

In this world, Furman disappeared. Among the teeming masses pushing and shoving their way to work, Furman embraced a life staring alternately below shoulder blades and at robust midriffs. He shuffled more than he walked, carrying nothing but an old brown leather briefcase. He rarely said anything more than the occasional "sorry" when colliding with his hurried co-commuters. Furman turned down a vacant alley and around a corner to stand in front of his store. Across the metal security door was the recently sprayed phrase: "Time stops 4 Newman." Though mildly irritated, he appreciated the overall feel of the work. The words had been painted to appear as though typed by a typewriter, with a gold under-shadow. And though he did not know this Newman, he could recognize wit when he saw it. Rolling up the door, he found his jewelry shop like he left it: dusty and empty. And thus, a new day began for Furman Barsky.

* * * * *

"This ring is one of a kind. I know what you are thinking, it's not a diamond, and you are right. Diamonds are more common for engagements. "

"That is exactly what..."

"No, no, no, wait, this is Alexandrite. Walk with me outside for a second...What color is the gem?"

"Green."

"Do you remember what it was a minute ago?"

"Well, it was red, but it must be the lighting."

"Let's go back inside."

"It's red now."

"Exactly. The color actually changes. This is no trick, it is not a mood ring. This is one of the rarest jewels in the world. A jewel of this size, 6 carats, can only be found in the Ural Mountains of western Russia. The ring is 24 carat gold and cast in 1864 by Alexander II, the man after whom the jewel was named. He made it for the soon-to-be bride of his son Nicholas, the Princess Dagmar. Tragically, Nicholas died the next year. This beautiful ring became mere history, lost in the passage of time. I have only recently acquired it from the great-granddaughter of Dagmar. The ring has spent the last two centuries seeking a love that would last. Imagine her eyes when you propose and you tell her that you found the most unique ring in the world for such a unique woman."

"Yeah, so how much is it?"

"Unique ring, unique price—$6,200."

"Wow, no, I am going to look for a diamond."

Furman almost dropped the ring, as his only customer in a week walked right out the front door, without even looking back. Instead he walked over to the glass case, carefully unlocked it, and placed the ring back in its place. After rolling down the graffiti covered security door, he walked down to the diner where he was to meet his ex-wife.

* * * * *

He lost track of what she was saying very early in the conversation. It was so good to be looking into her eyes again. They were absolutely spectacular. When people say that, they usually mean light eyes, he thought, green or blue. Her eyes are brown, but not simple brown. Deep within them is an indescribable complexity of facets, very much like a diamond. When he looked into her eyes, it was like…he felt calm. He felt like things were going to be OK. And he never felt that way, not anymore.

"…so, we have decided that the best thing for all of us is to move to Colorado. I am not saying that it will be easy for you, Furman, I am saying that it is best."

Her voice did not quite match her eyes, a little bit too nasal. Hardly noticeable, in fact, he didn't notice it until they had been married for a year. After that, he got a little too good at tuning her out.

"Are you even listening to me? Furman…" She chuckled a little bit, he loved it when she did that. "Furman, you're sweet when you look at me like that, but this conversation is really important."

"What? Yeah, no, I know that, Stacey."

"Did you hear what I said."

"I heard the word Colorado. Were you talking about a vacation?"

"No, Furman." She reached over and touched his hand. "Furman, we are moving to Colorado."

Reality rushed upon him. It was as though he were standing in front of a terrible car accident, knowing somehow he caused it, but not knowing how.

"We?"

She laughed. "Well, I have to take Sarah with me, you know."

"Take Sarah! But how will I ever see her?"

The conversation went on like that for a while. You can guess how it ended. As if it could not be worse, there was another man, too. Furman knew he was not a great guy, but he loved his wife (well, ex-wife) and he loved his daughter. Was he so easily replaced? Stacey said she thought it would be easier for Sarah if he *not* say goodbye. What could he say to that? Really, he did not say much. He walked away from the diner feeling raw.

* * * * *

After an indeterminate amount of time, he found himself stumbling down an alley, looking up at an old apartment building. Not his. In fact, he did not know where he was at all. He also didn't care. Furman worried about his safety fairly regularly, but right now, there was nothing that concerned him less. A misty rain began to swell around him. It was not cold, but neither was it comfortable. Most annoyingly, it fogged up his glasses, which he had to wipe with the corner of his now-untucked dress shirt every few seconds. The fifth clean-wiping permitted him to see a homeless man sleeping on the sidewalk, just before he stepped on his leg. Actually, he wasn't sleeping, just lying and staring. It was then that Furman's self-concern returned.

"Where are you going?" the Man's voice was startling, deep and powerful. It was not the voice one would expect coming from a semi-dormant vagrant. "There's nothing down this alley. There is nothing for you here."

"Yeah, you're right. I...I'm in the wrong place."

"I'll say." The Man shuffled, turning his face to the bricks of the apartment. This would have been a perfect exit for

Furman, if he had any idea where to go. Caught in indecision, he remained looking down on the Man's filthy back.

"Go home, Furman. It's down there." The Man reached his arm out and pointed to the other side of an overpass. The mist cleared a bit and Furman could see an overhead light illuminating the street on the other side. He could not tell what street it was, but the light was encouraging. It definitely seemed like a good...

"Wait, how do you know my name?" Furman asked, furrowing his brow until his glasses almost slipped off. He turned to look at the Man who now actually seemed asleep. Furman shook his head. *He probably said something like, "Go home, turban."* Furman thought to himself. Not that that would make any more sense. He wasn't wearing a turban. And he stumbled toward the light.

The lit street was not home, but it was somewhere he knew, five blocks from his apartment. After unlocking the sticky deadbolt, dropping his briefcase in the living room, and taking off his shoes, Furman collapsed in bed. He thought of Sarah, who had received so much more genetic information from her mother. She was beautiful. And he didn't know if he would ever see her again. The despair clumped with his fatigue, and he fell asleep face down in his pillow.

* * * * *

In his dream-world, the King-who-was-Furman was still hovering over his kingdom. Even here, it was hard to shake off his depression. He realized he was wearing armor now, with a sword on his belt. He drew the sword, which was far too long and glowed with fire on the edges. And he yelled. He yelled at the trees and the sky and the mist. Now his voice was powerful and with his scream went out the fury that was in his heart. And he watched everything burn around him. *Everything.*

The Darkness Behind the Light

He fell to the ground, kneeling. But he wasn't outside anymore. He was inside his castle again. Another throne rose from the floor because he willed it to do so. He threw his sword against the wall, where its fire lit a series of torches surrounding his throne room.

"You can do whatever you want here."

The voice was not startling, but awakening, coming from the darkness behind the torches.

"I know!" Furman replied, indignantly.

"You want to be alone?"

A figure stepped into the pool of light. He, for it was a he, was not clear, like the first time Furman opened his eyes in the morning. Everything else was sharp, real, even tangible, but not this man.

"I do."

"So, I will leave you alone." He bowed, as if before a king and began to step back into the darkness.

"Wait...how are you here?"

"I'm here because you want me to be." He said, still bowing, arms out as if holding an invisible cloak. And he was familiar, or something about him was familiar.

"Approach."

"At your pleasure."

"What do you want?"

"Sir, the question here is always, 'What do *you* want?'" The King tried to focus on him as he approached. But every time he focused on an aspect of his face, it became blurry. You could only see his features in your peripheral vision. And suddenly he knew it was the homeless man. Not here, *this* wasn't the homeless man. But that was who Furman was thinking of. It was him, but it wasn't. Furman was sure it was his voice.

The moments of silence that the King passed in thought did not seem awkward, but natural, as though time did not flow in the same way here.

"My times here are too short."

"That is because they are dreams, sire. Dreams can never last. It is their nature. But of course, that is your choice. I have the power to switch them."

"Switch who?"

"Switch your lives. This could be your reality if you wanted it, your other life just a dream."

"Why wouldn't I want that?"

"That is only for you to decide."

The King suddenly felt very tired. He put his head on his chest. He realized he had a really great beard. He had always wanted a beard. He smiled and closed his eyes, "Yes, that is what I want." He said sleepily, "I want to be here. Make it so."

The voice of the once-homeless Man was softer now, as though the King was hearing it through a tunnel.

"At your pleasure."

His voice echoed and repeated and began to get louder and yet less distinct. In fact, it became quite annoying. Then, a little hand slapped Furman in the face. Furman looked up to see that Chris's full arm was through the hole in the wall, flailing madly. The Man's voice swallowed up by Chris's faint screams.

* * * * *

From there it was as though someone had hit fast-forward. Furman's phone rang, it was Stacey. She sounded terrified and said that she needed to see him immediately, at the diner. She said that she needed him. Furman did not remember dressing, but when he looked in the mirror he was fully clothed. He actually looked pretty good, he seemed to stand up a bit straighter. His clothes looked cleaner. *She needs me.*

On the walk, Furman used his elbow much more than usual, not willing to waste a second. And surprisingly, after a few minutes, the people seemed to part for him, letting him through.

Turning toward the back of the diner, he saw her in a booth. Stacey was a mess. She had clearly not slept the night before and her hair was sticking up in random tufts. Furman smiled at her and she burst into tears when she saw him. He ran over to her, and knelt next to her, as she wrapped her arms around his neck. He stayed there embracing her as she sobbed out the story of her night. New Guy heard that she went to the diner with Furman and was jealous. He hit her, and yelled at her. She had tried to explain, but he would not listen. And she was most desperate, they were supposed to leave today for Colorado. She had already moved out of their apartment and their belongings were in a truck outside the diner.

"Can we move in with you? At least for now?"

"We?" Furman asked, wiping the hair out of Stacey's face. Stacey turned her eyes toward the other side of the booth. Furman turned to see Sarah sitting innocently. She looked up at him and beamed, "Daddy!" How had he missed her? He stood up and she jumped out of the booth into his arms.

"Of course!" he cried, and laughed, and cried, "Of course you can stay with me!"

Furman convinced them to walk with him to the apartment, it was not far. They could go back for the truck later. And so they walked, hand-in-hand. The crowd had diminished for some reason and they walked together without any resistance. Furman told Sarah about Chris, and said they could play together, or at least stare at each other through the hole in the wall. She laughed.

They need me, Furman repeated to himself over and over as they got closer to home. And he smiled as he looked at them. But his gaze drifted up, to a quiet apartment building on the corner of the street, before the overpass. There on the ground was the Man, the homeless one, not the one from the dream. He was still laying down, but propped himself up on his elbow. Furman tried to look at his face, but he couldn't focus. And he heard his words from the other night, "Go home, Furman." Of course, he didn't really hear them, he just remembered them, and was distracted by what he remembered.

Furman's shoe caught a crack in the sidewalk. He didn't even have time to put his arms out to break his fall. But he didn't feel any pain, everything went black.

He woke up with a jolt, and realized he was sitting up. He ran his fingers through his long beard. Light streamed through one of his throne room windows, warming his face. And from the darkness behind the light, he heard a voice.

"Good morning, Sire."

The Darkness Behind the Light

Dave Hare

Dave Hare and his wife Stacey are missionary linguists in Cameroon, Africa. They have four children and live among the Kwakum people. When not in Cameroon, they spend most of their time in Dallas, studying and researching at the Graduate Institute of Applied Linguistics. If he's not studying, teaching, killing snakes, or planting trees, Dave enjoys reading and writing. "The Darkness Behind the Light" is his first published short story.

The Turnspit Dog
by H. J. Hill

Hot.

The wind rises and even my stunted nose catches a new scent on the air as it drifts past. All I must do is face the breeze. That is how I picked up her scent from afar the first day, the morning she rode into the dying town on her handsome horse.

Had I not been so scared, had my feet not hurt so much, had I not been panting just to stay alive on that treadmill, I would have barked to grab her attention. As it came to pass, I did not have to. My long groaning to be free had fallen on unseen ears. My answer entered my narrow world on a dignified animal the color of a night sky without stars.

She did not understand that she was there for my sake. She thought the whole thing was her idea. Humans make that mistake often. It is part of their arrogance. To be able to recognize your rescuer a mile off is a gift. If your rescuer recognizes herself, even better—less to mess up, less to get wrong.

I locked my eyes on them, the lady under her wide-brimmed hat, and the horse decked out in fancy trappings. Closer, closer. Watching their approach kept my thoughts off my bleeding feet, my parched throat. The bowl of dirty water sat forever out of my reach. The Hard Man placed it so that I would always be tempted and would keep on moving the treadmill in disappointed hope.

The water was filthy. Still, water is water.

The lady tightened her reins. The mighty horse pulled up short. They see me, I thought. The lady's face froze in the heat. She threw one leg over the horse and dropped. A single step toward me. She stopped. The sun streaked her hair and lit up the silver strands sprinkled through it.

How ugly I must have looked. Matted hair. Caked mud. Once, in my young days, I saw my reflection in a glass on a

The Turnspit Dog

human building. Crumpled face. A large patch of short black hair encircled one eye, brown and white over the other one. Broad shoulders. Low slung. Not sleek or shiny like the hunters. Made only for hard pulling or wearisome work too small for the horses and that the humans did not favor.

I lowered my eyes and kept treading my wheel, turning the spit that held the roasting meat over the fire coals. Two boots materialized in front of me, the toes pointed in my direction. Then they disappeared. Oh, well, I thought. I had made the whole thing up in my head.

Water splashed on the ground. The pump handle clanked. Water splashed again, this time against metal. Light hit the clean, full water bowl that appeared under my muzzle. I stopped my treading and ducked my head, daring my eyes to peek upward, my coward's glance.

She knelt beside me. "Try that," she said, running her hand under my belly. "Girl."

The sweet cool water unglued my tongue from the roof of my mouth. I drank the bowl dry. The tight metal links that tied me to my treadmill eased, loosened. She drew the chain over my head and threw it away. It rang against the iron stake that held its other end prisoner.

Change.

She put her hand under my neck. The track of my treadmill wheel ran dark down the middle, stained by my bloody prints. I took a free breath and stepped from it.

"You! Woman! Just what are you fixin' to do with my dog?" The harsh voice belonged to Hard Man who ran the turnspit and me.

"I'm fixin' to buy her from you." The lady slipped a shiny flat rock from a pouch in her trail skirt and held it up to catch the sunlight.

"Pig's not done," said Hard Man.

"Yes, you are," the lady said, none too loudly. I was the only one who heard it and I did not repeat it. "Twenty-dollar gold piece for the dog and a decent slice off the overdone underside of that pig. The coin's good. Go ahead. Bite it if you want to."

Hard Man snatched the shiny rock and bit it. Biting shiny rocks must be a human game. I have never played it. His mouth twisted the way it did right before he would beat me for being slow or not understanding what he wanted, so I stepped back.

"Twenty dollars, in gold." He spat on the ground at my feet. "You made a mighty poor bargain." He drew his long knife, looked at the lady, looked at me, and sawed a hunk of meat from the carcass, slapping it onto crinkled paper. He tossed it to the lady and she made a good catch. Of course, I would have caught it for her happily had she missed. "There. Worthless dog's yours, too, and good riddance."

The lady patted the side of her leg and I limped behind her as fast as I could. After the treadmill, the soft red sand felt like cushions. She walked her horse to the back of the stable next to the shed where the blacksmith made hot, bitter smells with his clashing metal.

Shade.

My night spot. I wanted to run, to catch up with the lady, but my legs rebelled against speed. I was afraid she might forget me. I need not have worried. She tied her horse to a rail and pulled a fat bag from her saddle.

While she dug through her pack, I slinked to a hidden corner of the building and forced my sore feet to dig for treasure. A shallow depth down I struck it, just as I had left it. My large bone, the one I had escaped with after the rough men finished one of their mighty meals. I've gotten good at sneaking. Had they caught me, they would have begrudged me even their scrap and my thieving would have earned me at least one booted kick.

That bone was worth the risk. I wondered if the lady would give me a kick for having it. But no, she didn't seem the kicking kind.

The sound of ripping tore the quiet. The lady sat by her pack, a lake of white cotton cloth overflowing her lap.

She wagged her head. "I don't know what I was thinking, bringing a full petticoat with me into West Texas. What do I need with such a garment out here? No family gatherings. No cotillions. No costume balls."

She gazed back toward where the sun rolled into the sky every morning, the direction from which she had ridden. She did that a lot. When I look back, it is to guard against being followed. The lady hungered for something she had left back there, maybe a treasure like mine.

"Come on, girl. This'll do to bandage those poor feet of yours. What've you got there...a bone? Bring it over. You can gnaw while I wrap."

I shied to one side. She held out her open hand. What if she stole it? But what did that matter? A naked bone was the least I owed her for setting me free from Hard Man. I halted with each aching step and deposited my only possession at her crossed feet.

She reached toward me, but let the bone be. Instead she caught a paw and wound a thin strip of the cloth around it, tying it so it would stay on, at least until I tugged it off, which I planned to do at the first chance. After she bandaged my front feet, I went to chewing on my bone, and let her fool with the back ones to her heart's content.

She pointed to the old puncture marks on my legs and touched them softly. "Scars. Well, we've all got 'em, don't we?"

I did not see hers. They must have been covered.

"I was going to spend the night in that little hotel down the street, but I've lost my taste for this place,"

The place never had tasted good to me.

She tied her pack behind the saddle and walked her horse to the far side of the smithy where the mounting block stood. After she settled herself astride the lovely beast and laid her rolled blanket across the front of the saddle, she motioned for me to use the block to launch myself aboard.

I climbed in front of her and we walked away—the lady, the horse, and me. Once in the clear, I looked back. The treadmill wheel stood still, empty. Turning the spit was a small boy, one that belonged to a woman that Hard Man talked to and laughed with and visited often at night. I wished that my lady had another of those flat shiny rocks, so she could buy the boy free. But no, humans do not let other humans go so easily.

I caught Hard Man's eyes. His face dropped. I looked away. Never lock eyes with a predator. That dog law had kept me alive. The humans should have such a law.

"What am I going to call you?" the lady asked. "How about Boney? I mean, you with your prize bone and you haven't exactly been overfed. Boney sounds about right."

I perked my ears forward. I had been called much worse.

"My name is Liberty. Folks call me Libby for short. Liberty means freedom. I guess I've been short of that for a while." She gazed into my eyes and laughed. "You, too, I reckon. Laugh about life. If we stop laughing, we may as well stop breathing."

We met a thin, shallow stream. After a meal for me and Libby and our horse, we rested. Libby changed my foot bandages and washed the blood-stained ones in the rippling water. One strip floated away, but she didn't bother chasing it.

When we mounted again, Libby headed our horse upstream in the middle of the river. After a while, we walked out of the water and made a trail before zagging back into the river and upstream again. Then we walked out of the river to the other side and zagged back in downstream. That must have been another human game that I did not know.

Night.

The blackest night. I couldn't see my paws in front of my nose, but I knew they were still there. They hurt. The moon would rise late. Then we would have thin light.

The Turnspit Dog

We settled in a grove of thwarted trees on the side of a tall flat-topped hill. Libby sliced up the meat chunk she bought from Hard Man and laid two large pieces before me. Salt and smoke. I needed neither sunlight nor moonlight to find them. I inhaled them without chewing. She bit off a few small pieces, then wrapped up the rest in the grease-soaked paper for later. Wise human. Wiser than a dog.

The moon awakened at last. I slept. When I opened my eyes, Libby still sat guard.

"I was uneasy. Decided to keep watch. You may have gotten the short end of this bargain, girl, staying with me. I'm scared and that's one thing I can't be."

Uneasy. The human word for what you feel when you walk in the dark and a greater darkness lurks beyond your sight. My hackles rose. A sour, mean scent polluted the air and roused close memories. Hard Man. Nearby.

Libby must have smelled him, too. She stood up. Her hand rested in the pocket of her trail skirt on a thing that smelled of wood and metal and oil. And a scent of something else. A sharp, burnt, stinging odor that I only ever found around humans, one that only ever meant danger. Her hand moved. The object clicked.

Hard Man's boot crunched and slid on loose rocks. I focused my nose and ears toward the sound. For a human, Libby was bright. She tracked my gaze. The moon had taken our part. Its light glinted off the crooked metal tool in Hard Man's hand.

"I know you're there, woman. This can go easy for you. Or hard. Makes no never mind to me. I came for them rich coins. I figure you got a sight more of them. Nobody hands over their last gold coin for a two-bit dog and a hunk of pork. That old trash dog still with you?"

He shot his eyes from side to side, looking for me. I stayed still and quiet.

"Yep. Run off, did he? Just like him. Don't think to hide from me. Sun'll be up sooner or later. I can tarry."

Then the moon betrayed us. I backed deeper into the shadows, but Libby shone. "She."

"What?"

"She, not he, the dog I mean. You should have at least known that."

"Well, there's that sassy mouth."

Libby stood straighter. "You're a gifted tracker."

He dangled a strip of cotton petticoat in the air. I scented my faded blood on it.

"Be careful what you leave behind," he said. "Now give over that purse of yours."

"I think not."

Hard Man sneered. "Never been robbed before, huh? There's a first time for everything."

"No, there's not." Libby's hand clamped down on the thing in her pocket. She pressed her lips together until the blood in them retreated. "I keep my words mostly between me and God. But I must warn you now, though you don't deserve it. A very dangerous thing is about to happen."

Hard Man laughed. "I know." He stepped toward her.

"Come no closer." Her hand never left her pocket. "This is your chance. Turn around. Take your leave. I forgive you."

Hard Man's mouth opened in a dry pant. He stepped back. "I heard that sort of nonsense when I was a kid. It meant nothing then. It means nothing now."

I don't know what forgive is. Humans understand more than dogs do. I thought forgive might be a big stick. I saw no new weapon in Libby's hands, but her words struck a blow to Hard Man's chest.

"Nobody will come looking for you. An old woman out here all alone."

"Who are you calling an old woman? As for alone, I'm never that."

The Turnspit Dog

It's a rough thing, being a coward. I have been one my whole life. No more time for that. Libby did a big thing for me. I would do a big thing for her. Hard Man recovered the step he lost. I recovered five and flew out of the darkness. The pain in my feet vanished as I jumped. From the look on his face, I guess all he saw were my fangs glowing in the moonlight.

My gripping teeth sank into the hand that held his crooked tool. I ground into one finger and twisted. He punched me with his other hand. Blood filled my mouth. His blood. He screamed and held his crippled hand up. The middle finger was missing. Not missing. The nasty thing lay on my tongue. I hadn't meant to do that. It must not have been attached very well.

I spat it out. He staggered on his feet, so I picked a new target. My fangs sank into his flesh, this time between where his legs joined his body. He grasped the hair at my neck, then choked on his own spit and gurgled as he fell at Libby's feet. I shook him a few times for good measure.

Libby studied him. He breathed, but that was all.

"So, dog eat dog. Well done, girl!"

I panted my widest smile. The night air helped sponge the nasty taste from my mouth. The lump of human clay at our feet groaned once.

"Now, what to do with this mess."

We rode back into the dying toadstool of a town under a red sunrise. As it turned out, Libby was good with ropes and horses. She used both his animal and ours to winch Hard Man up and over his saddle. She lashed his feet to a stirrup so he wouldn't fall off onto his ugly head. Why she bothered, I didn't understand. The fall might have knocked some of the mean out of him. Libby was nicer than I was.

The town's two laziest men strolled out of the smithy. Libby tossed Hard Man's reins to one.

"You don't appear to have any law around here. This man came out to rob me and leave me dead and done. He failed and has earned his reward." She pinched another flat shiny rock from her purse and flipped it to him. "Here's a coin for his upkeep 'til he comes to himself. Any more than that, he can pay for on his own. Considering all the trouble he's caused us, that's generous."

The man who caught stuff snorted. "Well, aren't you the Good Samaritan!"

"No. I'm not. I'm about half good sometimes. Maybe."

Libby rode us straight out of that town but much slower than I would have liked. I didn't look back. We walked steady until we were clean out of their sight. Only then did Libby stir up our horse. We jounced along until we met the thin, shallow river again and she pulled up.

By sunset, we were treading higher ground. Libby set our camp on the side of another flat-topped hill. She sat beside me and threw an arm over my shoulders.

The big, whirling bowl overhead filled with streams of stars. White fire shot from one side of the sky wheel to the other. Libby breathed in deep, so I did, too.

"Lord, we're out here by ourselves, but we're not alone. Remember us and how small we are."

The turnspit wheel above us kept spinning, and there we sat beneath it, small but remembered.

H. J. Hill

H.J. Hill used to practice law but found out that she likes writing short stories a whole lot more. She resides in Texas with five bulldogs—none of whom write—but all of whom do provide fodder for her blog, "Bulldoggy." In addition to those involving dogs, her dark fantasy and steampunk stories have appeared in anthologies published by Emby Press, Pill Hill Press, and other publications.

Marshmallow Dragon
by Dana L. Horton

The dragon egg hatched, late in the night, deep in a forest, far from anyone. Dragon mommies and daddies do not raise their babies, because they don't stay babies for long. Slimy and white, the tiny dragon tumbled forth into the world, knowing himself to be called, Marzipan. The name came to him like a thought, and he knew it was his. The marshmallow dragon started out the size of a toaster. With each breath, he grew bigger. Moments later, he was the size of a bathtub, a dinner table, a car. An hour later, a properly-sized dragon lay on his side, resting from the work of being born.

Once on his feet, the young dragon lolloped through the forest until he came to a clearing. He felt strange in his skin. Something needed to be done. His body didn't feel quite as he thought it should. Sinking his belly low to the ground, he swayed his back and tilted his chin toward the stars. Clear, syrupy liquid oozed from his skin as he stretched. *Ahhh.* He arched his back toward the night sky. A sticky noise came from behind him, like thick tape being pulled from its roll. *Fwap-Fwap!* He craned his neck to see what had caused the sound and found a large pair of scaly, marshmallow wings sticking out of his back. He watched them thicken as the moments passed until they were hearty and strong like the rest of him. *Ooooooh!*

He ran in great circles around the meadow, thrashing wildly—until finally, with a few great flaps of his wings, he left the ground below. As he flew through the night, his body cooled in the brisk air, stripping him of the slickness of birth. He felt wonderful! Coasting high above the forest, dipping and gliding, he felt his body growing stronger. He could also feel something else. *Hunger.* His great stomach rumbled and growled, needing food. Marzipan stretched out his neck, lowered his head, and directed his body to follow.

The dragon was no longer a wet baby. He landed as a fully grown, young, marshmallow dragon. And that is another thing entirely. His huge feet touched down softly not far from where he took off. *Hungry.* He lumbered toward the tree line. With each step, however, Marzipan noticed clumps of grass were sticking to his feet. He shook a leg. The grass still stuck. He shook his other leg in turn, but the grass wouldn't budge.

Sitting on a log, he tried to get the grass off. Stomping and shaking his feet did nothing. Rubbing them together just created thick rolls of grass, but they were still stuck to him. Using his teeth, he gnawed at the grass, until he decided it was too much work to do on an empty stomach. Besides, using his teeth made his mouth feel itchy. He stood up and found his bottom felt heavier than before, but hunger had taken over, and Marzipan didn't want to stop anymore. Not until he found food.

Roaming through the forest, grassy feet and all, he was abruptly stopped from behind. Something was holding him! Marzipan peered behind himself into the darkness, but couldn't see anything. He pulled hard, but couldn't move. Digging his feet into the forest floor, he pulled with all his might. *Rrrahhhhhhhh!* A great ripping sound came from behind him and he was free. He ran, barreling forward through the trees. As he went, he bumped things and things bumped him.

An unmistakable smell wafted into his large nostrils. *Food!* He skidded to a halt. Head low, he sniffed the ground until he found a patch of delicious little fiddlehead ferns. He ate them all. He could see a big green leaf was now stuck to the side of his nose. As he breathed in and out, it fluttered. Marzipan shook his head and pawed at the leaf until finally it came off and stuck to his foot. He furrowed his puffy brows and squidged up his mouth in frustration. *Rrrrrrrrrr*

With a belly full of fiddleheads, Marzipan now found himself very *thirsty*. He listened to the sounds of the forest and followed them to a fair-sized lake. Frogs hidden in the tall reeds croaked loudly. Like a mirror, the surface of the lake reflected everything around it. The dragon's feet sank into the soft mud near the edge of the water.

He stretched his long neck out over the water. *Rrrrrrrrrr!* He backed up quickly! A monster as white as he, with a bright green, shaggy mouth was in the lake! He sat in the mud waiting. When nothing happened, he peeked into the lake again, tilting his head left and right. The thing in the water tilted its head, too. As Marzipan leaned down for a sniff, so, too, did the thing in the water, until their noses touched, and the water rippled. *Me?* He realized the big, white monster was his reflection and that shaggy green beard was nothing more than grass and fiddleheads stuck to his face. *Nuwft-nuuwft! Nuwft-nuuwft! Nuwft!* He couldn't help but laugh at himself.

Upon further inspection, he saw that all sorts of things were stuck to his body and wings. There were leaves and twigs stuck to his neck. Bugs and vines pasted to his sides. Sticks, toadstools, smashed wild berries and dirt were glued to his underbelly, and a small cluster of bats were trying to extract themselves from his wings. He thought of his heavy bottom and turned it to face toward the water. *Bark.* A thick stripe of brown bark, freshly ripped off the log he had sat on, was stuck tight across his backside! Everything he touched seemed to be sticking to him. *Uhhhhhhh.*

Licking the bats repeatedly, he managed to remove them from his wings. He discovered that once they were covered in dragon drool, they slid right off. Not happy with being licked, the bats screeched loudly and flew away into the forest. Feeling a bit low about his situation, Marzipan curled his tail around his body, but quickly discovered not only did he stick to everything around him, he also stuck to himself! He plopped his bottom on the ground and dragged himself along like an

Marshmallow Dragon

itchy dog, trying to remove the bark. He rubbed his backside against rocks and tried pulling at his tail, which only stuck more of him to himself.

Nothing worked, so he threw himself into the lake, where he promptly popped back up to the surface. Marshmallow dragons don't sink. He just bobbed around, trying to rid himself of everything that had stuck. Marzipan enjoyed the water. He sloshed around, taking gulps of water, to quench his thirst. Rolling over onto his back, he poked at his wet belly and then at his swollen feet. *Squishy. Not sticky!* A milky white circle grew around him. He gazed at it curiously. A thought occurred to him. *Am I melting?* He rubbed his tail against his belly and held it over a dark area of the water. A single milky white drop of waterlogged marshmallow juice dripped into the lake. *Aaaaahhhh!* Marzipan clambered out of the lake as fast as his puffed-up, squishy legs could carry him! *Melting!!*

He lay on the mud bank and dried in the night air. He could feel the water run back out of his swollen body. When he stood up to leave, the smooth mud was stuck to him. He dipped his feet into it, coating them thickly. Then he walked around in the grass. After a moment, he inspected his feet. While there was some brown grass stuck to him, it was not nearly as much as before. *Not sticky. Not melting.* Marzipan covered himself from head to toe in mud. Gazing into the water, he realized he looked more like a chocolate dragon than a marshmallow one. The sight of his face covered in mud made him snort loudly again. *Nuwft-nuuwft! Nuwft-nuuwft!*

He squelched off happily through the forest, dripping mud. The leaves and vines slid along his sides as he walked, but they didn't stick. In the clearing, he took to the sky once more. This time he struggled to get off the ground. The mud had made him less sticky, but it created another problem—it made him a lot heavier. The wind began drying the mud as he flew. Marzipan felt himself getting lighter and lighter as the water evaporated. The mud on his wings dried first and fell away in chunks. His broad chest heaved as he flew. His lungs swelled, and the mud on his chest burst into pieces and showered the ground below. The more he flew, the drier the mud became. Wind pried the dried clumps of mud from his skin, flinging them into the darkness. By the time he landed in the meadow, he was mud-free and sticky once more. Exhausted and disheartened, Marzipan slept.

By morning, a shaggy, grass-covered dragon was sprawled on his back, with his big pink tongue dangling from his mouth. He awoke and looked around him. Everywhere the dragon rolled while asleep was bare. He inspected his belly and legs, then the rest of himself. Every inch of the formerly mud-covered dragon was now coated in bright green grass. It stuck out all over. He swashed his tail from side to side. *Not sticky.* But imagining what he must look like sent him into a fit of snorting laughter. *Nuwft-nuuwft! Nuwft-nuuwft! Bush Dragon! Nuwft-nuuwft! Nuwft-nuuwft!*

He was a mess of dirt clods and green tufts. After the laughing died down, Marzipan realized he felt *itchy.* He scratched himself in a few places. He inspected his itchy arms, then his big belly. Bugs living in the grass, which was now stuck to his skin, were crawling all over him. *Bugs!* Marzipan sped back to the lake as fast as he could go! This time, he only stayed in the water long enough to wash off.

Clean again, he decided to try something new. Kicking his feet very quickly and flapping his wings, he took flight, right from the water. High in the sky, he coasted lazily, examining himself. *Clean.* And he was. Marzipan was as clean and white as a cloud and being a marshmallow dragon, he blended in perfectly with them. He spent the day flying across the land, this way and that. Higher and higher he went, until the air grew unpleasantly cold. The wind changed and began to stiffen his wings. A thin coating of ice covered him. He worried he might freeze solid if he kept flying. *Cold.* He felt his skin. *Not sticky.* Landing meant things would stick to him again, but flying

Marshmallow Dragon

forever was impossible, as impossible as keeping things from sticking to his marshmallow skin.

In the distance, something orange flickered on the ground below. Dragons, being curious creatures, can't help themselves sometimes, so Marzipan swooped downward toward the light. The thin layer of ice on his skin melted as he flew lower again. Without thought, he folded his wings back, against his body and sped up. His eyes narrowed against the wind. The dragon aimed his body straight for the lights, which grew brighter as he flew nearer. The air smelled of trees, and grass. And something else. Swiftly, he closed in on the area, watching the lights as they changed, dancing in the night. Hypnotized by the colorful show, Marzipan zoomed downward! Yellow, red and orange streaks leapt from the trees, spreading like...*Wild Fire!*

The dragon was headed straight for the fire, intending to turn quickly just before going through the flames. That is not what happened. Marzipan had forgotten about his wings. They were folded back against his body. *Hmffftp! Hmmmmmpt! Stuck!* Using his head, he turned himself, just enough to miss the center of the flames, but he didn't miss one of the taller pine trees.

Huummmpt!! Ooph! Ooofph!! Hmmmmffpt! Ooooorlll! The sticky dragon banged, bumped, and tumbled his way down the tree. He dangled from a sturdy lower limb for a moment —stuck until its bark pulled off, landing Marzipan in a heap on the ground. Pine needles and wood clumps on his body showed every place he had hit the tree as he fell. An empty owl's nest sat upon his head like a tiny, squashed hat.

A very angry woodpecker tried unsuccessfully to pull its beak off one of Marzipan's legs. After a moment of watching the frantic bird, the dragon leaned over and licked it helpfully. The woodpecker was furious and poked the dragon with its beak. Marzipan snorted and snuffled, laughing at the bird, which was now stuck to and dangling from his nose. After he stopped laughing, he kindly licked the woodpecker into freedom again. The angry bird buzzed by his head, just for good measure, which tickled the dragon to no end! *Bird! Nuwft-nuuwft, Nuwft-nuuwft! Nuuuuuuwft! Nuwft-Nuuwft!*

Crackling and popping sounds from the fire filled the air. Evaporating water hissed from trees. Marzipan sat on the ground not noticing. He was busy, trying to unstick himself from the forest. His tail was feeling strangely warm. He looked for it, but being such a long tail, it was further away, trailing behind him. Circling around on himself, he looked down the line of his tail, which had grown much warmer now. Marzipan knew there was a fire and that it was warm, but he couldn't understand why his tail would be *hot!* Curling it toward him, a ball of fire on its tip came with it. *Tail! Fire!*

The dragon thrashed his tail on the ground, but the flames didn't go out. He pulled it to his mouth and gave a few quick puffs of air to blow it out. The flames flickered, but didn't die. He drew a deeper breath. *Huuuuuhhhhhh. . .*Flames leapt from his tail into his open mouth. He swallowed them. *Guuuulp?* His belly instantly felt weird, like it did when he was hungry, but different. He jammed the flaming tail in his mouth and slobbered the flames out. Something was different inside his belly now. *Mmmmmm?* Taking his tail out of his mouth, he could see his usually pure white tail was now a pretty golden-brown color. He screwed up his face trying to figure out why. A loud bang came from somewhere deeper inside the fire.

Billowing smoke and flames raced toward Marzipan. He decided he should probably do something to stop the fire. His toasted tail dragged the ground as he turned in circles deciding what to do. He looked back and realized the end of his tail that had turned brown wasn't sticking to things now. He curled it closer for a better look. *Clean.* He swashed it left and right over the plants and leaves on the ground. *Clean!* The fire had fixed his tail. It wasn't sticky anymore! But, too much fire made him feel hot, like he was right now. Marzipan knew it was time for action.

Marshmallow Dragon

He took off and soared high above the flaming forest once more. Using wind from his wings, he put out a few small pockets of fire but the bulk of it raged on. *Blow.* Marzipan drew a deep breath and lowered himself until he was just above the tree tops. Then, with all his dragon might, he blew toward the fire. White, orange and red flames shot from his mouth like a cannon of fire! *Rrrraaaaahhhh! Huh?* The feeling in his belly rumbled harder, like thunder, tumbling and churning. Smoke curled from his nostrils. He blew at the fire again and created an even bigger fire. *No!* He gave up blowing and flapped wildly at the fire with his wings. His marshmallow skin grew hotter and hotter as he flew close to the flames, extinguishing them. He battled valiantly until the flames were dead.

By nightfall, he landed on a small patch of cool grass still left in his meadow, miles from the smell of burnt trees. He slept through the next morning and into the afternoon. He awoke to the sun high in the sky and inspected his whole self. *Clean.* His skin was copper-brown from the fire, but it wasn't sticky anymore. He looked at the grass around him—it was all still on the ground, as it was the night before. He rubbed himself against things throughout the forest, testing for stickiness. Even the bats didn't stick anymore! *Not sticky!* He galloped to the edge of the lake and looked at his reflection. No grass. No bark. He was beautifully browned, and *NOT STICKY!*

In celebration, he threw himself into the lake! *Woooo!* He floated smiling until he felt himself puffing up again. Sloshing his way out of the water, he sat on the bank where fallen leaves and a bullfrog promptly stuck to his shins. The lovely color had melted off. *Too wet.* He was sticky again. Frustrated, he let out a big sigh. *Huuupppptttt. . .* Flames shot out across the water. *Fire!* He needed fire to brown himself again so he could stop being sticky!

He jumped in the lake, washed quickly, pulled off the bullfrog, then flew straight up from the water, clean and white once more. The marshmallow dragon twisted, turned, and made loops in the air, blowing rings and clouds of fire to fly through. He went on and on—until he was the most beautifully toasted marshmallow dragon anywhere. When he landed, he knew that this was what marshmallow dragons were meant to do. And he would never have to be sticky again.

Dana Horton

Originally from Philadelphia, Pennsylvania, Dana Horton moved to Texas in 1994. She and husband Ron have two children and one grandson. For a decade, Dana worked with children in the United States and England. She is a Certified Activity Director and majored in Elementary Education in college. Dana enjoys travelling, reading, and playing ukulele, quite badly. She always wears flowers in her hair.

Life Motto: You have to grow old, you don't have to grow up!

In Search of the Big Trees
by Eldon Irving

With such a title, you might expect a story about redwoods or sequoias, but this adventure takes place in Texas, and although the word "big" is a modifier of almost everything in Texas, there are no redwoods or sequoias here.

After retiring from forty-three years of ministry, my wife and I do volunteer work at state parks. It is a win-win situation. We do some hours of volunteer work, which is a win for the state, and we are given a free site for our trailer, which is a win for us. Wherever we serve, on our days off, we search for interesting things to see in the area.

At Garner State Park in the Texas Hill Country, we heard that in the area, there were three of the biggest trees in Texas. Since most of the trees near our site were pecans, and the hills around us were covered with cedar and smaller trees, the word "big" sounded a bit incongruous.

"But these big trees are not in the park," we were told. "One is in Rio Frio, another in Utopia, and the third is in Concan."

All these places are tiny dots on the big Texas map, but we set off in search of the big trees.

Our first stop was the larger town of Leaky (population 387) to get more specific directions. Several people didn't know anything about the Rio Frio tree, but finally one person told us, "To get to Rio Frio, go down here and turn left at the Texaco station, then take the first right on a little country road. You go for a spell, you cross the river, then there's a church on the left, and the tree is on the right."

The first part was easy. We found the Texaco station and the little country road, but when we crossed the river not once but three times and there was no church, I began to wonder how long "a spell" was. Finally, we came to a small building

In Search of the Big Trees

with a sign "Rio Frio Post Office," but no one was there. Oh, well, it was a beautiful day and a nice drive. After we crossed the river yet again, I thought maybe the directions were given like some cooks give their recipes—a bit of this, a bit of that, with nothing really precise, but be patient and it will all work out. And it did.

We finally came to a church on the left, and back off the road on the right near an old house was a huge Texas live oak, the trunk partially hidden by the long branches hanging almost to the ground. You would have to get closer to really see it. The old house looked abandoned, but next door, a woman was working in her back yard.

"Excuse me. We heard that this big tree was one of the largest trees in Texas. Is it all right to walk on the property to see it?"

"Sure," she said, as she picked up a little puppy that was dancing around our legs. "Go ahead. No one has lived there for years."

As we moved closer, the big tree came into full view. As compared to all the other trees around, it stood as a mighty king rising above all the pawns below. However, it was a benevolent king, for even though it dwarfed the other trees and the house itself, it allowed one of its huge branches to hold a rope swing on which children had probably sat.

Near the tree was a plaque informing us that the tree had been a meeting spot for settlers to gather in the early days of the area, and a school had been built near its shading branches. Because of its huge size, the tree was used as the reference point for the first lot of the town, and since all additional lots were tied to the first, this oak is a reference point for the entire town. The plaque was respectfully signed, "Friends of the Big Tree."

After several pictures and a prayer of thanksgiving for the beauty of the big tree, we set out on our second search—on to Utopia.

Even if there had not been a big tree in Utopia, we would have had to go there. How can you not visit a place with the name Utopia? The town is small, but the tree is big. We were directed to a bed and breakfast, and the nice lady inside pointed us to the river, where less than a hundred yards away stood a tremendously huge bald cypress. There were other cypress trees around, but we didn't notice them at first, for our eyes were drawn to the size of this overpowering magnificent tree. As we stood there in awe, I wondered how old this tree might be. Just at that moment, one of the gardeners appeared, and I asked him.

"I'm not sure. My guess would be 400 or maybe 500 years. The lady inside would know."

And indeed she did, for when we approached her with this question, she responded, "It has been estimated at 860 years old."

I thought to myself, *This tree was here over 500 years before we became a nation—over 400 years before the Pilgrims landed on Plymouth Rock—over 300 years before Columbus discovered America. This tree is not only big; it is ancient!*

We took pictures. I wore a red shirt that showed up as a small red speck against the massive trunk. I felt like a Lilliputian sitting under the arm of Gulliver. Yet, underneath the tree, was a sign that read, "This is not the biggest tree in Texas!"

So on to the biggest tree in our search. This tree was reported to be in the town of Concan. The directions I got were even vaguer than those for Rio Frio, but I thought, *Concan is tiny. Just go there and ask someone.*

The first couple of tries brought only blank stares, and I thought, *How can people be living close to something so big and so unique and not know about it?* Then I remembered stopping to get information at a service station a few miles from the Grand Canyon, and the person said, "I'm sorry. I don't know anything about the Grand Canyon. I've lived in this area all my life, but I've never been there."

Eventually, I found someone who knew someone next door who knew about the tree. "Hey, neighbor, there's a gentleman here who wants to find the big tree. Can you tell him?"

He looked at me and said, "I can tell you where it is, but it's on private property. The lady used to let people come see it, but they began to litter. You can ask her, but I'm pretty sure what she'll say."

"What if I told her I'm a retired minister and promise not to litter and not to hurt her tree?"

He paused, thought for a moment, and then said, "That just might work," as he reached for the phone and dialed.

"Ma'am, there's a gentleman here who is a retired preacher, and he's doing volunteer work at Garner State Park. He wondered if he and his wife could come see your big tree. (Pause) Okay, I'll tell him."

The answer was "yes." He gave me directions and mentioned that a friend of hers was there doing some work for her. A short drive took us to an entrance with a sign "Big Tree Ranch." Immediately, a young man approached us with the look that said, "This is private property."

"You're the owner's friend, right? We just talked with her and she gave us permission to see her tree."

He smiled, nodded his head, and we drove past a sign that read, "No trespassing."

We found a small one-lane road, and at the end was "The Tree." I have used up all my superlative adjectives on the other trees, but if I had any left, they would certainly fit, for this was certainly the largest tree I had ever seen. There was a plaque claiming it to be the largest bald cypress in Texas. If I open my arms as wide as I can, the measurement from fingertip to fingertip is sixty-six inches. That means if there were six of me wrapped around that tree, we still couldn't touch hands. In addition to its massive size, it is claimed to be the oldest tree in Texas. One of the locals said that the tree was 2,000 years old. That means when Jesus was praying in the Garden of Gethsemane, that tree was here.

There are many wonderful unique things to see in this world. While doing volunteer work at Garner State Park, I saw three of them.

The Grand Tour
by Eldon Irving

It was "The Grand Tour." But not like most people dream about—reading travel brochures with that title, and saying to themselves, *When I retire and have enough time and enough money I'm going to do that*—travel to Europe and do the grand tour.

This was at the other end of the spectrum. I was in my early twenties, far from retirement. Because of a scholarship, I was in school at the University of Edinburgh in Scotland. It was summer, in between classes, and the rest of Europe with all the ingredients of a grand tour was just across the English Channel. I had the time, but not the money—or very little of it.

Ron, my Irish roommate, who was in the same monetary predicament but eager to travel, came up with a three-part-solution.

"If we travel on my old motorcycle, stay in youth hostels, and fix our own food, we could do the grand tour very cheap."

"Sounds good to me."

So we prepared to set out.

What to take? On trips in the States, I had pondered the same question. On one trip, which was only a week, I took a large suitcase with several changes of clothes. *You never know what you might need*, I thought. This was way too much. On another trip, which was three weeks, I took a small suitcase. On this trip, which was to be three months, I took what would fit in the compartment on the back of the motorcycle: One change of clothes, toiletries, and a towel.

I hadn't traveled very much while growing up, so this was a unique adventure. I remember when we took the ferry to Calais and began to motor through France, it was the first time I had been in a country where they spoke another language. I thought to myself, *What a strange and yet wonderful experience.*

This first part of the grand tour solution—the motorcycle—was certainly an economical one. With seventy to eighty miles per gallon, we passed by Mercedes and BMWs as they stopped for gas. It was also fun. When I was a boy, I always dreamed of one day owning a motor scooter, and here I was on the back of a motorcycle zooming through Europe.

The motorcycle was especially fun when we drove through small villages with narrow streets and houses so close that the rumble of the motor echoed and sounded like a tank or an approaching beast. It was also fun when we roared to a stop in front of a hostel, and the kids came running to see who was on the bike.

We did discover, however, that not everything about a motorcycle is fun. Sitting on a motorcycle is not a happy place to be when it rains…especially, on the highway. It's not what's coming down that is so bad—it's what is splashing up from cars in front. We soon learned: when it rains, stop.

We also learned not to ride the brakes going down a mountain. I was sitting on the back of the bike, taking in the mountain air and beauty when all of a sudden I heard the piercing sound of Ron down shifting—once, twice, three times, as he tried unsuccessfully to manage a sharp turn. The bike left the road and finally came to a stop about five feet from a ledge that went straight down several hundred feet.

When Ron stopped shaking, he finally said, "The brakes went out."

After a moment, we continued down the mountain in low gear, thanking our guardian angel for that extra five feet.

The second part of the grand tour solution was staying in youth hostels. I don't know what the situation is now, but in the 1950s, when this trip took place, there were youth hostels set up all over Europe, about a day's journey apart. Young people on their way to visit grandma, or students just wanting to

The Grand Tour

travel, could join the international youth hostel organization (you had to be under twenty-five), and stay at youth hostels for less than a couple of dollars per night. It was dormitory style, and the showers often did not have hot water, but it was cheap. Each place had a "Mom" who set rules and hours, and saw the kids off in the morning. Some hostel Moms were hostile and very strict, while others were more lenient. We experienced one of the strict ones when we arrived fifteen minutes after her posted arrival time. That night we slept on a park bench.

We were fortunate to find a more lenient Mom one evening when we misjudged time and distance. We were heading into Switzerland, and decided to stay at a hostel about ninety miles away. We didn't realize that we were heading into the mountains.

The switchbacks sometime slowed us to twenty miles per hour, and it was after dark when we arrived and knocked on the hostel door. We were both tired and road weary, and we must have looked like bedraggled orphans, for she opened the door and let us in. Exhausted, we went straight to bed.

The next morning brought one of the magic moments of our trip. The ride up the mountain had been so dark we could see nothing but the light on the road immediately in front of the motorcycle, but the next morning we awoke to discover that the youth hostel was at the top of the mountain and on the edge of a cliff. As we stepped onto the balcony, spread out in front of us was the whole magnificent range of the Swiss Alps—awesome!

The third part of the grand tour solution was fixing our own food. This, of course, meant buying it first. Rather than supermarkets, we found small "mom and pop" shops. I learned the phrase "What's the name for this?" in three languages. I would look all over the store, and when I found what I wanted, I pulled out that phrase, and then knew what to ask for next time. This meant, however, that I had to find the article first.

One time I was looking for eggs, but couldn't find them. I went to the shop owner, and like charades tried to act out what an egg looked like. I pantomimed breaking an egg and dropping it in a pan. This brought nothing but a blank look, although it did cause other people in the shop to gather around and try to guess. The shopkeeper would go get what they guessed. I would shake my head. This happened several times. Finally, I flapped my arms and clucked like a chicken. This was too much for Ron, who was shyer than I, and he quietly slipped out of the shop. But I got the eggs. In case you're wondering, we were in Germany and the word is "die Eier."

We cooked in the hostels and made sandwiches, which we ate on the road. In France, we bought long loaves of French bread, which were so fluffy and good that we ate them with cheese and wine in one sitting. In Germany, there was heavy dark bread, which lasted several meals and ended up being fried. In Austria, we drank dark beer. In Italy, we fixed pasta with the locals. In Spain, we picked oranges from trees along the Mediterranean. In Switzerland, we ate chocolate. In Denmark, we ate something I can't pronounce.

We visited museums, castles, and churches all over Europe. We saw paintings that I had only seen in books. In cities, we would go to Gray Line tours, look at their brochures, and then go on our own to see the sites. We walked up the Eiffel Tower. (Cheaper than taking the elevator). In Vienna, I saw my first opera. (Standing room ticket.) In Brussels, we saw the World's Fair.

Everywhere, I took pictures: Children playing and dancing in village streets, fishermen mending their nets by the sea, women hanging their washing out to dry, old men fishing by the river, artists painting by a flowered hillside. We saw things and met people that most tourists do not. In three months, we traveled over 4,000 miles through more than a dozen countries.

Forty years later, I traveled once again to Europe. This time I had hot water showers. I ate in restaurants. I traveled

The Grand Tour

with Gray Line Tours to see the sites. I sat in a seat to see an opera. It was nice, but it was not nearly as special and magical as that first student grand tour.

Rain Check
by Eldon Irving

In my forty-three years of ministry, I have performed the wedding ceremony for lots of couples, but this one was unique. The bride was an arborist, working in and loving the out-of-doors. She wanted the ceremony to be outside, so she and the groom chose to have it in a little courtyard at the Belmont Hotel in Dallas—a sixty-year-old establishment, which has managed to maintain its 1940s charm.

During the premarital counseling, I asked the couple if they had any alternate plan in case it rained. They looked at each other, and after a long pause, one of them offered, "Well, sort of...I'm sure the hotel has a place inside somewhere in case it rains." Then quickly and briskly, the bride added, "But it isn't going to rain!"

During the evening of the rehearsal, the sky was overcast, but there was no hint of rain. The forecast for the next day was a twenty percent chance of rain, but that had been the forecast for several days earlier, and no rain had materialized.

The day of the wedding was again overcast, but as the day crept along, no rain. I was to meet the groom in the hotel's lounge at 6:15 pm. We were to move into the courtyard at 6:30 where we would be given a signal that the bride was ready to come in from the other side, and I was to nod to the musical ensemble to begin the wedding march.

At 6:00, when I was about to drive into the hotel driveway...you guessed it. It started to rain. However, it not only rained; it was a deluge! I had to drive up close to the small overhang at the front door of the hotel and crawl over to get out of the car on the passenger side, while the valet attendant got soaked getting into the driver's side.

Inside the hotel, the groom was nowhere to be seen, but the small lounge was quickly filling up with wedding guests

Rain Check

and musicians who scrambled in from the weather, awaiting information where to go now. Wondering what was the "Well, sort of alternative plan," I asked the hotel clerk, "Now that it is raining, where is the wedding to take place?" She momentarily looked blank, but then suggested, "I suppose it could be in the lounge." The only contact I was able to make with the wedding party was by cell phone with the groom's parents, who agreed that the lounge would be the best place. Quickly, several wedding guests were recruited to rearrange the lounge furniture so the ceremony could be held there. Then further word came—again by cell phone—that the bride desperately wanted the ceremony outside as planned, and couldn't we postpone, hoping the rain would stop. Evidently, several people in the wedding party had opinions of what was the best plan of action, but the wishes of the bride won out as we waited for the rain to cease. Meanwhile, the musicians, who were booked for one hour (6:30 to 7:30), announced that if we postponed, they would need more money.

At a few minutes after seven, miraculously, the rain began to slow down, and as it momentarily came to a stop, frantic efforts were made to dry the outside chairs, set up the musicians under an eave, get the guests to come quickly outside—all in order to begin the service before it started raining again.

Just as we were getting ready to start, sirens went off. Was this a tornado warning? Everyone searched the skies, divining whether to go back into the hotel or wait it out. No one moved. Then, after what seemed like an eternity, the sirens stopped.

"Let's do this thing!" I said frantically.

The groom was ready. The wedding guests were ready. The musicians were ready. But as we looked to the area where the bride was to come out—no bride. More cell phone calls. Then after another eternity, the bride appeared in the doorway, I signaled the musicians to begin, the bride came down the stone pathway on the arm of her father. She dropped his arm, she took her place beside the groom, and now the service could begin.

But all of this had taken its toll on the bride. This beautiful and delightful young woman, who every other time I met her radiated joy and happiness, now stood before me stone-faced, as if in a coma.

Before beginning the service, I offered her a warm smile, hoping to assure her that now everything was all right. No response; no recognition.

Maybe the words of the service will help, I thought. *They are beautiful words.* I spoke of the beauty of marriage. I spoke of the love of God. I read from the love chapter of the Bible—beautiful words from the Apostle Paul, which often brought tears to the eyes of those who stood before me in past weddings. Still no response; no recognition. During the exchanging of the vows, she spoke the words as if they came out of a text-to-speech computer. The exchange of rings was just that—a mere exchange. No apparent emotion.

Then, finally, I spoke the words, "For as much as these two have consented to live together in holy wedlock, have pledged the same before God and these witnesses, and have sealed these vows with the giving and receiving of these rings, I now pronounce them husband and wife."

There was something about that last phrase "I now pronounce them husband and wife" that broke the spell. The stone face was broken. The problems produced by the rain were gone. Like the sun that breaks through the clouds, her face brightened and she let out a little squeal, and everyone cheered.

Normally it is the kiss or the statement, "Ladies and gentlemen, may I present to you Mr. and Mrs.____" that brings a reaction from the wedding guests. But in this case it was that instant—when this bride realized that indeed she was now married to the one she loved—that marked a magic moment. Everyone there recognized that, and at that moment, everyone cheered.

The bride was back to her beautiful and smiling self, and for the rest of the evening and all throughout the outdoor reception, it never rained again.

Eldon Irving

Eldon Irving is a retired minister, having served as a pastor for forty-three years. He has degrees from the University of Washington, Yale Divinity School, United Theological Seminary, and Brite Divinity School at Texas Christian University. He is the author of *Personalities in the Pews (Stories of Inspiration and Humor)* and *The Life of Christ in Masterpieces of Art.* He has had articles published in *Yale Alumni Magazine*, denominational magazines, and newspapers in Ohio, Colorado, and Texas. He has three stories in *Texas Shorts*: "In Search of the Big Trees, "The Grand Tour," and "Rain Check."

Stained Glass Pews
by Angela Jones

    Eight-year-old, tall, slender, dark-skinned Pete enters the front door softly marching to the bathroom. Wearing faded denim knee-length shorts and a gray t-shirt—both filled with dust from rugged play under the Texas sun with his friend, Andy. Collapsing his knees with flailing arms, he lands softly on the toilet, still dressed, and forcibly blowing invisible smoke through pressed lips. He thinks, *I'd better get up before she opens the door.* Tightly curling his fingers into his palms, he extends his elbows with all his might, and wrinkles his forehead. "Damn-it! I'm not going! I'm not going!" he says in a loud whisper.

    "Are you freshening up, Pete? We'll leave after supper."

    Startled, he relaxes his body and inhales sharply, as if catching his breath. "Yes, ma'am, had to use it first."

    Eventually rising towards the washbowl, he stares at himself in the mirror. His eyes fill with water, he looks away, then downward and swallows hard.

    Big Momma, is 69 years young, four feet five inches tall, with soft, mostly gray, tightly-coiled hair. She has big brown eyes, bronze skin, a remarkable smile, and whimsical laugh. Most others in her family were near, or full-blown, overweight but she remained petite. She speculated that perhaps when you're the cook, you don't eat as much. Prior to retirement, she cooked for the mayor and was known by most city employees for her often-requested cuisine. She has plenty of friends at church and cooks as often as the pastor will eat. Big Momma still drives, lives alone, and occasionally toils in the yard. Something her peers aren't able to do. Being energetic comes in handy—since caring for Pete after losing her daughter and son-in-law to a violent crime just a year ago. That night still haunts her. Big Momma believes that God makes no mistakes.

She often talked to God, celebrating Him for no reason. Seemingly out of nowhere, like now.

Preparing dinner plates for herself and Pete, she hums one of her favorite songs. Now on her third or fourth rendition, she realizes Pete is seated in the family room.

Still humming, she pulls out a chair to sit, "The plates don't have legs, it won't walk to you."

Free of dirt, in jeans and a collared shirt, Pete takes a seat with raised eyebrows, "Whatcha cook?"

"Smothered pork chops, rice and green beans"

Laying his head on the table. "Urgh!"

"What's the matter with you? Also made your favorite—cornbread!"

"My dad doesn't like pork chops."

"Your mom loved smothered pork chops. You did, too, young man!"

Exhaling deeply. "Where's the cornbread?"

Shrugging and taking a bite. "Pick up your bottom lip, you'll see it on the stove. Get some food in you, can't be late for service."

"I can be late and show up like never!" he chuckled while biting cornbread.

"Your cousins are coming tonight—TomTom and Eugene—not sure if April showing up, cause her momma let her do whatever she wants."

Upon arrival at church, Pete sat a few rows back from Big Momma, as usual, and surveyed the small crowd for his cousins. Shortly afterwards, his head rested on the back of the pew with eyes half-opened. Jumping, as if spooked, he was jarred from a lethargic state by a woman's loud voice. Releasing an audible breath, he thinks, *This isn't singing, it's yelling. Jumping Janet on the radio can sing, nobody in this stupid church can sing. Nobody. Doesn't matter, I won't be coming here that much anyway.*

Stained Glass Pews

Noticing the increasing piano tempo, he turns toward the music stand. Familiar with the lively scene to follow, the pianist will gradually play faster and the people will dance for what seems like hours. She'd soon be standing, swaying, jerking, and stomping while violently pressing the black and white keys. Members stood, clapped, and joined the choir singing. Shaking his head, he thinks, *I hope her wig doesn't fall again, or maybe I hope it does. Fine by me, just wanna go home.*

A defeated Pete positions one elbow on each knee, drops his head into both palms cupping his chin. He closes his eyes as the dancing begins. Thankfully, TomTom pushes his shoulder hard.

"Are you sleeping? Big Momma gonna get you."

Eugene reaches around his big brother to push Pete as well. "Ooh, I'm telling."

Dodging Eugene's hand, "What took y'all so long? It's boring."

TomTom crossed his arms. "Didn't wanna come, but momma made us."

"Yeah, we had to, too. But April at her daddy house."

"Cuz she fast! Momma sick and tired of her!"

"Shut up, Eugene! You talk too much. I'm telling April so she can punch your head off!"

Pete and TomTom laughed, one holding his belly while the other patted Eugene on the shoulder.

Eugene stared at them—not appreciating the joke or the possibility that April may very well punch his head off. Pointing at Pete, he said, "April says you're the ugliest in the family. You're too dark and your lips are bigger than everybody's—combined!"

Silently he compares his forearm to theirs. "I'm not that much darker."

Finally, service ends. Remembering April's comments, Pete struggles to recall his dad's appearance. Once home, he hurried to his room to grab a photo. He found comfort viewing photos of his parents and wondered how life would be if they were alive.

"Night, Pete."

Yawning, "Night, Big Momma. I'm in the lead, throwing rocks. Andy been beating me, but I'm gonna win tomorrow."

The next day, Andy knocks about mid-morning. He's a short, round guy with pale, freckled skin, and carrot-colored hair. Pete is nearly dressed and immediately flees the family room to finish up.

Yelling over his shoulder, "Can I go out?"

Smiling, "Guess I don't have to ask you to get dressed. Huh?"

"Nope. I'm winning today. He's beat me like a gazillion times."

Casually, rising from her Lazy Boy chair. "I'm coming, Andy. Hang tight."

Andy steps side to side twiddling his thumbs. Staring at the door, he reaches for the handle, then stops. He reaches again and stops. Exhaling, he grabs the door handle and opens the screen door at the same time Big Momma opens the door.

"Hi, there! He's getting dressed, Should be out in a minute."

Like a ninja, Pete appears in blue basketball shorts with matching t-shirt. He poses like a performer awaiting applause. "I'm ready, Big Momma!"

Big Momma steps aside, allowing the boys to see one another.

Andy takes a half step and is inside. Smiling big, "I'm wearing basketball shorts, too. My lucky ones! I'm gonna whip you again!"

Heading towards the door. "You wish, I'm already doing my touchdown dance."

"They don't let cheerleaders in the end zone."

Stained Glass Pews

Pete's comment produced a hearty laugh from the three of them.

"You boys get on outta here!"

Once outside, they resumed the rock throwing contest. Pete came out the winner after several rounds. They laid face up on the green grass in an L-shaped formation, breathing hard, each one using one hand to shield his eyes from direct sunlight. After a short while, Pete rolled on his side, stretched his arm to firmly tap Andy on his forearm. Quickly rolling himself to his feet and yelling, "Tag! You're it!"

Andy got up as quickly as he could to join in.

A few days later, the boys played video games in Pete's family room. Big Momma was busy preparing dinner. Hearing running water and pots and pans rattling, they remained focused on the video shooting game.

Standing while still engaged in the game, Andy asks, "Why do you guys go to church today? It's not Sunday."

"Don't know," Pete shrugs.

"We go to mass on Sundays."

"What?"

"Mass. Our church is mass. I mean when we go to church, it's called mass. What's yours called?"

"Church." Says Pete while fist pumping after hitting his target.

"I like Mass. Why don't you?"

"Whatcha mean? Never been to Mass to not like it."

"Well, why don't you like church?"

Holding the PlayStation remote with both hands, Pete aims it downward. Staring at Andy with a wrinkled forehead and eyes looking down, "I can't tell you."

"Why not? We're friends, aren't we?"

"Yes. Just can't say."

"Why? It can't be that bad. Not as bad as your end zone dance." Andy joked.

Pete stared at the TV, holding the game remote, not pressing any buttons.

Andy playfully tosses the game remote on the sofa. "It's Over!! Game over. I knew I could beat you."

The following Saturday, after supper, someone knocked at the door. *We're not expecting guests this evening and it's a little late for Andy to be out,* thought Big Momma, as she made her way to the door, yelling, "Who's there?"

Pete had come running to see the surprise guest and stopped short of entering the family room—opting to look from afar.

Opening the door slowly, then faster with a big smile. "Hello, Anna, I haven't seen you in a while and sure appreciate you letting Andy play with Pete as often as they do. It's been good for him. He's still getting used to the changes."

Anna, a tall, well-proportioned redhead with hair in a ponytail. "Andy really enjoys playing with Pete. I couldn't keep them apart if I wanted to. In fact, Andy would like to invite Pete to church tomorrow. We'd love to have him."

Slowly shaking her head, while gradually looking up from the floor, "I don't know. I'm not sure if he's ready to venture out to another church. Our church was his parents' church, you know."

"Big Momma, I wanna go." Pete slowly comes around the corner wringing his wrist. "Please, Big Momma."

"Pete, we'd love to have you. They're good playmates, right, Miss Ella?"

"Yes. I suppose they are, and looks like this here fella wants to go. Your family leaves about 7:45, right?"

"Yes. Tomorrow is our monthly brunch after service. See you tomorrow, Pete. Good night, Miss Ella."

Pete stood there a moment longer, wondering, *Big Momma's name is Miss Ella.*

The next morning, Pete yawns after breakfast. "What time is it? They coming at 7:45."

"It's 7:40, young man. You got time. Go grab a sweater, might be chilly inside the church. Go ahead—the blue one—it's clean."

Quickly rising, he practically power walks to his bedroom. "Got it! They here yet?"

Moments later, a well-dressed Andy knocks at the door while a shiny red full-sized SUV with chrome wheels waits for their return. Giddy and laughing, the boys jump in.

"Good morning, Mr. and Ms. Cooper," Pete says, as he searches for his seat belt.

"Hi, Pete," says Mr. Cooper. "Good to see ya again. I'm usually working when you guys are playing." Turning to his wife, he continues, "Thankfully, she keeps things in order until I'm home."

Ms. Cooper smiles while adjusting the radio volume up a bit. "Buckle up, please."

"We did, Mom."

Leaning towards Andy, "What are we going to do at Mass?"

"You know, church stuff. Probably same stuff as your church. Sing, pray and stuff. We have dinner after service today."

Smiling big, "I'm just glad to be away from my church."

Anna listened to the boys, as she often did to ensure appropriate dialogue, while pretending to apply make-up.

Forcefully crossing his arms, "You never told me why, Pete"

"Why what?"

"Why you don't like church. It's fun. It should be fun."

"Just being away from my church is fun."

Firmly placing his palm on his forehead, "But why?"

"Okay, I'll tell you, but only you."

"OK, what? What?" Andy leans in.

Pete motions him to come closer. "They killed my parents."

Wide-eyed. "Who? Why? Are you sure?"

"Yep. I saw it. My mom and dad in pink and blue boxes at the front of the church. Dead."

"That doesn't mean they killed them." Says Andy.

"The pastor said they gave their life to the church. Now doesn't that sound like someone from the church did something bad to them? Big Momma says they're in heaven with God. But I know they would rather be here with me. There! Now I told ya."

"We should tell someone. But who? The police?"

In a loud whisper, "No! I'm getting away from that place. Just wait and see. Don't know how, but I will."

"You could stay in my room with me."

"And sleep on the floor? No way, Jose!"

Having heard all of the boys' conversation, Ms. Anna flips her hair as they park. The sound of the radio fades, as she peeks over her seat. "We're here. Andy, be sure to introduce Pete and show him around."

Once inside, Pete meets several people and is amazed by the size. He touches the plush cushion on the pews, and wonders what the books are in the holders on the back of the pews. His church had stained glass windows but nothing to the likes of these. Service starts with soft music and a welcome greeting. Pete noticed Andy was missing. He thought. *Where'd he go? And why didn't he take me with him?*

Seeing Pete's concern, Ms. Anna says, "Andy is an altar boy. He'll be back soon."

Half-smiling, he says, "Okay."

Moments later, Andy and others appear adorned in white robes. A few carried something, while others had nothing. Pete watched in amazement. They walked to the front, bowed down and completed a series of hand motions. The choir sang a few short songs and before long the pastor was up. He talked for a little while, followed by money collection. Moments later, to Pete's surprise, service was over! No dancing, no extreme pianist, nothing! He hadn't noticed when Andy returned and he hardly had time to get comfortable to doze off.

Upon exiting, several people waited to shake the pastor's hand. Person after person shook his hand and called him "father." This confused Pete a great bit. He couldn't imagine that the pastor was everyone's father. He waited to see what Andy would call him. Pete was certain that he wasn't Andy's father.

Andy's turn had come, he stepped forward, extended his right hand for a handshake, nodded his head, and said, "Thank you, Father."

Pete couldn't wait to ask Andy if he had two dads. He wondered, How can he have another dad? Then would I need another mom, too? Whoever he was wouldn't be as good as my dad. If I had one.

Andy grabs his shoulder, "Come on! We have brunch today. Pancakes are my favorite. Are you hungry?"

"Pancakes! You'd better believe it."

"We have to grab our seats first. Follow me and stay close."

Waiting to be served, Father Millison visits most tables and comes to their table. Ms. Anna stands, "Good morning, Father. Thank you for a beautiful message today."

"Bless you, dear. Every opportunity to serve God's people is a blessing. Who do you have with you today?"

Smiling, "Andy, please stand and introduce your guest."

Andy stands. "This is my friend, Pete."

Extending his hand for a handshake, "Welcome, Pete. It's lovely to have you visit us. We hope you will visit again."

Pete stands, "Yes, sir. I want to come back."

"That's great! You're welcomed anytime. We'd be honored to have your family join our parish."

Going up and down on his toes, Pete says, "I want to join. Can I join?"

"Well, sure, we welcome everyone. Have your parents visit with you next time."

Clearing her throat, Ms Anna says, "Father, Pete's parents are in heaven…with God. Pete's our neighbor and lives with his grandmother, Ms. Ella."

"I see. My parents are in heaven, too. I was a boy about your age when I lost them." Grabbing Pete by his shoulders, he pulls him in for a tight hug and points at him. "I know what you're going through. I tell you what. Invite your grandma, Ms. Ella, right?"

Pete nods. "Yes, sir."

"Invite Ms. Ella and tell her Father Millison would like you to join our youth activities and prepare you for training as an altar boy. Would you like that?

Wide-eyed with mouth open and nodding, "Yes. Yes, sir. Yes…Father?"

Pete quizzed Andy on the ride home about what's it like to be an altar boy. Once Mr. Cooper parked, the boys jumped out. Pete rapidly makes his way to Andy's side and pulls him towards the back of the car. "Told you I'd get out of my church. Told you."

"You think Ms. Ella will let you?"

"I don't know, but I'm going back to Mass and I mean it. Don't know how yet."

Ms. Anna approaches, "Pete, you'd better get on home."

A few days later, the boys are out playing. Big Momma answers a knock at the door. "Hi, Anna! Has the boys gotten into some trouble?"

"No, ma'am. I was hoping to talk to you while they played. It's about our Sunday service a few days ago. May I come in?"

"Sure. Have a seat. Can I pour you some tea?"

"No. No, thanks. I, um, overheard a conversation between the boys and want to share it with you. It's important."

Leaning forward and scratching her forehead. "Go ahead. Anything dealing with Pete I'm interested in. He's gone through enough."

Angela Jones

Angela Jones, once a contributing writer for *Star Athlete Magazine,* has authored several articles covering elite professional and collegiate athletes. A certified speaker with the John Maxwell Team, she is a licensed minister and an enthusiastic writer. Angela enjoys creating fictional characters facing modern dilemmas, and finding clever ways for them and those around her to hear God's voice. She's joyfully married to her childhood sweetheart—with a blended family of five children and six grandchildren.

Dada, Do Dat 'Gin
by André King

It is said one cannot go home again. Yet our memories take us there. We all have had things happen that take us back to happier times. The memory of a school dance, the boy who stole a kiss, and we touch our face and smile. A piece of music takes us to an orchestra field trip, and how we loved that composition, or the song that reminds us of our wedding day. The list could go on forever, but each sparks a memory. This is mine.

It was the summer of 1958. We lived in the small town of Poplar Bluff, Missouri, nestled in the foothills of the Mark Twain National Forest, just across the state line from Arkansas on State Highway 67. Mom was a petite four foot eleven, with tiny and delicate hands, the kind that belonged on a porcelain doll. She had piercing blue eyes and flaxen blonde hair that cascaded to her waist. Poplar Bluff was her hometown. Born the January after the stock market fell in 1929, she grew up there, and became a young woman during World War II.

She had three children. I would turn eight in March that year. Joe was the middle child. Dad called him his tow-headed dare-devil. He had blonde hair and blue eyes, sometimes referred to as bedroom blue. Tall and lanky for his age, he turned six in June. Billy was born in February and turned four a month before my birthday. He was a few inches shorter than Joe, but shared the same lanky frame. Billy's eyes and hair were both brown. His eyes were different...darker than brown. I heard the term Raven Eyes as an adult, and immediately thought of Billy. A happy-go-lucky kid, he was curious with a sharp mind, and wanted to learn.

I was tall for my age, almost taller than mom. As the oldest, I had to make sure the boys stayed out of trouble, especially Billy. He followed his older brother and tried to imitate whatever he did. I quickly learned how to climb trees, throw a knife, and traverse the woods. I got the nick-name Tomboy and it stuck.

My primary responsibility was to keep Billy safe. Born with Cerebral Palsy, it left him challenged physically and mentally. His speech impediment sometimes made it hard to understand him. Letters would get scrambled or left out altogether. For example, a *B* became a *V,* a *D* became a *T.* He also had physical limitations. His left side was underdeveloped, with his arm always bent at the elbow across his chest. The left hand twisted at the wrist permanently in a downward bend. It never stopped him, however, from doing what he wanted. Billy took his first steps when he turned four and never stopped. Chasing him was a full-time endeavor, even with his left-sided limp.

Our house sat on a hill where two streets met and formed a *T.* It was a two-story abode with bedrooms upstairs, the kitchen and living-room downstairs. An S-curved gravel driveway led to the street below. From spring through early fall months, we had electricity. Winter snow storms could drop the temperature below thirty-two degrees in a hurry—freezing lines and knocking out the electricity. No electricity, no stove, no heat. When that happened, we used oil lamps for light. A wood-burning stove provided heat for cooking, and a Ben Franklin pot-bellied stove heated the rest of the house. My job was to light the pot-belly to warm the house if the electricity went out. I would let Billy stomp on the wax milk cartons or crumple up the newspapers for the fire starter.

Behind our house, a fence separated the yard from the slope of the hill and the distant valley below. Lots of trees provided shade in the hot summer. One oak had purple and white Wisteria entwined in the branches that hung almost to the ground. Billy and Mom planted it the previous spring. He took responsibility for his plants, and faithfully watered them as they grew. One day we noticed, he was twisting the vines together as they encroached up the tree. Each day he added another twist. The final result was a purple, green, and white cascade of color through the foliage. One section might be purple, green, and then white. The section above would have white, green, and then the purple. This went throughout the tree. People stopped to take pictures; it made a beautiful photograph. Dad put a sign at the end of the driveway saying: *Take Pictures On Foot. No Cars Allowed In Driveway*—just to keep the driveway clear and protect the lawn.

Each fall, before the leaves began to turn, Dad purchased two cords of wood. He split the wood himself, claiming it was cheaper, and the work gave him exercise. Dad was a field engineer. His six-foot-plus frame, dark brown hair and eyes, chiseled jaw-line, and high cheek bones, made him very handsome. Dad had an infectious smile and eyes that twinkled when happy. He loved the outdoors and, when there was time, took us camping and fishing. He loved to spend time with his family away from the phone. A call meant he had to go into the field.

In early September, our house on the hill gave us front-row seats when thunderstorms rolled into the valley. This fall day started with a gentle breeze rustling through the trees. Puffs of white clouds floated in a blue sky. Mom watched with a smile while Dad played with us in the yard. Toward afternoon the breeze stiffened, the temperature suddenly dropped, and Dad searched the sky. The clouds over the valley indicated a storm was coming. He stopped playing with us and began to urgently chop what was left of the cords of wood. Billy held up the tarp while Joe and I furiously stacked the wood, Dad's voice in the background, urged us to hurry.

The wind really picked up around three in the afternoon. Unseen hands battered tree tops as the wind grew in strength. The valley clouds were no longer friendly, but had become an angry mass of grays and blacks, a fight in the sky for control. In the distance, lightning and thunder broke the stillness. The birds and the crickets silenced their songs and huddled against the approaching storm.

We watched as Dad chopped wood with an anxious eye on the coming storm. A couple of times lightning flashed as the axe roared into the wood. Billy watched with the wide-eyed innocence of a child looking at the wonders of nature. Dad would smile at each giggle he made. Billy stared, trying to catch the magic of the storm all at once. The clouds rolled over each other, getting more ominous with each tumble. Thunder roared and lightning flashed in its advance. The swing of the axe quickened. Joe and I kept a close eye on Billy as the axe chewed into the wood. He ran around excited, and we were afraid of flying chips hitting him. Once he stood frozen, watching the sky, oblivious to the axe behind him. Dad reared back with the axe. I picked Billy up just as a very sharp wood chip stuck in the ground where he had been standing. He could've been seriously hurt. Pop never knew how close the axe came to him.

The storm grew closer. Lightning streaked across the sky, shattering into small shards. Billy giggled with each flash. Dad had one final log to split. A brilliant streak seared across the sky and splintered into dozens of small fingers of light. A second flash, more brilliant than the first, instantaneously lit the horizon. Three fingers of light pointed at the earth, just as the axe slammed into the wood. Billy thought Dad made both flashes happen. He danced around yelling, "Dada, do dat 'gin! Do dat 'gin!" Once we understood what Billy meant, we all laughed. Dad finished the last piece of wood and placed it safely under the tarp. He picked Billy up and wrapped him in his arms. Together we watched the spectacle in the sky until the first raindrops fell.

Time passes, seasons change, we grow older, and childhoods are forgotten. A distant echo among the stress each day brings... living...work...raising a family. We make memories for our children, while ours fade into the bridgework of life. Our parents and Joe have passed, now it's Billy and me. A thunderstorm accompanied by fractured lightning takes me home, to that stormy September afternoon with my family, and I still hear a four-year-old say, "Dada, do dat 'gin! Do dat 'gin!"

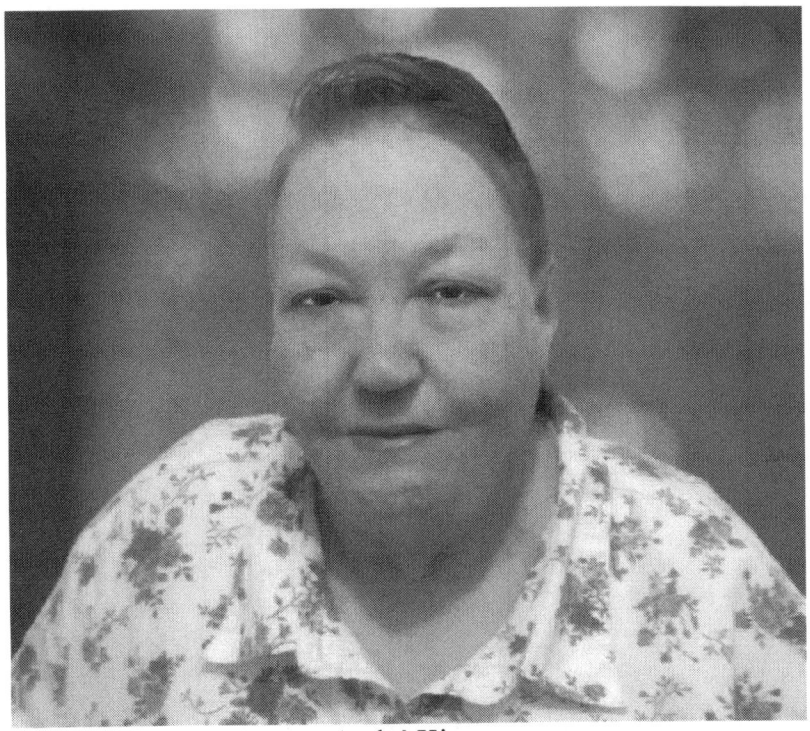

André King

Writing beautiful stories and poetry has been a part of André King's life since the age of twelve. Recognized by several awards—including the 1988 World of Poetry Golden Poet Award—she won the 2015 Irene Emerson Poetry Contest and was third place winner of the 2016 Writers Guild of Texas Flash Fiction Contest. André has thirty years of rich experiences and education in criminal justice and the legal field to draw upon for her writing.

God's Glimpses for the Future
by Pamela Flynt Knight

Faye was a twenty-year-old standing in the door of a new life. Excited, she held tight to her brother's arm as she stepped forward down the aisle to the wedding march playing. Before her was her husband-to-be, in his Navy Dress Whites. Her parents were poised on the first row to the left and his on the front row to the right. Her brother would walk her down the aisle, her dad would not allow anyone else the privilege to give her away. It had only been a month since his heart attack, and she was delighted he was there.

The ceremony was over quickly and after walking down the aisle as husband and wife, they slipped to the side. One passionate kiss in the corner while awaiting the church to clear out so they could take pictures. Starting a new life was exciting, but everything moved quickly, and later just seemed like a blur. The pictures and reception seemed to be no time at all, then they were able to get away for their honeymoon.

Of course, the wedding held memories they will never forget. Friends thought it was cute to tape "Help Me" on the bottom of his shoes to be read by everyone as they knelt to pray. Dan's father was angry with the inappropriate decoration being drug behind the car as they departed, although many others were amused. And then there was the struggle to actually see to drive because of the white murky detergent on the windshield. The windshield washer and wipers were of no help with this mess. Carefully they made it around the corner to a gas station where it could all be washed away, and they could continue on their way.

It would be a couple more decades before Faye would begin to understand the small glimpses that God would give her over the next several months. The biggest lessons were the ones where God taught her to stand alone, shoulder responsibility alone, and to wait and depend upon Him.

They had only one glorious week together before Dan had to report and head overseas for his first duty station. But anxiety would not be allowed. They had made their plans. As soon as he arrived, he would get the paperwork taken care of and, very soon, they would again be together.

But world events and governments do not consult with young lovers before making changes that will affect their lives. Faye was naïve and never connected how a world of chaos around them would affect their lives, as she and Dan were hit by world events. The Vietnam War was in full swing and Dan would be thrust in the middle of it. He was a radioman and headed to the communication center for the war. However, it was neither Vietnam nor America that impacted their lives and separated them for the coming months.

The Republic of the Philippines, where Dan was stationed, was friendly to America, but it was run by a dictator, Ferdinand Marcos. He wanted control of everything in his country. The free love, hippie lifestyle of the day would not be tolerated under his rule. Marcos declared martial law! Military rule was the rule of the day.

Dan arrived in the Philippines just weeks before the dictator made his declaration. He had Faye's paperwork ready to be signed for her travel, but the dictator's announcement squashed their plans, and put a halt to her joining her new husband overseas. Their hopes and plans were set aside, along with her command-sponsorship.

An unexpected and heart-breaking blow for the newlyweds. Dan was set to stay at the duty station overseas for the next 18 months. The week they had spent together was not nearly long enough. They did not expect such a long separation. So, they began looking for ways that Faye could join him—yet there were obstacles. Now there was no way for them to get base housing. As long as there was martial law, there were no sponsorships being approved for non-commissioned personnel. San Miguel was a small facility where almost everyone knew each other but command-sponsorship was critical to housing.

This left housing in the small town. Most locals lived in poorly constructed wooden and/or metal framed structures—often with a thatched or metal roof. The streets were mostly dirt roads and the market was a huddle of open air vendors under one big roof. It was a big contrast to the large Naval Port where U.S. ships were serviced for the war. Not a great option for a new husband and wife from America. In the limited brick constructions, the electricity was not well controlled. Throughout the day, most 110-volt items were easily used although the country was on a 220-volt system. You had to watch carefully in the evening when the power jumped. Warnings were the lights would dim and brighten. Light bulbs had to be changed and an eye kept on the power converter. If the switch wasn't made in time, the light bulbs would blow out, and the converter could blow out appliances.

Safety was also an issue. When you did find a little apartment, it often had a brick wall surrounding it with broken glass concreted to the top to prevent people from climbing over. With martial law, this was more of an issue than before, because people would hide to avoid the streets. Patrols shot first and asked questions later.

Living "in town" was very different. Living conditions were different from anything Faye and Dan had known stateside. Dan's duty hours were different, and Faye had to stay alone at night. It was scary. But, even with the obstacles ahead, they were determined to be together. Once Dan found an apartment he could rent, they began to plan on Faye's arrival.

Their first obstacle was the fire Dan experienced. He had been asleep when his apartment caught fire, but he was fortunate to get out with the clothes on his back and his paycheck that he grabbed off the dresser on his way out. That was all the money he had, and everything had to be replaced, including his uniforms. A very unexpected cost for the young couple. And another delay.

The next obstacle for the young couple was travel. Not being command-sponsored, they had to pay for her round-trip airfare. Mileage between Manila and the duty station was rough, too. Although it was not a great distance, the road conditions made the travel between points much longer than you would expect. You could get a car and driver to shuttle you, but that, too, came at a cost. The time meant that Dan had to be able to take leave to make the trip.

Meanwhile, back home, Faye had settled into an apartment of her own and a temporary job to pass the time. She waited patiently for word from her husband. Once she received word they had a place to live, she was able to start making arrangements. She had a lot to deal with in getting prepared. There were medical exams and shots and even some dental work before she could head overseas. Not being command-sponsored, these costs fell on their shoulders, adding an additional burden. She also had to get her passport and travel arrangements in place. There was no one-way ticket to a country with martial law. Faye had to purchase a round-trip ticket. With all the obstacles and issues, the whole process took Dan and Faye six months to coordinate.

Although she was excited about her trip, the day she was to leave, it was like the sky began to fall in. There was a rain storm that did not seem to want to stop, so her flight was delayed. By the time she had rearranged flights to try and meet her connection in Hawaii, her luggage was unable to be retrieved, and left on the delayed flight. She took a deep breath and remembered her mother always saying, "God will take care of us." Her parents were there, so they knew of the delay and about her new connections. However, there was just enough delay that when she landed in Los Angeles, her connecting flight had taken off about five minutes before she arrived. The airlines had to reschedule her flights and book her into a hotel for the night.

Another deep breath. Instead of heading for Hawaii, now Faye was scheduled to head for Japan and then the Philippines. As she arrived in her room, she quickly called her parents to let them know what had happened. But, she was unable to call her husband who would soon be on his way to Manila, on leave, to meet her. She called the Red Cross for help. Due to the turmoil of nations, the person at the Red Cross that evening did not believe she would be able to even enter the country. No explanation was sufficient. Faye desperately tried to explain that if a message were not sent immediately, her husband would be on leave and headed to Manila. The time difference was critical. If they missed him at the duty station, they could leave a message for him at the USO in Manila. The urgency of the moment was lost on the person handling her call—they determined it could wait until morning—when a supervisor could establish if she could actually go. Dan never got a message.

The next morning was beautiful. The California sunshine could not have been more beautiful. This was wonderful. Now, everything would fall into place. Faye was up, dressed and on her way quickly. She was excited as she settled in to board her flight. Time to board came and left. She patiently waited nearly an hour before those waiting to board the flight were informed that there had been an issue. They were using the plane for another delayed flight. An additional hour now loomed ahead of her after they were able to secure a plane for travel. The wait was frustrating. She was afraid of missing her connection in Japan. It was a long flight and when they finally touched down in Japan, Faye was again faced with a missed flight. Her connecting flight had left just minutes before she arrived. The process for rearranging flights started all over again! Of course, the airline was happy to put her up for the night and rearrange her flight for the next day. Yet again! Here she was, already two days late to arrive, in a foreign country and did not know if her husband had received word through the Red Cross. She did not know how to reach her husband and, with the time change, the only call she made was to let her parents know where she was.

She was not prepared for the night ahead of her. Although she was booked by the airlines into an international hotel, communication was difficult. The broken English spoken by the Japanese workers at the hotel was as difficult for her as her southern accent was for them. Cold and tired, after several hours of waiting and flying, Faye finally headed to her room.

Once she decided to settle in for the night, she discovered that the one blanket in the cool room was wool, and she was allergic to wool. In an attempt to turn the heater up she was frustrated to only find controls for the air conditioner. Communication with the front desk for help was futile. The few hours of sleep she managed to get were curled up under her coat. It was morning before she understood "air conditioner" was exactly that. It conditioned the air. The heater was at her fingertips and she did not know it. One more trouble faced on this journey of mishaps. Like most everything about this trip, she didn't seem to be in control of anything and it was miserable. What could she do but keep going?

The next day, she was able to get to the airport and her flight was on time and she had no more connections. Just before she arrived in Manila, her husband had discovered when she would arrive. He had spent two anxious days wondering where she was. He had spoken to her parents and knew she was delayed in Los Angeles, but it seemed the airline that put her up in Japan and rescheduled her flight also lost any information about her. They told him they had not seen her since she left the plane in Japan. Obviously, the communication breakdown in Japan was wider spread than between the broken English and southern accent. The airline didn't seem to know about the bus ride, hotel or return trip to the airport. Dan actually found his wife through an airline she never boarded.

Finally, husband and wife were delighted once they were reunited. They did not want to let go of one another. The one week together in the six months of their marriage seemed forever ago. They found Faye's luggage locked in an office for safe keeping. It seems it arrived on the original flight. Now they had to hurry. There was no time for any pleasure or overnight stays. Dan's leave was quickly coming to a close. They had to return to San Miguel right away.

Weeks later, Faye and Dan were happy to get her a visa where she could stay. They would be together for the remainder of his time at that duty station. The return ticket was cashed in and never used. A year later, when it was time to return home, Faye was able to fly back on a military plane.

They lived in town and learned how to accommodate their lives under martial law and in a foreign country. Dan's work schedule was crazy, and Faye adjusted to often being alone. It was different from anything they had known—difficult at times, yet at other times, it was easier. Their small salary at home in the U.S. would barely get them by, but here, this young couple was "rich." They could afford luxuries like a house girl. Faye loved watching her polish the concrete floors with wax polish, a rag and a coconut hull. Certainly nothing she could have done herself, especially standing up!

Looking back and remembering, over several decades, Faye wishes she knew then what God had taught her. Hindsight helped her see the glimpses God gave her into the future. They had short times of meaningful events quickly followed by long periods of separation. Out of necessity, she learned to do everything alone. Being a Navy wife meant she would, at times, have to be responsible for everything. It meant watching things fall apart. She would deal with sick kids and house issues and finances all alone. It meant sorrow swallowing you while you watched a ship disappear in the distance, and great joy in holding tight to that sailor when the ship docked again.

If only she had known then what she knew now! But she knew if asked to do it all again, she would relive each trial and each joy because it taught her how to depend on God and how good He is. That was a lesson far greater than any delayed travel experience, lengthy separation or difficult occurrence.

Pamela Flynt Knight

Pamela Flynt Knight is the author of six non-fiction books. She dabbled with poetry and writing when she was younger, but it was not until 2010 that she began publishing. Since then, she has self-published and published through traditional means. Pamela has a wide variety of non-fiction works but enjoys focusing on spiritual lessons. Her books, *Living in the Fire* and *Why Are You Here?*, emphasize the importance of God in everyday life.

We Break From Inside Out
by Lisa Moak

It was Friday morning, April 13, 2011, but inside his 50s' style ranch home, John was unconcerned with the weather. Nestled in his recliner, where he slept each night, he searched through the morning gloom to find a pack of cigarettes. His motivation to stand came only after spotting a pack on top of his dusty entertainment center. Pulling out a smoke, John made his way through a tiny pathway, pushing through empty Burger King bags, beer cans, and mounds of paper products to his kitchen and bathroom. These last paths through the garbage in his home were guarded jealously, as they gave way to important areas. As he moved stiffly through the dark, a cold fist enclosed his heart sending tremors to his toes.

Something turned in his stomach, it felt edgy and hard. His liver, ever the quiet organ, suffered alone from endless nights of poison from cheap beer and greasy fast food. Things were beginning to brew inside him, a sort of mutiny that would make *the Bounty* pale in comparison. His lungs spoke up first, sending spasms of coughs through the house.

John washed himself in the dim restroom, ignoring the smell of urine and mold. His clothes from yesterday hung neatly over the kitchen table chairs. He hadn't seen the inside of his bedroom since July 2010, the day his paper and trash collection took over the floor, blocking the door; thus, his recliner became his sleeping quarters and the kitchen, his closet.

After his morning toiletries and dressing, John headed to his car. His pudgy frame was buttoned up tight in a leather jacket, gloves, and a soft, woolen cap that covered his bald head. The fog that appeared each time he breathed reminded him he should fix the 1998 Plymouth Voyager's heater. Outside lighting illuminated the building that housed Emerson

Marketing Group, casting a pale glow upon the white stucco as he eased into a parking space. Passing security, he made his way down the stark, white hallway to the glass enclosure that held his cubicle. John felt as if he were walking into a meat locker as he entered the room. The brick in his stomach jumped.

Throwing off his jacket and gloves, he fell into his chair which squeaked in resistance to the weight thrust upon it. John checked his voicemail, the weather, and stared at his to-do list. At 8 a.m., he started opening the mass of messages in his inbox. That was when the tightly closed box holding his reality broke apart and fell away.

He clicked on a message from *friend@yourcomputer.com*, read it and read it again, mouthing the words this time, trying to comprehend the lines:

Dear John,

I know you hate your job. I know you are truly miserable. I know you hate your life. I just want you to know that it is okay. I am your friend.

Sincerely,

Your computer

John raised up from his chair and slowly poked his head over the cubicle wall. Squinting, he scanned the office. No suppressed giggles. No movement at all. Shaking as he sank back down, he decided he must be experiencing nicotine withdrawals, so he left for a quick smoke.

When he returned ten minutes later, the office was full of people and noise. John nodded at a few co-workers lolling outside their cubes as he slipped back into his own. He stared at the computer keyboard. The same email sat there like an obedient dog waiting for a command. He commanded *delete*.

To John, his work was full of monotonous tasks and endless meetings. At 10:15, he felt a low growl in his belly, the brick was turning. He grabbed the jacket on his way out to the smoking area, and stopped at the vending machine for his morning chocolate donuts. Barely noticing how difficult it was to separate his wallet from his back pocket, he pulled out a crinkled dollar and shoved it at the mouth of the machine. The dollar shot back out at him like a baby spitting out peas. He tried to straighten the dollar across his thigh. Once more he shoved the dollar at the machine, which sucked it in, but the excitement was short as the digital lights blinked at him "ERROR!" He pondered sticking his arm up the vending machine slot for the beckoning treat. Since his bulgy arm would never fit in that tiny slot, he looked carefully around, then reared back, and karate-kicked his right foot into the front of the device. The lights blinked harder at him, but now the message was different:

HEY....THAT....HURT!....YOU....DON'T....NEED....THIS....JUNK!....LOVE...YOUR...COMP...UTER

John slammed his fist into the money return button. The dollar flew back out at him, seemingly from the force of his blow. The "ERROR!" light blinked innocently again. He looked around confused. Putting the dollar back in his wallet, he headed towards the smoking area without the donuts.

When John returned, his boss was waiting. Mr. Freeman was a thin man who wore a thin tie. He carried a thin mustache above his upper lip because he thought it looked chic juxtaposed with his thin wire-framed glasses. Mr. Freeman spoke with a nasally voice that sent John's spine into convulsions.

"Hey, John!" he whined, "Is that marketing strategies presentation ready? I need to run it up to the top for approval today."

"Sure. Just let me tweak it and I will shoot it over to you," he answered.

John slipped back into his cubicle, intending to complete the task before him. Yet again, another curious message waited:

Dear John,

Look, I know you don't believe this, but you are worth something and I just wanted to let you know. Even the miserable person you have turned into deserves to be loved. I am your friend.
Sincerely,
Your computer/friend

John sighed. He didn't have time for jokes with so much work to do. A tiny splinter of fear spiked inside. The iron fist gripping his heart closed tighter. He couldn't explain the messages, and he wouldn't try. John squeezed his eyes closed, like a child hoping the unwanted plate of peas would disappear when they reopened. He blew out a breath to calm the sea inside and opened his PowerPoint application. He needed to refocus his mind, and aimed for two productive hours of work before lunch.

The computer clock read 12:00 when John paused for his lunch of Cheetos and Marlboros, then returned to his desk exactly thirty minutes later. Not ready to work yet, he decided to check his Facebook page. His teenage kids, John Jr. and Sandy, had created the profile for him. They had even uploaded his photo, an old picture of a young father with brown hair, grinning as he wrapped his arms around two wiggly toddlers. A mixture of college and high school acquaintances made up his fifty friends. They were all successful with beautiful families. Their happy lives infected his lonely page, reminding him of his defeated life, but he needed to stay in touch with his kids, so the humiliation was endured.

Putting in his password, he opened his Facebook page. John had a new friend request. Icy prickles scraped his skin as he read:

Your computer – Hey, John, don't avoid me! Please friend me and you can see what a great friend I can be! Love, Your computer friend

Nausea gripped his stomach, as the brick spun rapidly inside. The claw squeezed his chest, and he let out a gasp.

Buzzing erupted from his company BlackBerry sitting on his desk, alerting him to an incoming message. John grabbed it and read the incoming text:

John, I am waiting for your answer. I want to be your friend!

Sweat broke out across his forehead as his hands started to shake. Just then, Mr. Freeman poked his head around the corner of the cube and started to speak, but stopped when he saw John.

"Wow, you look awful, John. What is it? The flu?" he asked, while backing away from the cubicle. "Look, we can work on the presentation next week. Why don't you go home and get some rest?" Freeman held his thin tie in his hand and was trying to shield his nose from the imagined germs floating his direction.

"Yeah," John said, "I think I need to go home."

John left his buzzing BlackBerry on his desk and made his way outside. The afternoon sun had finally brought the temperatures up above freezing, but he shivered as he made his way through the parking lot towards his rusted minivan. He could see the bright pink "Goddess" window sticker glaring at him from the back window of the van. It reminded him that this was once his wife's. She had driven the kids to and from school, soccer games, and ballet recitals all while he worked. She was frustrated with him working so much, but he had assured her that his next big promotion was coming, and that it would all be better soon. Soon never came, and the wife eventually left him for his son's thrice-divorced soccer coach.

He rested his arm on his chest as he drove, as if protecting what was inside. The object in his stomach seemed to grow larger, leaving no room for food. He sped past the Burger King on the corner for the first time in a year without driving in.

Dead grass surrounded the driveway as he eased the Voyager home at 101 Mercy Street. John walked up the dilapidated steps to the front door and flicked away his spent

We Break From Inside Out

cigarette butt as he searched for his keys. Once inside, he made his way to the kitchen, stepping lightly over the trash and Walmart bags full of paper plates and cups. He thought of the day he bought the plates and cups in the first place. It was the last errand he had done for his wife—pick up the items to use for his son's upcoming 10th birthday party. Only now, he was not invited to the parties. He wondered why he kept buying bags of unused plates and cups. Shaking his head, he opened the refrigerator. The shelves and bins were full of blue and silver cans of Coors Lite bought in bulk at the local Costco. He made his way back to the living area and his recliner.

Falling into the chair with his armload of cold beer, he scanned the lamp table by the chair for the remote. He eventually rescued the device from under a pile of newspapers, and aimed it at his most prized possession, the 52" HDTV, with built in WIFI, Netflix, plus satellite and a surround system by BOSE that hung like an award on the far side of the living room.

John chugged his beer while mindlessly flipping through 400 channels. News, sports, romantic comedies, reality TV, entertainment news, *Telemundo*, *Sci-Fi*, *History*, *Home and Garden*, food stations. Nothing caught his interest until he finally landed on the *Discovery* channel and a show about busting scientific myths. He settled down to watch, as he popped the top of his sixth beer. The myth-busting team was playing with a microwave, trying to discover if standing near it while it worked was harmful to humans. John's eyes became heavy as he watched. Something jerked him awake, sending his cigarette into his lap. He wiped ash from his pants as he listened.

"Of course, there are those that think microwave, or even radio waves, pulsating through the air, can mess with your brain. We are going to see if there is any truth to this."

John focused on the screen, as if a great revelation had occurred to him. Now the pretty myth-busting maiden was speaking. Her green eyes looked out from the TV, like she was talking directly to him—and she was!

John, stop looking for answers that aren't there. Don't you get it? Your computer has been trying to talk to you all day and you are just ignoring it. The message is simple. All you must do is accept the message. You are loved. You are valuable. You just need to look outside yourself and you will find the answer. Your computer is your true friend.

Practically frozen in disbelief, John switched channels. An aging male local news anchor was talking about a recent warehouse fire and the damage it had caused.

"The damage could be estimated in the millions, reported the fire department,"...John, seriously, all you need to do is accept...accept you are worth something. It is so simple. You are worth love! Listen to your computer friend!

John quickly flipped again. Conan was beginning his monologue.

"Good evening, folks. I was just walking about today and noticed...I noticed this poor sap driving home in a beat up Voyager, staring blankly into space like aliens had taken over his brain...(audience laughter) Imagine his surprise when his computer tried to tell him he loved him!"

Peals of laughter filled the room.

John hit the power button and the screen went dark. Confusion and weariness melted over him. All those emotions he had sent to the depth of his soul welled up inside: his dead-end job, the lost days with his kids, the forgotten smiles of his wife. The clamp on his heart gave way. He softly moaned as he felt release.

The TV crackled and came back to life. A voice boomed at him from his Surround Sound.

John, I have been trying to reach you all day. I just wanted you to know there is hope, but we break from inside out. Don't fear me, I am your friend!

We Break From Inside Out

Tiny fissures spread across his brain like the ice on his window panes. The aneurysm lurking silently in his head burst like an explosion of fireworks. He grabbed for his cell phone before the darkness engulfed him.

On a Saturday, one month later, bright rays of warmth landed on John, as dawn crept in his living room windows. John had just returned home the night before, after a lengthy stay in Our Lady of Mercy Hospital. He opened his eyes and scanned the golden-hued room. John felt—different. The brick in his stomach was gone. With simple clarity, he saw the content of his home: beer cans, cigarette packs, full ashtray, and trash piling around his feet. Picking up the pack of cigarettes, he crunched them into a ball before flinging the whole pack onto the floor.

His intentions were clear as he moved quickly to the kitchen, lunging through the garbage that stood in his way. His prize awaited under the kitchen sink, trash bags. A white sheet of plastic flung open as he wrenched it out. This will take time, he thought, but he planned to take a break soon and walk down to the local diner. There he would order eggs over easy, toast and coffee. He hadn't been to the diner in so long, but he knew they would remember him, and how he liked his coffee. Or, at least he hoped she would be there and remember him. The thought of talking with the pretty brown-haired woman in the diner made him feel different. He liked the feeling.

Out the kitchen window, bright sunlight lit up the frozen yard. John paused, inhaling deeply, he breathed in yellow rays with the air. Squirrels ran across the patchy ground vainly searching for nuts. Focusing on the dirty windowpane, he barely recognized the image staring back at him. Moving in closer, he let out a quiet gasp—he was smiling.

Lisa Moak

Lisa Moak is a writer, musician, yogi and former expat who currently resides in Texas. She has worked more than 20 years in marketing and corporate communications, but has never strayed far from her first love of writing. Lisa writes poetry for *MadSwirl.com*, inspirational articles for *ElephantJournal.com* and essays and short stories for publication. While not working or writing, she also plays trombone in various concert/ jazz bands, gardens and raises chickens.

The Mysterious Gift
by Ray Reed

The old man stirred as he woke from his nap on the hard park bench. The shiny new green plastic bench the park department had recently installed was not as comfortable as the weathered bench with its sagging wooden slats he had slept on for years. As the fog of sleep dissipated, he instinctively looked to the bench beside him to ensure that his backpack was still there. It contained nothing that would be of value to anyone else, but it was all he had.

He didn't notice it at first, but as he sat up and looked around, something caught his eye. A piece of paper, a note perhaps, sticking out of one of the outside pockets. Who would leave him a note? His only friends, acquaintances really, were other members of the homeless community. He reached for the note, then recoiled in shock. It was a note all right—a one hundred-dollar note.

Where had it come from? He looked around. There were people in the distance walking their dogs, jogging, strolling down the track that wound through the park. The bench he was sitting on—*his* bench—was in a secluded part of the park, far from the popular trail. It offered an alluring view—azaleas and roses in the Spring, the leaves of the maples, oaks and elms creating a palette of red, yellow and orange in the Fall.

He was an anomaly among the homeless of the city. He had no sign announcing his need for money, did not wear a veteran's hat, did not spend his day standing on the street corner weaving between cars waiting for the light to change. He had cultivated relationships with a few business owners who paid him cash, or oftentimes food, for doing various jobs—picking up trash from their parking lot, rounding up stray shopping carts, scrubbing pots and pans. He didn't begrudge those who solicited publicly—most days they made more money than he did. He simply could not bring himself to beg. Circumstances had brought him to this point, but he still had his pride.

He looked again at the bill in his hand. He turned it over, held it up to the sky, looking for signs that it was fake—play money that someone thought would be a funny joke. Ben Franklin stared back at him, but in the light, he could see the other image of Franklin in the oval on the right side of the bill and the large numeral "100" visible vertically on the left. This was genuine.

Some days he made twenty dollars doing odd jobs, but that was rare. He had difficulty remembering when he'd had one hundred dollars. His memory of better days when he had a full-time job was fuzzy. There had been a time when having a hundred-dollar bill in his wallet was not unusual. Thoughts of home, a wife and family swirled through his mind like a vapor that just as quickly vanished. That one tragedy had changed all that.

What should he do with it? Unlike most of the homeless he encountered, he did not have an alcohol or drug problem, and that was one of the reasons he preferred being alone, rather than frequenting one of the shelters. He sympathized with those whose addictions drove them onto the streets, but he did not have a connection with them.

The brilliant midday sun warmed him as he pondered his good fortune, but the autumn evenings already had a chill in the air. He looked at the old blanket, worn thin by years of use, strapped to his tattered backpack. A new blanket, perhaps even a sleeping bag, and, oh…a pillow. What a luxury that would be on that hard, plastic bench. He grabbed his backpack and headed off to the Walmart several blocks down the street.

He returned an hour or so later with a large shopping bag in each hand. He would have a good meal this evening and then a great night's sleep. He was dismayed, however, when he saw a young man sitting on one of *his* benches, talking on his

The Mysterious Gift

cell phone. Occasionally, someone invaded his space, but mostly people avoided this secluded area of the park, which is why he had chosen it. Here was this young man not only sitting on one of his benches, but talking to someone on the phone.

He set the bags down and stood off to the side. He wasn't interested in eavesdropping on someone's conversation, but this was a common social norm these days. Despite people's protestations of privacy concerns, they posted personal information about their daily activities and carried on conversations in earshot of total strangers. The old man couldn't help but hear one side of this exchange.

"The doctor gave us a prescription for her, but the pharmacy said it would be eighty-five dollars. I don't have the money to get it filled," the young man explained, his voice almost cracking, as he shared his dilemma with the voice on the other end.

"I know, but I can't even provide for my daughter. It will be two weeks before my next paycheck, but she needs the medicine now."

The old man was only hearing one side of the dialogue and had no idea to whom he was talking, but the problem was clear.

"I couldn't help but overhear," he said as the young man clicked the phone, ending the call.

"Yeah," the young man replied, almost in tears. "My five-year old daughter has a severe infection, and the doctor prescribed an antibiotic for her, but when I went to get the prescription filled, they said it would be eighty-five dollars. I'm ashamed to say, I don't even have enough money to take care of my daughter's health."

"I heard you say you had a job."

"I do, but it doesn't pay much. We live from paycheck to paycheck, and I won't have enough money for her medicine for two more weeks. She needs it now. I had a second job at night, but I got laid off a few weeks ago and haven't been able to find anything else."

The old man stared at the young father who had his head in his hands. He was wearing jeans and a T-shirt and a worn-looking pair of sneakers. Nothing fancy, but clean and neat. He looked at the shopping bags he had placed beside his backpack. He thought of the contents that would provide comfort and warmth, then looked again at the young man. He recalled a young daughter of his own—a distant memory that still haunted him. He knew what he had to do.

Not wanting the young man to leave, he hesitatingly entrusted his entire possessions to this stranger. "Can you watch my backpack for a little while?"

"I guess," the young man replied. "I came out here to think, and I guess to avoid going home and facing my wife and daughter. A man is supposed to be able to provide for his family."

"I'll be back in about half an hour. Just keep an eye on my backpack."

The old man headed down the street. When he returned, there were no bags in his hands. He reached in his pocket and pulled out a crumpled hundred-dollar bill.

"Here," he said, as he proffered the bill to the young man. "Take this and get the medicine your daughter needs."

The young man stared at the bill. He looked at the old gentleman holding it. He glanced at the ragged backpack beside him. He was trying to process what was happening. A homeless man was offering him one hundred dollars. He had obviously returned whatever was in those bags, gotten his money back, and was now trying to give all of it to a perfect stranger.

"I can't take your money," he said. "One hundred dollars must be a fortune for you."

The Mysterious Gift

"I found the money sticking out of one of the pockets of my backpack when I woke up from my nap. Now I know why. It was so I could give it to you."

"But what was in the bags?"

"A pillow and a sleeping bag. This bench is nice—long enough for me to stretch out—but my backpack is not the most comfortable pillow, and there has been a chill in the air the past few nights. I do odd jobs during the day, though, and I can earn enough to buy what I need."

"How do you know I'm not scamming you?"

"I don't," the old man admitted. "But if you are, you must need the money more than I do. I may be homeless, but I still have my dignity. And if you do have a daughter that needs medicine, I'm glad that I can help you get her what she needs."

"Well, I have a confession. I don't have a sick daughter. In fact, I don't have a daughter at all."

The old man was still extending the bill. He looked directly into the young man's eyes. *Why was he telling him this? Did guilt change his mind and prompt him to tell the truth?*

"I do have a *YouTube* channel, though. Do you know what that is?"

The old man had heard of it, but wasn't familiar with exactly how it worked.

"I film people in various situations and then post the videos on *YouTube*. In fact, we've been filming you ever since you woke up from your nap. See that man with the camera crouched down in those bushes? I put the hundred-dollar bill in your backpack while you were sleeping. We've been videoing you ever since." The old man looked where he pointed and finally saw a man surrounded by azaleas with a camera in his hand.

"I must confess that I was trying to demonstrate why people should not give money to the homeless, but when we followed you and saw you go into Walmart rather than a liquor store, we quickly revised our strategy."

With that, he reached for his wallet and pulled out four more new Ben Franklins. "This is for you. I'd like to have your permission to post this encounter on the internet, but regardless, the money is yours."

The old man looked at the crisp new bills, the young man, the cameraman, the park bench, his backpack. Tears began to roll down his cheeks. He and the young man embraced.

"I had a young daughter once," he said, as his voice cracked with emotion. "She was sick, too. I would have paid any amount of money for her medicine, but there was none that would help her." Then he added, "You can use your video however you like."

"Can I come back and check on you from time to time?" the young man asked.

"I'd like that," the old man replied.

The Mysterious Gift

Ray Reed

Ray Reed is a retired firefighter who, along with his wife, enjoys traveling, spending time with their seven grandchildren, playing golf, reading and writing. He is active in his church, where he and his wife teach a young adult Bible study. Ray has written two novels, but "The Mysterious Gift" is his first attempt at a short story.

Christmas Lights in July
by B. K. Shaddick

Heels were a poor choice.

When I take a few steps from my car, my sole hits the loose gravel. My ankle twists. Stumbling, gravel crunching under me, I manage to stay upright by holding my arms out like a seabird hovering on the wind.

This day has not started well.

Under the shell of my pantsuit, I swim in sweat that covers my body like an ocean—at least the suit is black. The color will hide my permeating perspiration. I press the button on my key chain, yet don't hear the click of the car door locks engaging.

Oh, I locked it already.

I need to relax, but the Jones's residence is so out in the middle of nowhere—this whole trailer park—so isolated. Steadying myself, I clutch my handbag closer and adjust the awkward, inches-thick file under my arm.

Weathered boards creak as I ascend the stairs onto the rickety landing. The door is closed. I lean forward to peer into the darkened interior through the fractured glass of the storm door and a tiny, grimy stained glass window. A potent whiff of ammonia prickles the inside of my nostrils even with the door closed. I jerk back, blinking.

What in the world?

When I stand upright, something grazes the top of my head. I drop my file. Papers explode around me when the folder hits the landing's railing. I ignore the file and scramble to brush the top of my head and the sides and everywhere. I'm sure whatever touched me is a spider or a wasp, but no arachnid, or insect, is forthcoming. I glare up.

A single, red, broken-off and dirt-caked bulb of white-corded Christmas lights hangs directly in the center of the doorway.

Grumbling to no one, I take care not to disturb the rebelling curls resting for once controlled on the top of my head. Momentarily, I squint at my reflection on the cracked glass of the outer door. After readjusting my graying flyaways, I sigh and squat to rearrange the papers for one "Bunny Jones," age five. None of the file fell over the side onto the gravel; I'll take that as a tentative good sign.

As I'm about to knock, holding the case file in front of my body like a shield, I notice a tiny hazel eye peering at me through a less than an inch-wide crack between the inner door and threshold.

"Bunny?"

"Miss Shaw?" she says, high voice hoarse, and widens the crack between the door and threshold to sandwich her perfectly round face.

The tracks of tears clear streaks down her cheeks through dirt. Yellow faded ducks swim through the sweaty front of her thick, blue flannel onesie.

"Yes." I crane my neck to peer behind her.

The interior of the trailer is black as a cave in the middle of the day. Someone had taped aluminum foil to the windows. I check my watch. 2 o'clock on the nose. Kayly Jones should be here—I confirmed with her weeks ago at the hearing and yesterday morning over the phone.

"Where's your auntie?"

The door shrieks on its hinges, as she pushes it wider. She pops her index finger in her mouth, and I cringe at the black semi-circles under her other nails and the pungent stench that escapes the trailer. Her hair is rumpled and dirt covers her flushed face like an oil slick. A chemical taste rolls over my tongue. My hand wavers around my nose settling just above my lips.

"Bunny, where is your Auntie Kayly?" I cough, covering it by clearing my throat.

She shakes her head.

I raise my chin, "Ms. Jones?"

"My daddy was here. I told him mommy is gone."

My eyes widen, and I swing my head down to stare at the tears welling in Bunny's eyes, "When?"

Bunny drops her hand and licks her pink lips, then pulls the hood of her onesie up and over her head to cover her eyes. She turns to bury her face against the wall near the door. Perspiration darkens the crease behind her neck—where the hood sat folded.

Screw this. I shift her aside and stride in. I tear off my blazer and toss my file on the ratty, stained couch. The acrid scent of cat piss and cigarettes assaults my senses. My mouth goes dry. Feces dot the carpet to the left of the front door and continue in a trail down the hallway to the two bedrooms, but there isn't an animal in view. I don't remember a cat or even a dog. Most concerning is the interior, which is the same temperature, if not hotter than the exterior. The outer shell has created an oven of the aluminum trailer. The residence wasn't like this my last visit.

"Ms. Jones?" I call out again.

The trailer's bathroom is down the hall with the bedrooms, the one littered with brown landmines, but the bathroom door is cracked. Sunlight streaks the dingy linoleum in the narrow hallway. The other bedroom doors are cracked open, but it's too dark to see within.

There's a tug at the outer seam of my pants. "Miss Shaw? It's hot."

I kneel in front of Bunny so that we're eye to eye. I want to tell her to get out of the trailer, but a 60-year-old pedophile with a taste for girls under five lives a couple of doors down. No way. She won't be out of my sight. "How about some water?"

"Can Mommy get it for me?"

My eyebrows come together so hard above my eyes, I'll get a headache if I don't stop. I bite the inside of my cheek and sigh. "Your mommy, she's not coming back. Not for many years. Not until you're big—until you're grown."

Bunny wilts, as if she hasn't heard this story a thousand times. God, this isn't fair—it's just not fair. She's a good kid. I'd considered adopting her myself, considered it long and hard and... I kept coming back to her, remembering how I'd felt in fleece-wrapped footies, existing in a hot trailer with an absent mother—at least Bunny has attended some school.

I dig my government phone out from my pocket, notice in passing a voicemail from an unknown number, and scroll through my contacts until the "J" section. I press the green call button on Kayly's number.

The ring at my ear is answered by the tune of a popular country song coming from the bathroom. The song continues through the chorus. When it starts again, I end the call, glaring at the white sliver of light.

I rub my hands together, then on my pants, and wipe the sweat from my brow. My face heats and tingles, though it has nothing to do with the roasting interior of this trailer. I step over the animal feces, and the ball of my pump slips on what must be piss. I remain upright.

"Dang shoes." I glance back at Bunny. She hasn't moved from her spot near the door. "Stay there, sweetie. Don't go outside yet."

I push the bathroom door open and shriek. As if the place is on fire—and I admit it's almost there—a black cat darts out and bounces around the room before it finally sprints at the cracked door. It mashes its body against the threshold, finally escaping into the afternoon light.

"Rufus!" Bunny holds her arms out to the cat, but he's long gone.

The storm door claps closed. A jagged triangle of glass falls out onto the landing and shatters.

"Stay there, Bunny! Don't go near the glass." I peek back into the bathroom.

When I push the door open again, further this time, it snags on a lonely shoe against the yellowing linoleum. Rounding the door, I pause. The image of a woman's pallid face, her eyes still, pupils pinpricks, flashes from my memory into the physical world. I crush my eyes closed. When I reopen them, the white fiberglass shower, dark green mold around the edges and peppering the wall, greets me like an unwelcomed guest.

All the years I wore the badge still haunt me. Sometimes, I can't help the death that my mind creates—the phantom sensory of death. And all those years, I'd been so lonely, grieving for strangers.

Afraid I'd die alone.

A red toothbrush rests discarded in the sink, the flat bristled kind that you get free from the dentist. The water dribbles down the drain, which lacks its stopper. A syringe, its plunger to the bottom, flashes into being for a split second on the counter, and then it's gone. In its place is Kayly Jones's cell phone.

And to think—I'd thought this job would be less death, more helping children.

But the death is still with me.

I need life in my life.

But first, why is Kayly Jones's cell phone here on the counter and not with her? I glance back at the face of my phone, remembering the voice mail. I'd told Kayly I don't do texts, which she'd insisted on sending at all hours of the night since she'd taken temporary custody of Bunny. I'm old school. This generation is all about avoiding human contact more than shooting off some words. Did Kayly finally listen to me and leave a message?

I press 'play.'

"This message is for Jennifer Shaw, CPS, uh." There's some shuffling, and Kayly coughs. "I'll tell her!" She pauses and inhales. I get the impression she's sucking on a cigarette. Her person always reeked of them. "I'm going to Mexico with my boyfriend. For good. I'm almost at the border. I can't take care of a kid, even if it's my sister. Our bitch-ass mother couldn't keep herself out of the pen, and I'm not going to let her pass my sister off to me like she did me to her sister—God rest auntie's soul. I hope that woman takes a stainless steel ride."

And then, as if forgetting who she was talking to, she adds, "I left Bunny with our neighbor, Pam, at my mom's old place. She enjoys a rush—you know, dope, uh, drugs." I glance at the sink, but there's still no syringe. It really was my imagination again. "But she means well. She said she'd watch Bun until the morning you got there. I left her a fifty." She exhales into the phone. "Sorry, Jen."

I save the message and glance back at the empty shower. My mind has been getting better, but sometimes the hard ones stick with you. The young ones. I'm glad I didn't actually see this Pam in the shower. I'm not thrilled that the woman is nowhere to be found, but at least I can get Bunny out of here.

I leave Kayly's phone and exit the bathroom. I'll have to call it in, but—

"Miss Shaw?"

My eyes meet the bright eyes of miss duck onesie. "Yes, Bun?" The nickname is odd but not unwelcome on my lips.

"Can I come with you?"

My chest tightens as I stare at those puff curls, rebellious on her head. Without thought, I touch the top of my head, and my mind wanders to the woman I once saw dead in the shower.

Over Bunny's head, my eyes settle on a tiny, three foot Christmas tree I recognize from my last visit. The plastic branches are flattened on one side as if it had fallen, but someone put it back on its little pedestal near the vacant space where a TV once sat. Not a single ornament decorates its branches. A red, sun-bleached tree skirt surrounds the base, and I mentally compare it to the Christmas tree I'd put up last year for nobody but me and Tina Turner, my Russian Blue.

Bunny likes cats. She'd love Tina. Tina would tolerate her, I'm sure, as she tolerates me.

"Of course, Bunny, of course. We'll have to go back by my office."

A grin widens her face, and I can't help the grin on mine that answers.

B. K. Shaddick

B. K. Shaddick is an attorney, aspiring traveling foodie, and a veteran. She enjoys writing sci-fi and fantasy—featuring powerful female leads. "Christmas Lights in July" is a nod to her year of clerking for a judge who handled child abuse and neglect cases. In her free time, B. K. attempts to grow tomatoes in Fort Worth and practices hot yoga. She owns two dogs, is owned by two cats, and occasionally shares her home with foster dog(s).

What the Heck Am I Doing Up Here?
by Stella Kittles Sikes

Have you ever been in a situation and had the strange, ominous feeling that you weren't supposed to be there? I have—once, and I hope I never have it again. Not as long as I live.

I'm number six of eight children, born to native South Carolinians who moved to the small East Texas town of Athens when they were expecting their third child. Money was always tight around our house. But every four or five years my parents would load all of us into a "new" used station wagon, topped with a suitcase-laden luggage rack and pulling a trailer full of luggage for a trip back to South Carolina to visit kinfolk and show off the newest addition to our family. That was the extent of my vacations growing up.

After graduating from the University of Houston, I wound up staying and working in Houston. I had never really been an adventurous type; but since marrying in 1978, I had been on quite a few adventures with my husband, Jim—camping, whitewater canoeing, motorcycle riding. We even went skiing in Colorado on our honeymoon. Well, Jim skied, since he had been skiing for a number of years. I mostly tumbled down the bunny hill in ski school.

Jim was a native Houstonian, an engineer and an only child. His parents had both come from very humble backgrounds and neither one had ever had the opportunity to venture out into the world. Alma, born in Schulenburg, Texas, was the granddaughter of German immigrants, and grew up speaking German until her family moved to Houston when she was eight years old. Jimmie was born in Houston, but his paternal grandfather had also emigrated from Germany. Jimmie and Alma were married in October 1930 in the middle of the Great Depression, but it was over 17 years before their son Jim was born. And they would do anything for him. They looked more like his grandparents than parents, especially when he started school. Now, as they celebrated their Golden Wedding Anniversary, she was 71 and he was 78 years old, and neither one had ever been on an airplane.

"We're going to take you to Las Vegas for your 50th anniversary," Jim announced to his parents. "We'll be flying there," he added.

His dad said, "Oh, boy!"

His mom said, "Oh, my."

I made all of the arrangements, booking two rooms at the MGM Grand Hotel during the week of November 17, 1980, and scheduled our return to Houston for that Friday afternoon, November 21. As we sat on the airplane waiting to take off, I could tell that Jim's dad had on a new shirt and pants, since his clothes weren't dotted with tiny burn holes from the occasional ashes that would fall from the ever-present cigar in his mouth. Alma, wearing her usual double-knit, pull-on pants with a floral cotton blouse, fidgeted with her seat belt. Soon we took off, not realizing the perilous situation that awaited us in Las Vegas.

Jim's mom was a huge fan of Anne Murray, especially her song "Snowbird," so I had reserved tickets for her show later that week. We also saw one or two other shows while we were there. His parents stared in awe at all of the neon signs and sparkle of Vegas. Neither had ever seen anything like it! We had rented a car when we arrived, so we drove out to see Hoover Dam and some other sights. After dinner that Thursday evening, we went to see Anne Murray's show and they were both thrilled. Alma hummed "Snowbird" all the way back to our rooms.

Friday morning, our magical trip took an ominous turn. I remember waking up early to the sound of fire truck sirens. As I lay there, I said, "There must be a really big fire somewhere." Jim wasn't curious in the least. A fire station sat catty-cornered across the street from the hotel, so we had heard fire trucks leaving several times during our stay. But the fire truck sirens just kept going and going. *Well, I'm going to see what's going on,* I decided. So I went over to the windows, pulled back the drapes, and that was it—that was the moment—the most terrifying moment of my life!

There was smoke pouring out of our building—close to our windows and there were fire trucks all over the parking lot with people everywhere—people who seemed to be yelling and pointing at me, standing there looking out the window on the eighth floor of a building that was on fire. *Well, if the hotel's on fire,* I deduced, *what the heck am I doing up here?* "Holy crap, our hotel's on fire!" I yelled. But, what about fire alarms, room sprinkler system, the front desk calling our room or banging on our door to warn us? There was none of that. It was up to us to save ourselves. I'll never forget that feeling as long as I live.

Jim finally looked out the window for himself. *Didn't believe me, huh?* I thought, *Hurry up; we gotta get out of here!* Then I remembered—*We have to get his parents down all those flights of stairs!* No matter. Jim had already switched into high gear and quickly dressed. Not knowing what to expect in the hall, he cautiously opened our door. Smoke was hanging around the ceiling of the hall. A stairwell door across from our room intermittently spewed people covered in black soot, allowing even more smoke to belch into the hallway. People were running first one way and then the other, searching for a safe exit. This was no school fire drill. We needed to find a stairwell that led to the outside, to safety.

Jim took off down the hall. In a minute, he returned and reported that there was a stairwell at the end of our hall that led to the outside. Confident of our escape plan, we went next door to his parents' room to let them in on our situation. They were up and dressed, unaware of what was going on just outside their door. Jim calmly told them that there was a fire and we needed to get out of the building. We couldn't take any luggage with us since we had to help his parents manage all those stairs. But we *assumed* that we would get back into our rooms after the fire was out and everything calmed down. We had no idea about the magnitude of the situation.

So off we went into the stairwell, Jim holding on to his dad's arm and me holding on to his mom's arm. And there I was, traipsing down eight flights of stairs in my nightgown and coat. I was definitely in a hurry to get out of that building! But we couldn't hurry—not with his aged parents. Step by step, we made our way down the stairs, staying to one side, while others rushed past us. Both of his parents had arthritis and had a lot of difficulty maneuvering the stairs.

When we finally reached the fresher air of the world outside, we couldn't believe what we saw. It was like a scene out of a movie. Helicopters were plucking frantic people from the hotel roof. A few desperate people had actually tied sheets together and were hanging out of windows. And, worst of all, there were tarps covering lifeless bodies on stretchers in the parking lot.

We could not get away from the carnage fast enough.

We learned that a triage center had been set up in another hotel across the street. So we made our way there to get Jim's folks checked out. Walking down those eight flights of stairs of a burning building had been quite an ordeal for them. Both of their blood pressures were elevated, so the emergency staff had them lie down and gave them medication. Unfortunately, we had left their train case full of medications in their room with the rest of their things.

Meanwhile, I found a restroom in the triage hotel and changed into some clothes I'd grabbed at the last minute. Jim went back across the street to see what he could find out about the situation. After learning that we wouldn't be allowed to return to our rooms for our things, we decided to go to the airport and return to Houston as scheduled—minus our luggage.

Back in Houston that morning...my brother-in-law Rocky had seen the newscast about the fire at our hotel and called my sister Betty at her school. "I don't want to alarm you," he told her, "but your sister's hotel is on fire." Rocky was friends with a newscaster at KPRC television station in Houston, so he told him we had been in the MGM Grand fire and would be coming back to Houston that evening. When we returned home, a news crew came to our house and interviewed us about our experience for that evening's 10 o'clock news.

In the following days, we learned that 87 people had lost their lives, mostly from smoke inhalation; another 700+ people were injured, including 14 firefighters. The fire was blamed on faulty wiring in the kitchen area. The sprinkler systems that weren't required at that time later became mandatory in all new buildings. We eventually received our belongings from our rooms, minus some of our jewelry. We were reimbursed for the "missing" jewelry and for our room fees, as well.

I haven't been back to Las Vegas since then, but every time I stay in a hotel now, I always check for emergency exits close to my room. Do you do that when you stay in a hotel?

After almost 38 years, the emotions still well up inside of me just thinking about it. I'm so thankful that we survived the ordeal unscathed, and pray that I never have that feeling again.

Stella Kittles Sikes

Stella Kittles Sikes is a mother of two, retired, and enjoys learning something new every day—including how to maintain websites. A graduate of the University of Houston, and a 35-year resident of Houston, she now resides in Athens, her East Texas hometown. Having lived through some daunting situations in her life, she is currently writing her memoir as a series of short stories.

I Am Nothing
by Mary Ann Taylor

Louis Bernard collected thumbs. Each day, on the metro, he would take at least four, sometimes five thumbs, from unsuspecting passengers. Paris could be a brutal, lonely city, but this was a good living. With him, he kept a few thumbs to sell each day. Tourists would buy them, of course, or a schoolgirl awed by his precision and skill. A good life.

One day in mid-March, Louis Bernard took his collection and fanned the works on the seat. No one needed the space as the metro was practically empty this time of year, after the early rush of the morning. It was a small fan indeed, only two thumbs, neither particularly new nor crisp. At a euro each, they would not be enough. He needed a baguette a day, a box of milk, and an orange or apple. He must work.

He carefully stripped some newly-found metro tickets of their written instructions, leaving a reasonable surface in yellow or an unfortunate green with tiny holes pierced two-thirds of the way down the edge. The size was good, the texture not so bad. One did what one must, for art. The peelings left some untidiness which Louis Bernard tucked into his coat.

He could tell it was bitterly cold outside, as the travelers had on gloves, scarves and hats. Only a few had their hands free for his viewing. A young group stepped on, laughing and loud. They were, of course, Americans. They were always so open, looking into one's eyes with such frankness that it still made Louis Bernard gasp. Three of them clung to the metal pole in the center of the aisle and none wore gloves. He decided to take all their thumbs; a boy said they had nine stops. Surely he would have to hurry.

From his pocket he removed a knife, opened it carefully, and placed it on his leg. Taking out a pencil, just a stub now, he coaxed the end into sharpness. Perhaps it was a cloudy day, suggesting to him that he should use the yellow. They sold better anyway. Louis Bernard hoped it would be his good fortune to sell some of the thumbs back to the Americans. Two euros and he could buy a baguette for breakfast, as well as that night's dinner, which he had not as yet arranged.

He went to work quickly. The first one was easy, a young man's thumb with no marks or wrinkles. It took only two stops, which pleased Louis Bernard. The second one belonged to a woman. The nail was carefully painted a deep red and looked odd, as if it had been a replacement. Who knew with women?

The third was nearing completion when one of the group exclaimed, "Wow! Look at that! The old guy's drawing that thumb thing." It was the thumb, *le pouce,* not a thumb *thing.* Americans rarely remembered that the French had studied their language, although, oddly, they expected fluency from strangers on the street. What awkward nonsense, he thought. Louis Bernard made the French with his mouth, silently, assuming no one would notice. He liked how the roundness of the ooh-sounds felt. Because they were ignorant, Louis Bernard would not look up, not even pretend to notice, until he was ready to show his works for sale.

It was not always so. As a young man, painting on Montmartre, he lingered lovingly on the angle of a nose, the shadow below an eye, even a single hair, as he joked with his customers. They were often ignorant as well, but he was bright, full of juice. His friend Paul routinely traded his work for the favors of the clients. Never Louis Bernard. At least once, a woman asked him if he would barter, and he calmly replied that he would not. He was not sure what she meant to exchange, to be honest, but he preferred to think she meant to give her watch instead of herself. And the years faded, cold and hot, spring and fall, until he was no longer young enough to paint at Montmartre and wait for the money to come to him. As for Paul, he never knew what happened to him, but rather liked to think the worst: he had married and moved to Florida.

This day, on the metro, he finished his tiny portrait. He looked up and smiled winningly, "Voila," he said, knowing the Americans would understand that much. "Two euros." The young man whose thumb it was, blushed.

"Come on, it's yours," Louis Bernard continued. "Two euros." He made the "two" very clear so as to be understood. The boy shrugged, then reached for his money. As he struggled to count something out, the train pulled into the next stop: Georges Cinq.

"Why do they call it that?" one of the American girls wondered. "George sank, George sank, time to pull a pretty prank," she giggled. Just as the horn sounded to close the doors, a French girl in a school uniform rushed past the other passengers and snatched Louis Bernard's cap, and as the doors slammed, her triumphant "Regardez! Regardez!" echoed through the metro. A prank indeed.

Louis Bernard refrained from crying out after the girl. What would have been the point? She was gone, and the train was pulling out. He handed the boy the drawing and absentmindedly put the coins beside him. He tried to sketch a bit more, but felt discouraged and weak.

Soon the Americans began looking at signs carefully, mumbling to each other that the next stop was theirs. Louis Bernard was not unhappy to see them go. It had been a poor morning's work. Suddenly he looked beside him at the coins that lay carelessly tossed on the seat, gold edged with silver. Ignorant! Two euros each instead of one. The extra must be returned. Louis Bernard looked around worriedly; the boy was at the front of the group. The door opened at the station, and the Americans straggled off. Louis Bernard stiffly behind them muttering, "Pardon, pardon."

The young people were much faster, but Louis Bernard was intent. This was a new station, unfamiliar to him. At one end was a section of escalators. The boy and his group headed toward them. Louis Bernard tried to call out, but it was no use.

I Am Nothing

As he reached the top of the rise, he saw the backs of the young Americans as they sprinted to the middle of a wide plaza. Sick at his own mistake, he turned to retreat to the train when he saw two things that would change his life: a statue and a tall young woman with a shock of bright blonde hair, gazing down at his Paris.

"No officer, I don't mind a few questions. My name is Louis Bernard. I collect thumbs. Drawing them—for a living. Each day on the metro, I take four or five to sell later. I have been known to sell the thumbs back to the very ones from whom I have taken them. I have done nothing wrong. No need for handcuffs; I shall come quietly in your foursome. But once you hear my story, you will understand that I was perfectly justified in my actions of today. In no way was I defiling art, as your alleged witness suggests.

"The thumbs? Ah, yes. A good place to begin. When I arrived in Paris, I hoped to study with someone of substance. But I had no money. What else? Teachers care for what they can get, nothing more. A few said I had promise, to get money and return. So I went to Montmartre. Money to study? No. Now I draw on the metro. It is a living.

"I had just finished a boy's thumb and another when the schoolgirl snatched my cap. As you can see, I have no hat so I am telling the truth. The boy foolishly paid me 4 euros, but with the excitement, I did not pay attention. The Americans cannot grasp the money, haven't you noticed? I wanted to return the coin, as I have always been honest, monsieur. In that manner I arrived at the stop called La Defense. Yes, that's it. I had never been there, of course. It was not my stop. It was not my choice, but it was time for my daily. So why not?

"Have you been to this...this atrocity? So horrible, impossible. Nothing but new this, new that. La Défense. Ha. Everything shiny and steel. The new French, the technophiles. Where it will end?

"Suddenly, there it was. On the right, I do not know how far from that old abomination, the *escalier roulant*. A great thumb posing as art. Monsieur, I ask you as a fellow Frenchman, why? Unspeakable, and what is more, it is my living to draw thumbs. Can you not see it now, what they have done? Surely you understand? Someone has taken my idea and stolen it, mocking me in front of all France. What I drew, I did for each individual, not for all the world to see in such a way. And there, on the esplanade, in bronze. It was too much.

"But then I saw her. Oh, what a vision, an angel surely. She was tall and glowing. Her long hair a perfect shade of gold, a halo. I walked toward her, of course, forgetting the boy. Her eyes were blue beyond earthly blues, blue as heaven itself. She had no need of a coat although it was bitter. She was an angel, monsieur, I assure you. Listen, I heard voices call her: "Ami, ami." And I knew what I must do. No, no, of course they did not pronounce it correctly. Americans never do the *a's* well. But I knew what they were saying. She was the Friend, the angel to whom I must go and tell my burden before I could continue against the enemy newly arisen.

"So I went to her and looked up—she was taller than I— and said, 'Friend, I must tell you of myself.' I spoke to her of all my training, the good, the bad. She knew it already, of course, but I understood I must tell her myself. Ah, my life. The disappointments, the joys. I told her of dreams of another Friend, all in white, whispering to me through the years. I spoke of metro wisdoms—the small ways to avoid uneasy glances, the great rewards of beauty and its study when no one else can see. I told her of her own high position, her soul's purpose to come to me and hear my confession. I could barely watch her as the sun made the light around her. How it gathered to her. I assured her that I was nothing. *Je ne suis rien*, from Paul. But she had come to give me hope and life. Surely you can understand.

I Am Nothing

"And then I saw her face, that it never moved, frozen in a perfect smile. Had it been other than an angel, I should have wondered how she could be so still. It was an artist's dream, for the corner of her mouth never once faltered, even when she stopped me to say in good French, 'Merci, merci' and turned to walk away.

"It was at that moment that I decided never to draw another thumb. It would be wrong. Why, they would think I was giving them the *statue*, *mais no*, the word is too good for the vulgar thing. That I was selling some silly souvenir. Unthinkable. I am sure you would agree. At that moment, I knew I must now draw the corners of the mouth. Not the entire smile, just that bit of angle where upper and lower lips meet. Like the angel arc that it was. Do you not see? Perhaps too *avant garde* for you to understand, monsieur, but I feel great excitement. At last, I have something new.

"Then I went for my daily. It seemed that I should include the enemy in my ritual. I never saw anyone. I know about the tourists, watching upward and out always. One takes care to avoid running into them. Perhaps, had I seen your witness... But, that's life. Surely, monsieur, you can understand. If it were art, perhaps..."

"You just don't know how glad I am you can speak English. 'Je m'appelle Amy.' That's all I can say, plus 'Merci,' for real. Madame says my 'Merci' is great. I mean, we've been here three days and it's so hard to get used to, you know? I guess we all thought y'all...all y'all...I mean, they all...Oh, well. I suppose we supposed the French really spoke English, if they wanted to. But no one will much, except in the expensive places. And the French words, man. We're all first semester pretty much, in high school, you know? Well, I've had Spanish myself, because in Texas—that's where I'm from—they say everyone ought to know at least some. This trip, though, what a ...What was the question again?

"Oh, right. We were taking a little break and getting ready to shop. I mean, that's fun anywhere, if you know what I mean. There's only so much museum hopping and culture a person can stand. That big cemetery, Pere Lachaise, counted as culture, too. When we got to La Defense, I couldn't really decide where to go, so I just sort of stood there. It was so cold I could hardly move. It's odd how it can be so sunshiny and still twenty degrees. I should have brought my coat. I looked at the Grand Arch and then down into Paris. It's really, really big, you know? Paris? The new Grand Arch at the top of this hill, then the Arc de Triomphe down in town—it all looked way cool, like they planned it that way.

"Then that old man walked up. Took him a long time to get to me, which was weird, because who would've thought he'd be coming to me, of all people. Really, he looked pitiful—almost white, like some sort of creature, you know? Like this albino salamander my little brother kept once for a Boy Scout project? He kept his eyes all squinty and started talking. He's short, so he had to look up at me the whole time. I'm not tall enough for basketball, but I do play volleyball at school and love to spike, although I'm not too good at setting, and I just hate to serve. But when you're that tall, it's hard to shop because the good things are all size fours and sixes. I get so jealous sometimes. Oh, where was I? Oh, yeah, the old guy. He went on and on, looking up at me, eyes practically closed. I could only catch bits of it. Some sort of autobiography, I think, about his life. And parts were about heaven, though my vocab is pretty much terrible and I couldn't get the connection between his life and heaven. French is just too fast. Am I speaking slow enough for you? Okay. I just wondered.

"Anyway, I listened as long as I could. I wasn't exactly scared, but he smelled so bad, you know? I thanked him with my best *mercis* and walked away. I hoped he wouldn't follow me, and he didn't. He went over to that statue thing, the thumb. I thought the French were supposed to be rude and here he is friendly as pie...Oh, I'm sorry. I didn't mean that like it sounded.

"He stood there and I watched from behind a column just to see what he was going to do. In our country people sometimes get guns and do things. I thought he was such a nice old man at first. Maybe he'd try to gum somebody to death but that's about it. Gum. . .gun. . .gum . . .gun . . . I never realized how close alike they were. Well, I tell you, it was totally yuck. He sort of started trickling. Le Pouce, right? The thumb statue. And, well, I know you know what he did. I think you do or none of us'd be here, right? He peed. Big as Dallas. He sat there and took out his you-know-what and went potty. All over the base of the statue. I mean, that isn't okay, is it? Even here in France? And he laughed the whole entire time. I couldn't see anything funny. Madame lectured us about dog poop and little kids going and how we shouldn't get all Puritanical about the whole thing. But grown men? And long? He must have gone for five minutes. It went everywhere, steamy like.

"Anyway, I hope you won't hurt him or anything. I thought he was nice at first but man oh man, that was nasty. I mean, don't you have places for people like that here? He didn't look hungry or stupid or dangerous crazy or anything. But peeing on sculpture? On culture? Too gross. Are you going to do anything to him, or what?"

The Eleventh Commandment: Three Candidates
by Mary Ann Taylor

Wake Unto Me

Cavan and Zoe entered the theater as the house lights dimmed. Their seats were on the right aisle, center section, halfway down. Heads turned as they passed, hand-covered mouths whispering to partners. There were knowing smiles of recognition. Cavan stood back as Zoe took her seat, settled in, and rearranged her skirt. He looked deep into her eyes as he sat, which always made her melt, and stroked the back of her neck with his fingertips.

The classic theater was beautifully refurbished. Stately trompe l'oeil arches framed pastoral scenes on the walls. Majestic columns, subtly painted on the proscenium, soared higher than real columns have ever gone, slender, graceful, strong. The new curtain was black velvet, the same material, really, as Zoe's dress.

As the curtain rose, the orchestra began a gentle overture with a solo flute, echoed by a French horn. The melody ascended slowly, in the modern way, like a Goreçki symphony, seeming to harmonize effortlessly up a never-ending scale. The bass notes were felt before they were heard, so soft was the dynamic, so low the pitch. Cavan's music, thought Zoe, his best work ever.

Zoe turned to look at him as he listened. He had long, dark blonde hair, caught at the nape of his neck. It was always so, never free. His forehead was high. His eyes, green and clear, glistened.

The first actor entered, stage right, and the sight thrilled Zoe. Actors were wonderful, to take words that lay on the page and make them live gloriously. And these actors knew their lines perfectly.

The Eleventh Commandment: Three Candidates

The opening speech was brief but startling. The plot complication involved a young nobleman who sought to convince his brother that he was serving an evil enemy. Their sister was to marry a prince of the kingdom. A traitor, in an effort to overthrow the plan, produced evidence of her infidelity and enlisted the sinister brother's aid in its disclosure. The noble brother pleaded with him, saying it was impossible to serve one who hates us. A disastrous conclusion seemed at first inevitable, and the tension allowed the audience to weep in fear. With the unexpected conclusion, a dramatic revelation of their sister's innocence, the audience wept with joy. The words were Zoe's, her finest play.

Before the applause ended, Zoe and Cavan slipped out. He took her hand as they hurried up the aisle to shouts of "Bravo!" and "Brava!" In the foyer, marble floors reverberated with even more music, a magnificent waltz. Cavan stopped, still holding Zoe's hand. They began to dance. She swirled, and the deep turquoise silk of her dress fell in waves around her. Her eyes met his again. In great, graceful circles they waltzed. Zoe was glad of the different skirt but couldn't remember changing.

When the music stopped, Zoe went in search of the lady's room. She remembered that the theater had a lovely one. In the farthest corner was a toilet just for little girls, half-sized and pink. She was disappointed to find that all the stalls were broken or locked. The child's was gone entirely. Leaving reluctantly, Zoe was surprised to see the audience now filling the foyer included old, dear friends. Some had died years before, she thought, but perhaps she'd been mistaken. She found Cavan.

He stood erect, thin and lean; his steel grey hair was quite short. His lips, sweet as ever, were in a bemused bow. As they left the theater, Zoe realized that her damask dress was covered in roses and wondered how she could have changed again without anyone noticing.

As Zoe took Cavan's hand, she explained that it was possible to walk above the trees. He looked at her silently, as if he knew what she intended. They walked down the wide steps to the sidewalk and then, without effort, without impediment, the two ascended above the street and over the aspens that swayed gently in the lightest breeze. It was effortless and wonderful to fly! Zoe felt happy and fulfilled. She decided it was best to return to the ground and search out another restroom. Coming down, she heard a dog yelping insistently. It was very close.

Oh, Schatzi, she whispered. We both need to go, don't we? Zoe sighed. Such a beautiful dream. She got up, let Schatzi out, and went to the bathroom and thought of the 11th commandment: Thou shalt not drink a Diet Coke before bed. It was still early. Perhaps she could find some of the dream.

Cavan was sleeping deeply, thankfully. Years ago, when he was himself and could speak with sense, he commented that he never dreamt. She knew he did, of course, because he'd laugh in his sleep. She'd laugh to hear him so amused by a dream.

Zoe strained to think of the plot of her play. It made such sense at the time. Was forgetting some strange punishment, for all those marvelous men named Cavan who, of course, weren't him at all, not now? And then the bathroom indignity. Unfair.

She unknotted Cavan's hand as she lay back into her pillow and put it under her neck. When he awoke and moved, she would feel something, even if he didn't mean the gesture.

The Collard Shirt

Wanting is the flavor of a nickel sitting on your tongue. It aches down the jaw strongly, and with a wrenching bouquet, settles in your stomach. Cassandra knew that flavor very well. She knew it when she was six years old and saw the dress in Sears. It was pink and white, the neckline trimmed in seed pearls.

The Eleventh Commandment: Three Candidates

"Mama, can I have that dress?"

"I don't know, Cookie. It looks a bit small." And so her mama took it off the rack and walked imperially, for she was a stout woman, to the counter. "My baby would like to try on this dress. Would you be so kind as to direct us?"

"Sorry, but colored is not allowed to try on." Mama blinked her eyes. This was not their beloved Chicago, but mid-sixties Dallas. "Then we'll just take it." She counted out the cash, and thanked the woman for her time.

"Mama, why you cryin'?"

"I'm not crying, baby. An angel was pinching my cheek for a minute to remind me to tell you how much I love you. Here, give me some sugar." Mama reached down and hugged her. Sears in Dallas also had colored water fountains, but Mama would never allow Cassandra to drink from them. And after wearing that beautiful pink dress once, Cassandra never saw it again, although she hadn't minded that it pinched her arms. She remembered wanting it but forgot how flavor faded once the object of desire was had.

When she was fifteen, she tasted that nickel again, but this time it was like raspberry juice, deep, rich, insistent.

Cassandra saw Lionel playing football one hot September night. He was shiny with sweat. Cassandra didn't understand the ins and outs that interested him, and four months later, when she feared she had a stomach tumor, her mama quizzed her at length. The baby was kept at home and Cassandra went to work.

"Cookie, class does not have color. Do right and be right. Everything will be fine."

And things were fine. As Khalim grew, Cassandra realized that the flavor of wanting could acquire a permanent status. All she wanted was for Khalim to succeed. Her jaw ached for him constantly. In elementary school, she went over his homework with him for an hour.

"Mama, Miz Hutchins said it was a five minute 'signment."

"Maybe so, Skeeter, maybe so. Read it to me one more time, baby." And then he could go play. She was not disappointed. His grades continued good in middle school. He had manners, never trouble. He played basketball and was popular and happy. She lost her Mama but found her place as one.

Cassandra was not surprised when he was invited to the Oak Cliff Country Club. Three of the basketball boys' families were members, the fathers all doctors. Golf was a class game, and anyone could play, though she couldn't offhand think of any brothers who were famous at it.

"Mama, they told me to wear a green shirt."

"What for, Skeeter?"

"They just said. OK? I don't know why."

Cassandra explained to him that tennis players wore white, so maybe golfers wore green, and she certainly didn't know any different.

"Now, Arthur Ashe is a brother, and he always wears white. Do you want to go?"

"Yes, Mama. What am I gonna do about a green shirt?"

"I expect any green shirt would do. Wear those white jean shorts we got last spring, and I'll run get you a nice T-shirt over at the K-Mart."

A few days later, the big day finally arrived. Cassandra never let on how pleased she was. She pulled the car into the gravel driveway at the club and let Khalim out. He told her Jason would bring him home.

On the drive back, Cassandra thought she felt pretty sassy. She wished she could call her mother and tell her about Khalim. They say it's what you miss most after they pass, being able to call them up. "Mama, he's a good boy, and today he's playing golf at the country club. Isn't that fine?"

The Eleventh Commandment: Three Candidates

Four hours later she heard the front door shut, and then Khalim's door slam. Puzzled, she went to his room.

"What is it, baby? Something wrong?" He turned on some music, loud. "Skeeter, what's wrong?" Cassandra began to panic. He had closed the door and propped an old bed slat against the knob. Cassandra usually didn't bother, but her mind was racing, and she couldn't stand the suspense. She unwrapped a hanger, knelt on the floor, and with her face near the crack, pushed until the slat fell. Khalim was on his bed. The green shirt was on the floor, apparently hurled away. Hot tears brimmed in his eyes.

"What's wrong, baby?"

Quickly, he wiped an angry tear. "Nothing."

"Just tell me. You know I'm not leaving this spot till you do, young man."

He cut his eyes around and looked at the opposite wall, where a poster of Michael Jordan stretched his arms an impossible distance.

"They said wear a *collared shirt*. I thought they were trying to talk jive, saying *collard*, like greens. But they were saying collared, like old men wear. Jason said he thought I'd know. It's like some sort of eleventh commandment, he said, only everybody who plays golf really obeys it."

Cassandra blinked her eyes. Her sides began to shake. She covered her face with her hands and tried not to laugh, but it came in great, swelling waves. Tears rolled down her face.

"Why you cryin', Mama?"

She wouldn't have told him the truth for anything. "I'm not cryin', baby. An angel pinched me, that's all. To remind me to say I love you." She wiped her face and stood up to leave. "I love you, baby." He was too big to hug, he'd said so not long before, so Cassandra planted a kiss on his head. If she'd noticed, she would have realized that the taste of the nickel had faded, but the joy of having, remained.

Parable of the King's Bridge

And it came to pass that the Old Man, foul for protection, foolish by design, became tired and longed for rest.

"I shall lay me down under the overpass there by the Federal Building," he said. And he took his pack and his Thermos and he went to the place where the walkers passed above him, from one building to the next. He laid himself down, and he saw there was a vent from which poured warm, sweet air into the January chill. And it was good.

Each two hours did the Old Man, putrid by neglect, sick by misfortune, move himself carefully from the path, for officers of the law enforced the kingdom's decree that no man, neither any woman, should lie on the vents or streets of the city. And so it continued throughout the day.

Nevertheless, the Old Man drank rotted gall which passed for wine, consumed for warmth, comfort, and ancient desire. In the fourth hour of the afternoon, the man roused himself not from the way, but remained while the watch kept its rounds.

And it came to pass that an officer of the law remarked to his fellows that the man seemed too still and might have left this life for another, which should be a blessing to the Old Man who smelled and ranted and hungered and drank the vile poison of his choosing. The officer called through the heavens to his brothers and sisters for aid in touching this miscreant who stirred not.

Other officers of the law careened through the concrete canyons of the city and, arriving, inquired of their brother what had come to pass. For all knew the rules of the kingdom forbidding his place of rest.

A sister officer set her face in stone and said that she would wake the man if the dead could be waked. And she shook him harshly and called him a name not his own, to no avail. Another officer, a youth, began to see that he was but ill. And the first officer said that the Old Man should be taken to the porch in the city wherein worked physicians who might

The Eleventh Commandment: Three Candidates

care for him until he was returned once more to the streets where he would dwell for the rest of his days.

And so it was that the Old Man was taken up into the officer's vehicle and the air was allowed to enter so that his stench should not remain within it. And the officers left hence to take him to the care of the physicians who would learn his name and give him broth and implore him to get himself to a shelter for the rest of the harsh winter.

And there was another man, who, from his high window amid steel and glass, watched the hours of the Old Man. "I thank all powers that be that I am not as this Old Man in the street," he prayed. "For I cleanse from me the sweat of my brow and bathe my body each day that I live, and I drink not the contamination that enters his body and passes vilely into the gutters of the city. I taint not myself with herbs that are not of exquisite refinement. And I sleep not under bridges." And through the day, he sought his papers with diligent concern and called heartily and happily to his brothers and sisters throughout the land.

And it came to pass, that the fellows of the man high above the street remembered that it was the day on which he celebrated his birth. And they did give thanks for his presence among them, bringing all manner of meats and sweet things to consume. The man ate and rejoiced and was glad. And the man did strive not to sleep after the feast for such was forbidden.

As the day was ending, the man and his fellows made light of the Old Man—fetid by choice—who had been removed from the grate of redolent air and said with mirth that the man knew not the eleventh commandment.

And the man reached low into his leathern pouch and removed a placard onto which had been engraved: "11. Thou shalt look busy." And the laughter was loud in the company of those who sat with the man.

And so it was that on that night, the man dreamt of white bedclothes. For he saw himself and all his fellows covered with their sepulchral stillness. And, in the dawn, the man vowed not to waste his time upon the earth, but to do and be good. He would seek out the Old Man from below the bridge and offer him of his silver and lift him gently. And he would carry him unto shelters and give of his own time and substance. His thoughts were kind and righteous toward the man, his vow pure and true.

But lo, in this day, came the leave-taking of the princely head of his fellows, and all was in preparation. The man remembered himself and wondered if he might gain in power and influence with his fellows. He sought high words and praise for his own great deeds, and inscribed them to those who reigned above him. And his vow of compassion was forgotten when he was found worthy to advance in station, to the unknowing sorrow of the Old Man, and many unto whom he might have done that which was good.

Yea, as the years passed, the time came for the Old Man to go down to his grave, on a cold night, as he lay himself under a bridge. And there were none to mourn him as he joined his generation of paupers beneath the earth.

In his old age, the other man was not taken down to the street nor cast under a bridge. And it soon became time when he would go down to his grave and join the Old Man beneath the earth. In the days before his passing, the man had grown weak and silent, in spite of his wealth and former joys.

And, as his days grew short, he cried out, "What lack I yet?" And his eyes fell upon the words of the inscription which he once thought held such wisdom: "11. Thou shalt look busy." Lo, he could not. Into his mind came the commandment with no number, yea, the one greater than them all: Thou shalt love. Yea, he saw the paths in which he had failed, for they were many. Yea, he longed for love and pity, and he hoped for grace eternal.

The Eleventh Commandment: Three Candidates

Mary Ann Taylor

Mary Ann Taylor lives in Duncanville but hails from San Angelo originally. Following dual careers as an investigator with Children's Protective Services and as a teacher at Mountain View College, she now blogs at BluebonnetSyrup.com and tries to be helpful to others. She has two stories in *Texas Shorts*: "I am Nothing" and "The Eleventh Commandment."

The House
by Mary Sue Tiffin

Absentmindedly, she drove to the back of her house. Grabbing groceries from the back of the car, she slammed the trunk shut. The day had been challenging, to say the least, and she was looking forward to a quiet, uneventful evening. She followed the stone path to her back porch, climbed the three steps and froze.

Her screen door had been ripped, the door pulled partially out of the hinges. The interior door was completely broken. A clear view of most of the kitchen and the hallway leading to the rest of the house was giving her adrenaline a major boost.

Quietly, she set down the groceries. Her detective senses heightened, she drew her loaded gun from its holster, and carefully entered. To her left, the laundry room was untouched. The kitchen didn't seem to be disturbed, so she pressed down the hall, pausing to listen for any unusual sound. Navigating the creaks in the floor, she arrived at the living area. All was good.

Still quiet, she proceeded across the living room to the hallway that led to the bedrooms. She checked them and the bathroom but found nothing out of the ordinary.

She turned back to the main room. As she started to open the massive wood-carved front door, someone shoved the door and sent her reeling backward onto the floor. Regaining her balance and grabbing her gun, she ran outside but found nothing. More puzzling was why. As a police detective, she seldom brought her work home. Her case files were locked up at the precinct. What were they expecting to find?

Jennie decided to phone her former partner who was now at a different precinct.

"Mark, any chance you could come over and help me bolt my back door?"

The House

"I guess so. What's wrong with it?" He didn't sound too thrilled.

"An intruder broke in and fled out the front."

"Jennie, are you ok? What was he after? What did he look like? How much damage?" His voice now showed his concern.

"I'm fine, have no idea what he wanted or what he looked like. He's gone now. The doors were the only things damaged as far as I can tell."

"I'm coming. You be careful."

Trying to figure out a reason for the break-in, she distracted herself by retrieving her groceries and putting them away. Still antsy, Jennie changed out of her work clothes and waited for Mark. When he arrived, he quickly walked around the house looking for clues. Finding none, he grabbed his tools and some barbeque he had picked up. Jennie laughed. That man did love his BBQ!

She was suddenly hungry and grateful for his thoughtfulness. They decided to have a less hurried meal before plunging into the repairs. He had brought both brisket and ribs. Fries and beans plus fresh rolls completed the dinner. She provided the drinks.

Jennie had known Mark since their days at the police academy. He was a few years older, but they shared many interests. Both had lost a parent at a young age, and both were 'tunnel-vision focused' with their work as detectives. It was nice to be able to relax with someone who understood the other. Both were dedicated to their jobs, so friendship was their only relationship. They seemed too busy for more personal matters.

After lingering over some chocolate chip cookies Jennie found in her freezer, Mark asked for a detailed account of her visitor. She gave him a step by step account, walking through the events of the evening. They looked inside for any clue of what the intruder wanted.

It was a futile effort.

Mark wanted one more look outside. Although the light was fading, he hoped they might find some overlooked clue. Jennie was feeling exhaustion creep over her, but was grateful that Mark was so particular.

The coolness of the evening got her attention, so she grabbed a jacket from the front door coat stand. Thinking that Mark might want a jacket, she called out to him. Getting no response, she hollered again.

"Mark? Mark? Where are you?"

This was unusual. She went down the front steps and around the corner of her house. She kept calling until she found him lying under some bushes. He was not moving. His head was oozing blood from a nasty gash. She quickly looked around to make sure the attacker was gone, and then focused on her friend.

"Mark, can you hear me? Talk to me!"

She knelt beside him and, finding him barely breathing, called 911—reporting 'officer down.' Usually this hastened the response and, within a few minutes, the ambulance and a police car arrived.

After the paramedics examined him, they said he would be taken to the Trauma Center. The 'TC,' as it was known, was reserved for critical cases. It was distressing news.

Jennie knew one of the patrol officers. Tristan had been in a few of her classes at the police academy. She thought at times he might have had a crush on her, but he had been a good student, and was eager to learn everything he could about police work. He wanted to be a detective, so she was always ready to answer any of his questions. He had real possibilities. She felt much better about solving this mystery with him being in charge. Tristan assured her that he and his partner Rick, whom she did not know, would be very thorough.

Jennie gave a detailed report beginning with her discovery of an intruder. The men checked the house inside and out. They found a place behind tall bushes and a few trees that seemed to have been recently disturbed. Coming to see what they had found, she noticed the area was nowhere near where Mark had been injured. Tristan suggested that the intruder might have been watching her. This had been in the back of Jennie's mind and was not a comforting thought.

When the report was finished, Tristan wanted her to stay in a hotel for a few days for safety reasons. She was reasonably sure the visitor wouldn't return, at least not tonight, so she declined. Jennie thought his concern was sweet.

She found Mark's tools and awkwardly braced the back door with the 2x4s. Although not completely secure, it would be fine for now.

It was curious, she thought as she drove to the TC. She had nothing of value in her house. Jewelry was minimal, with most being passed down from her mother and grandmother. Keepsakes, really. Not any value except sentimental. The same could be said for any decorations and pictures. So, why her house? It was just a nice, basic, older home with some lovely acreage. She had admired it for years.

When she had moved to the area, it was one of the first houses she had seen. It had seemed to be abandoned, but she couldn't find any records. The clerk at the courthouse explained that there had been a fire about eight years before and many of the records were lost. Eventually, it came up for auction and she was able to grab it. As she had slowly repaired the house, it had become her refuge—until now.

When she arrived at the TC, she discovered they weren't prone to sharing details about a patient unless it was family. She tried to use her badge for information and all it got her was that Mark was resting but unconscious. "The next 48 hours…" She had heard this comment before and it was difficult to wait, because this time it was a friend and not an unknown victim.

Since she couldn't see Mark, she returned home and tried to get some sleep.

After lunch the next day, Tristan stopped by her office and asked if she knew anything about the previous owners of her home. Jennie referred him to the courthouse records.

"Why?" she asked.

"In checking around, we found that the house had once been owned by the daughter of an eccentric millionaire. Her father also had shady dealings in financial 'areas!'"

"So you're thinking that there might be something in the house that would indicate him in a crime?"

"Not so much that," continued Tristan. "He just vanished and everybody figured he had been murdered. Maybe his body was hidden under the house or on the property."

Jennie shuddered. This was not anywhere in her ideas of why she had an intruder.

"Is the daughter still alive? When did she move out? Was she the last occupant? Where did you find this information?"

"Slow down," Tristan replied. "We don't know if she is living because when she left here, she left no trace. Can't find records anywhere. You got the house on auction because of two years' back taxes. That's the only thing we have been able to find out."

Jennie sighed. What was happening to her little piece of 'happy', she wondered. The intruder must have been watching the house for some time. Now she considered what Mark might have found before he was hurt.

Since she had not been able to see Mark, she asked Tristan if he could check and see when Mark might be able to tell him what had happened. A policeman investigating the injury would have more influence with the TC staff.

It was two days before Mark regained consciousness and Tristan could question him. Mark didn't remember much, but had a vague memory of a disturbance under that window where he was found. He had bent over to inspect it in more detail, but that was his last memory. He was still groggy with a very bad headache.

The House

Later that day, when Jennie turned the corner to her house, she was stunned to see lots of activity. She parked when she got closer and went to see what was happening. There were guys digging, a few dump trucks, even a backhoe.

"What the heck is going on?" Jennie asked Tristan.

"We found some unusual disturbances around your house. We had the x-ray guys over, and now we are following up on what they think might be under your house."

"Such as…"

"Bodies," Tristan reported.

"You're kidding, of course." Jennie was shaking her head. "How did you get this idea? Where is the search warrant? You can't just start digging on a property regardless of what might be there."

Trying to distract her, Tristan said, "I finally got to talk to Mark."

"He's awake and ok? What did he say? When can he leave the TC?" She was now more interested in Mark's recovery than the digging site at her house.

"Mark is still in a fog about most things but he did remember seeing an unusual disturbance beneath the window where he was found. He remembers bending down to look more closely and then, nothing else. That's why we decided to check again to see what we could find."

"If it's just one area, why are your guys everywhere making a huge mess. Is this really necessary?" Jennie was confused, curious, concerned, and annoyed. She wanted answers. She wanted them off her property! Now!

She quickly discovered Tristan was not going to be forthcoming with any information.

Mark. She returned to the TC and found him resting, so she decided to just sit down and close her eyes. She was beginning to realize how much she would miss him if he didn't recover.

Jennie awoke to the sun on her face. Mark was sitting up and grinning.

"Mornin', sunshine."

"Oh, wow. I must have been tired. How long have you been awake?" she yawned.

"Long enough to have phoned the precinct to see what was happening with the case."

That woke her up. She wanted an update.

"Something doesn't seem right about this whole thing. They said they were digging at your house. What does that mean?"

Jennie rolled her eyes and told Mark what Tristan thought he had found and then had called in 'The Cavalry' without warning, or asking her permission. She thought Tristan was moving a bit too quickly.

"There is something about this that isn't right," Mark stated. "Let's go to the Court of Records at City Hall and maybe find some answers."

"Are you nuts? You've been in this bed for several days. You said your head still throbbed. You were unconscious most of the time. We aren't going anywhere. Besides, the records were probably destroyed in a fire."

"We're going. I may have had my eyes closed, but I've had lots of time to think. Several things Tristan and Rick asked me were odd, I thought, but I figured it was the fogginess that was causing my questions. It wasn't. The more I thought about it, the answer seemed to center around former owners of your house."

Realizing that she would not win this battle, she helped him put on his shoes and jacket. They asked the nurse for a wheelchair so they could go to the atrium in the lobby for a change of scenery. She found one and they took it to the elevator and down to the lower parking level.

When they got to City Hall, Jennie signed in, entered the records area, and went to the back to let Mark inside. Mark had been on the force when the fire had occurred and remembered an obscure cellar room that had been spared. Since it was in an older part of the library, he hoped it might have some older records.

Amazingly, they finally found the deeds to Jennie's house going back over a hundred and fifty years. It was quite fascinating to read how things had transpired. More interesting was not how, but what.

They looked at each other, stunned and amazed. Without a word they made a hasty exit, but only after making a copy of the records with their phones. They would need the photos for verification. Jennie drove, and Mark called his boss after sending him the photos. The captain listened, not quite believing what he was hearing and seeing. It was enough to mobilize the SWAT and Rescue teams. They would meet down the street from Jennie's house. No one was to approach the house until everyone was in place.

When everyone had gathered, plans were clarified. Jennie then drove to her house on the guise of checking on the 'dig.' She pulled around to the back and almost before she could get out of the car, Tristan ran to meet her.

"Have you found anything of interest?"

"No, not yet, but I think we're getting close. You really don't need to be here. I'll call you if something turns up."

"That's ok. I need to pick up some things from inside since I obviously won't be staying here for the next few nights. I'll let you know when I leave."

Jennie went inside ignoring Tristan's protests. She went to the attic and signaled the assembled police.

Immediately, troops were swarming over the property. Gunfire came from the side of the house. Some of the 'diggers' had machine guns. Jennie stayed in the attic, as it seemed much safer than the main floor. After a few of the 'diggers' had been wounded, the rest retreated toward a ravine about a hundred yards from the house. A few were carrying and dragging something with them. SWAT advanced directly, while the Rescue squad circled around to inhibit their retreat.

More gunfire. More 'diggers' down. Two made it to the ravine where they threw their bounty over the edge and then proceeded to jump.

The pursuers made their way to the edge. It was not a pretty site. The ravine dropped dramatically and ended with an empty, rocky streambed.

Tristan and Rick were dead.

Jennie came down to join the others, knowing what she would find.

"Why?" the captain asked. "What's going on here?"

Mark had gotten someone to wheel him down to the scene.

"When I had begun to check the outside of Jennie's house on the night of the break-in," Mark explained, "I found places where someone had been under the house and had done some digging. I was just going to go under the house when I was hit. While I was recovering, Tristan and Rick came to ask me if I remembered anything or could identify anyone."

"They were overly curious about how much I knew about the house. They asked if Jennie knew anything about its history. I pretended to drift off, so they left. Their questions made me curious and I had lots of time to think. When Jennie came and told me what was happening, it started to make sense."

"We left the TC and found our answers at the Court of Records," Jennie continued. "Tristan and his brother Rick were descendants of a late 1800s smuggler. Since the property was situated not far from an inland coastal waterway, the smugglers landed their treasures, rum, and slaves at the site of my house. The river to the house dried up years ago."

"Tristan must have been searching for this treasure a long time. He became friendly with Jennie when he discovered she now owned the property. No one knew Rick was his brother so they could get paired as partners and have time off together to find the bounty. The intruder was trying to find a way to access a closed area under the house to make their search easier."

Mark paused and added, "Seems greed always has harsh consequences. However, when we find everything, the value should be staggering. Guess you're now a 'woman of means,'" he said as he turned to Jennie.

"Maybe I'll tear down the house and really dig up the area!"

The mood lightened and the clean-up began.

"Ever think of taking an extended vacation?" she asked Mark.

"Maybe," he grinned.

Mary Sue Tiffin

Mary Sue Lollar Tiffin is a native "Dallasite" who was first published in her high school anthology. A musician by profession, she currently plays drums for a choir and sings with a country/gospel group. Married to Doug for 38 years, they have a son and daughter (plus spouses) and four grandchildren. Mary Sue's hobbies include travel, photography, and sports. Recently retired, she plans to spend more time writing.

The Top Hat and the Feather Boa
by Catherine Tucker

"Ugh!" Christopher pulled the pillow over his head hearing his mother call his name for the third time. "I wish I were a dog," he mumbled. "Dogs are lucky. They don't have to go to school. And if I were a dog, I'd be a pit bull so I could bite Devin "the devil" Martin on his marshmallow behind."

"Joel Christopher Grant," his mother yelled from the bottom of the stairs. "If I have to call you one more time, I'm going to come up there and drag you out of that bed by your ear."

"Yes, Mother." Hoping his mom would think he'd already gotten up, Christopher used his cheeriest voice. He tossed his pillow to the side, only to see Mater's buck-toothed grin and Lightning McQueen's smiling face beaming up at him. "What are you two so happy about?" he said to the *Cars* movie characters on his pillowcase. "I'm replacing you with Spiderman on my next birthday, just watch."

"Christopher!"

"Coming, Mom." Christopher quickly slipped on his clothes, then hurried into the bathroom and washed his face and brushed his teeth. He ran a hand through his thick brown curls, then bounded down the stairs.

"Chris, you need to hurry and eat your breakfast, otherwise you're going to miss the bus," his mom said.

"That wouldn't be the worst thing in the world." He plopped into the chair in front of his breakfast.

"It would be because you'd have to stay home by yourself," his sister, Pepper, said with a smirk.

"In six more months I'll be nine, so I can take care of myself."

"Why do you hate school so much, honey?" His mom took a sip of coffee, her brows furrowed.

Christopher shrugged. "I just do. That's all."

"Tell her," Pepper whispered.

"Chris, is there something you need to tell me?"

"I'll tell you later, Mom. The bus is here."

"I love you both. Enjoy your day." Hannah kissed her kids on the forehead as they darted from the house and raced down the walkway to the bus. She worried about them being treated unfairly because of their mixed heritage.

"If you're not going to tell Mom, at least stand up for yourself."

"He's bigger than me, and he hits harder."

"If you want someone to stop picking on you, you have to act brave even when you're scared until you aren't scared anymore."

"Easy for you to say, you're not the smallest kid in your class."

"Just remember, act like you're not scared. If that doesn't work, pick up something big and clobber the jerk."

* * * * *

After school, Pepper saw a crowd begin to gather near the bus stop. As she got closer, she heard, "Fight! Fight! Fight!"

"Oh, Jeez, this can't be good!" She raced over, but the fight was over. She saw Christopher scrambling to his feet, wiping blood from his nose. Devin Martin towered over him.

Swinging Devin around, Pepper punched him hard in the chest. "Pick on someone your own size, meatball."

"Ow! You're lucky you're a girl." Picking up his books, he scrambled in the opposite direction.

"Pepper, don't tell Mom, okay?" Christopher dusted the dirt off his jeans.

"Why not?"

"If she comes up here, everyone will know I need my mom to fight for me. Bad enough my thirteen year-old sister has to. But if Mom comes, I'll be called a chicken for sure or worse— a baby."

"I'll think about it. Lucky for you I have an entire week since next week is Spring break."

* * * * *

Christopher and Pepper loved going to their dad's parents' home in North Carolina for Spring break. It wasn't as hot as Texas, and they lived in a huge house built around the turn of the century. After eating lunch and visiting with Grandma Jules and Grandpa Joe, Christopher and Pepper started looking for something fun to do.

"Let's go down to the basement," Christopher said. "We've never been down there before."

"That's because Grandma Jules said never to go down there."

"I think it'll be fun, besides, I'm bored. I've already advanced to the fourteenth level of *Mario Party Star Rush*, and I don't have any more new games. Anyhow, Grandma Jules is playing bridge with her friends, Grandpa Joe won't be back from playing golf for hours, and Mom and Dad are at the hospital visiting with Aunt Jeannine."

"Okay, let's go, but only for a few minutes. It's probably creepy down there anyways."

When they opened the door and crept downstairs to the dusty basement, the smell of cat pee and old socks made them almost turn and go back. But they became fascinated with what they saw: an old rocking chair with a one-eyed doll, a telescope, a ladder, paint supplies, and a big brown leather trunk.

"I wonder what's inside that old trunk?" Christopher said.

"I don't think we should..."

"What could it hurt?" Christopher lifted the lid.

"It's just a bunch of old clothes." Pepper held up an emerald green cocktail dress, a man's silk smoking jacket, and long white ladies gloves. "They're beautiful! You think these belong to our grandparents? Ooh-la-la, look at this beautiful red feather boa. I think I'd look gorgeous in this, like a movie star from the 1920s." Pepper tossed the boa around her neck. "Hey, did you see that?"

"See what?"

"A streak of light flashed around me when I put the boa on."

"Naw, you're imagining things." Christopher flicked lint off an old top hat he'd picked up. "I bet I'd look cool in this. Whoa! What was that?"

"What?"

"Don't tell me you didn't see those bright specks of light when I brushed the lint off this old hat."

"Now, who's imagining things?"

"I think we both are." Christopher laughed, placing the hat on his head.

Grabbing her cell phone, Pepper said, "Hey, let's take a selfie."

"Okay."

Snap. Snap. Snap. "Now a funny face." *Snap.*

When Pepper looked over at Christopher, she leapt three feet off the floor.

"Chris, you're a ...a...you're a ...dog!"

"Look who's talking." Chris cast a baleful glance at his sister. "OMG! Pepper, you're a ...cat!"

Pepper looked down at her gray paws. Her eyes became as big as saucers. Her stomach twisted into a knot. She felt something tug at her bottom that she'd never felt before. Slowly walking around in a circle to see what it was—she screamed, "I have a tail!"

"What's happened to us?" Chris asked, looking bewildered, his four legs trembling.

The Top Hat and the Feather Boa

"I...I...I don't know. But let's not freak out."

Suddenly realizing his wish had come true, Chris said, "Hey, I'm a dog! Yes!" He pumped his paw in the air. "What kind of dog am I? A boxer?"

"No." Pepper stifled a laugh.

"A Doberman?"

"Nope." She snickered.

"A pit bull?"

She shook her head. "Uh-uh."

"What kind of freakin' dog am I?"

"You're a Chihuahua," Pepper squealed, rolling on the floor, laughing and holding her stomach.

"Hmpf! You're no prize yourself.*"*

Pepper suddenly stopped laughing. Rolling over to all fours, she blinked.

"What kind of cat am I?"

"I don't know. You have a gray face and those same annoying blue eyes. Your hair is mostly white and gray."

"I'm a Siamese cat! I hate cats! Why couldn't I be a dog? Even a Chihuahua is better than being a silly cat."

Christopher and Pepper were so preoccupied with their new transformations, they didn't hear the approaching patter of white satin slippers.

"Milo, Misty, what's all the hissing and yapping about? Are you two fighting again?"

Shocked and astonished, the two stared up at the tall brunette wearing a white satin robe. Her blue eyes were dazzling.

"Silence is all I get now that you've already awakened me?" She smiled, lifting the cat from the floor. "It's okay, my sweet Misty." She scratched the cat gently behind the ears and kissed her on the head.

"What do I do?" Pepper looked down at Christopher.

"*Sh-h-h,* moron! She can hear you," he whispered. "Oops!...uh...wait...she's looking at me."

"My darling, Milo, you want some attention, too?" She placed the cat on the floor, then picked up the dog, stroking his brown fur and kissing him on the top of his head.

"Are you two going to play nicely together for mommy?" She placed the dog on the floor. "I know dogs and cats aren't supposed to get along but..." Suddenly she noticed the top hat and the feather boa on the floor and gasped, "Misty, Milo, you naughty pets! How many times have I told you not to play with our things? Nicholas will be furious if you damaged his favorite hat." Grabbing the two items, she stalked from the living room and headed up the winding staircase.

"What are we going to do now?" asked Misty. "I think we just lost our way of getting back home."

"If those things belonged to her and this Nicholas, how did they get in Grandma Jules's basement? And who are these people?"

Misty and Milo strolled from room to room. "Look at this strange furniture. There's no TV or computer," Misty said.

"What kind of refrigerator is that? Is that a stove? I'm starting to get really worried," said Milo, with his tail tucked between his legs. "Have we traveled back in time or something?"

Then they said in unison, "The newspaper!" Dashing from the kitchen back to the living room, they jumped onto the sofa to read the newspaper on the side table.

Misty slowly read the headline out loud, *"Alexander Graham Bell Makes First Telephone Call."* Her eyes became huge and glassy following the black print to the date, *"March 11, 1876."*

"What? 1876!" Milo said, his legs trembled like tiny tree branches in a blizzard.

"Misty, Milo, it's time for lunch." They heard the angelic voice call from the kitchen.

"Dog food, no way! Not this guy!" Christopher grimaced.

The Top Hat and the Feather Boa

"And I'm not eating no stinking cat food," Pepper said, her nose turned up.

"Misty, Milo, where are you?"

The two walked reluctantly into the kitchen to their respective bowls. Each took a big whiff, shook their heads, and walked away.

"Aren't we finicky today. I'll have Juanita prepare you some chicken and rice. You like that?" Milo barked and wagged his tail in agreement. Misty licked her lips in anticipation. "I've absolutely spoiled you two rotten." After Sophia instructed the maid on what to prepare, she called them to go for a walk. Milo wagged his tail excitedly with the prospect of going outside. Misty was excited, too.

"Let's get your leash on, Milo."

"Huh! A leash? Uh-uh, not me! I'm not wearing that thing." He hid behind the sofa.

"What's the matter with you today, Milo? You're behaving quite strangely. Okay, you win, but I promise if you don't stay right by my side, this won't happen again."

She opened the front door and Misty was the first to rush out into the warm overcast day. Milo followed. He trotted beside Sophia, content to be outside in the fresh clean air. But suddenly he heard a familiar sound that sent shock waves through his nervous system. Then he saw it.

A huge black boxer had broken away from its owner. It charged in their direction. Paralyzing fear froze Milo in his tracks.

"Bruno, come back!" called the owner, a short portly man wobbling after the dog.

Misty leaped in front of Milo. Her back bowed, she bared her teeth and hissed at the muscular beast. The boxer snarled, baring its razor-sharp teeth. Milo barked weakly, but when the dog growled ferociously, he whimpered and ran behind Sophia who swung her parasol repeatedly at the dog. Finally, the owner grabbed the dog by its collar.

"Bruno, no! Down, boy, down!" the owner said, pulling the snarling animal away. "Ma'am, I am so sorry. Are you hurt? Did he bite either of your pets?"

"No, I'm fine, and they're fine, too. And you're very lucky they are."

"I apologize again, ma'am. You have a nice day." He tipped his hat.

Sophia picked Milo up and stroked him. "My poor baby, you're trembling. That big ugly beast scared you so. It's okay now, Mommy's got you." Milo felt Sophia's heartbeat, and he felt loved and protected. She looked down at Misty as she lowered Milo to the ground.

"Misty," she said, picking her up and kissing her. "You were brave today. You stood up to that big bad dog. I'm so proud of you. Well, I've had enough excitement for one day. Let's go home. Your lunch should be ready."

The next evening, Sophia's husband, Nicholas, took her to the theater. Milo and Misty were excited. With Sophia and Nicholas gone, they'd surely be able to find the hat and boa.

But their excitement was short lived. When Sophia exited the bedroom, Nicholas pulled the door snugly closed behind them.

Sophia got up early the next day to walk Misty and Milo. Misty loved the warmth of the sun as it washed over her face, and she adored watching the orange sunrise break through the lavender sky. Milo enjoyed their walks, too. He loved chasing the birds and butterflies and wallowing in the soft grass. It was a great day.

Until it wasn't.

Milo smelled the sweat of another dog. The portly man and his boxer were coming toward them. Panic started to grip him. His first instinct was to run. But in that moment, Milo made a decision. He would stand his ground. He might die, but he wouldn't die a coward.

The boxer barked and growled. The man pulled at his leash. The leash snapped. The dog charged straight at Milo, Misty, and Sophia.

Milo snarled. He growled. He bared his razor sharp incisors.

The boxer growled viciously. But as Milo advanced toward him, the boxer began scooting backward. Eventually, it turned and ran back to its owner who was running toward him.

"Ma'am," he said, gasping for air as he grabbed the dog by the collar. "I'm so..."

"Save it, buster! You need to get a better leash for that animal of yours before someone gets hurt." Sophia waltzed past the porker of a man.

"My hero," Sophia said, beaming at Milo. "You were so brave today! I'll have Juanita whip up a special treat for you again."

Milo trotted to the house with his tail wagging high. He was a small dog but that day he felt ten feet tall.

* * * * *

"Chris, Chris, wake up!"

"What? What's wrong?"

"Nothing's wrong. We've finally got a chance to get the hat and the boa and go back home."

"Really?"

"Yes, the door is open to Sophia and Nicholas's bedroom, and they're both asleep. Come on."

Milo followed Misty as she tiptoed from the living room and up the stairs to the master bedroom. She eased the door forward. It squeaked. Nicholas grunted, rolled over, then continued snoring.

The two crept into the room. With the moonlight beaming though the window like a silver ribbon, Misty spotted a wardrobe and knew the hat and boa had to be inside. But the doors were closed and the knob was at least three feet from the floor. Instinctively they knew what to do. Misty bowed low and Milo climbed on her shoulders. She stood up on her hind legs, lifting him up. When he eased the door open, his heart jumped for joy. He grabbed the boa and handed it to Misty, then took the top hat from the shelf.

"Let me down," he whispered. "On the count of three, put on the boa. One, two, three..."

* * * * *

"Christopher, Pepper, we've been searching for you for hours!" A look of concern creased Grandma Jules's face. "Your parents are worried sick. Have you been in this basement all this time?"

"Yes, Grandma Jules. We must have fallen asleep," Christopher said sheepishly.

"Well, let's get you something to eat. You two must be starving. Your Grandpa Joe grilled hamburgers, and I cooked those crinkly fries you love."

"Hamburgers, oh, boy!" Christopher said, leaping to his feet.

"French fries! Yummy!" Pepper said.

"You kids must be hungrier than I thought." Grandma Jules laughed, leading the way up the stairs. "Take off those old clothes and leave them in that trunk."

"Grandma Jules," said Pepper, "Who did these things belong to?"

She chuckled. "That top hat belonged to your great, great, great, great grandfather Nicholas Grant, and the feather boa belonged to his wife, your great, great, great, great grandmother Sophia Grant. I'll tell you all about them later. They were the toast of Raleigh-Durham high society. This house actually belonged to them."

The Top Hat and the Feather Boa

On the ride home, their parents gave them a stern talk about sneaking off without letting any of the grownups know where they were. Christopher and Pepper hardly heard any of it, knowing that something magical had taken place that weekend at their grandparents' house.

For Christopher, Monday morning meant returning to school and falling back into the routine that he'd left behind before Spring break. And it didn't take very long before that routine meant having to face Devin Martin after school. Pepper watched a short distance away.

The usual crowd gathered as Devin stepped into his path. "Fight! Fight! Fight!"

"Going somewhere, weasel head?" Devin's two smaller companions burst into laughter.

"Yeah, I'm going to my bus if you'd get your wide load out of my way," Christopher said.

The laughter stopped. Devin's cheeks turned beet red. "What did you just say to me?"

"You heard me, blubber butt. Get out of my way!"

Devin pushed Christopher. He stumbled back, but he didn't fall. When Devin charged at him, Christopher kicked him hard in the abdomen. Grabbing his stomach, Devin dropped to his knees, coughing and wheezing. His friends walked away, shaking their heads.

The crowd started chanting, "Chris! Chris! Chris!"

From that day forward, Christopher remembered the lesson he'd learned during Spring break. He loved school, and he was never bullied again.

Catherine Tucker

Catherine Tucker grew up in the Mississippi Delta surrounded by rows of cotton fields. For amusement, she read the dictionary from cover-to-cover. She later discovered a better escape—reading books. After earning a B.A. Degree in English, Catherine enjoyed a successful career with the federal government, retiring in 2015. As a full-time writer, Catherine has penned two novels, and the short story "The Top Hat and the Feather Boa." You can find her writer's blog at catherinetuckerwriter.com.

Amy Calling
by Judith K. Werner

Amy hadn't really wanted to come home for Christmas. Too much hugging and crowding her personal space, overheated rooms, forced smiles...all that. She'd been gone for two years now. Gosh, was it really that long?

Two years to lick her wounds from her failed marriage with Kevin. She'd thought, at the time, that it would have been better if he had died—instead of running off with a woman in his tennis class. With a death, it's flowers and kind words. With a divorce, it's becoming a third wheel in a society of couples.

She'd moved away, found a new job, made a new life. Doing pretty well, actually. Oh, she'd emailed friends and family once in a while. Phoned her mom dutifully. That kept everyone at arm's length, just like she liked it.

But now, with her mom's just getting over a bout of pneumonia, she felt she had to go home for the holidays. She'd made the flight reservation, then bought gift cards for those who'd be there, clamoring for her attention. Mom had said not to get her any presents—just be present. She could do that. Just add in a bigger sum for Mom's generic gift card. And please stay with me at the house, Mom had said. Hmm. That was a bit harder, so Amy had come armed with a plan. She had reserved a room at a local motel she'd recalled from childhood. She'd never needed to stay there before, but it would at least be familiar and close. Amy figured Christmas season at a motel would be noisy and hectic. She could stay in her room and order in. She could always cancel if things weren't all that awful, and if she decided to stay at Mom's after all. Not likely, though.

Now it was Christmas Eve. She arrived late enough that it was already dark when she stopped the rental car in front of her childhood home. Stepping cautiously up the cleared front walk, Amy figured Uncle Mike had shoveled it, just like always after Dad had died. She could see traditional Christmas tree lights through the window and a wreath on the door.

Should she ring the bell? After all, she hadn't lived there for years. Before she could decide, Mom threw open the door so wide that the wreath bobbled around.

Boy, Mom was a bit thin and pale. But her embrace was still the familiar Mama Bear hug.

"Let me look at you!"

"Hey, Mom. How are you?"

"Oh, I'm just fine now. Totally on the mend. It's so good to have you back home. Come in! Come in! Everyone can't wait to see you. How was your flight? Are you hungry? We have tons of food and lots to drink. Here, give me your coat." Mom's chatter hadn't changed, either.

On cue, Amy shed her coat and purse, gave her a kiss on the cheek, and murmured,

"I've missed you, too, Mom." She inhaled the bouquet of roasting turkey, freshly-cut fir tree, and candles, a smile forming despite her hesitation.

But then the torrent began—aunts, uncles, and cousins huddled around Amy, each trying to talk at once.

"It's so good to see you." Thanks for not saying finally.

"How do you like your new, uh, life?" How do you answer that?

"Are you seeing anyone?" Sheese, let's not go there.

"How have you been?"

"Fine, and you?" Anything to deflect the attention from her. She was beginning to feel a bit cornered, as they swarmed in and around her.

Mom saved her by calling everyone into the dining room. Places were taken, grace was said, food was passed. After a few seconds of silence, Amy smiled weakly and said with less gusto than she felt, "It really is nice to come back during the holidays. Thanks for waiting for me. You all look great. The house looks great…let's eat!"

As the meal continued, Amy was grateful that with her mouth full, she'd not have to field the usual barrage of nosy questions. Then her tween cousin Jenny asked, as Amy knew she would, "Have you seen Uncle Kevin lately?"

"No, he lives in Cleveland now. But tell me more about you. What are you studying in school these days?"

"Just boring stuff, as usual. That's what I like most about Christmas—no school. The thing I like least, though, is trying to stay awake at Midnight Mass."

Amy laughed, thinking how she had felt the same way at age twelve. Then her mother asked, her brow furrowing, "You'll be going with us to Mass tonight won't you, Amy?"

Amy had prepared for this. "Well, by that time I'll be pretty beat. I've got some computer stuff I should do, and I've got a room booked here in town. I can rest and see how I feel later." She sipped some water, comfortable that all she had to do was get through the meal, then bow out gracefully. She would excuse herself to the bathroom, get the gift cards from her purse, distribute them, and scoot out the door chanting, "Merry Christmas." She excused herself to do just that.

But Mom, at least, deserved an explanation, and Amy found her in the kitchen. She explained she just felt claustrophobic here. Everyone meant well, but she felt like she was getting the third degree. All she wanted was some solitude to relax and catch her breath. She'd come back and stay with Mom early tomorrow when it would be just the two of them.

Mom sadly shook her head, but agreed not to stand in her way. Amy kissed her mom on the cheek, then allowed herself to be shooed back into the dining room, where all eyes fixed on her as she entered.

"I'm really wiped out with the travelling, and now with a full stomach. I'm going to stay at the old motel, rest, get some work done, and maybe come back for Midnight Mass, if I possibly can."

"But they're working on that old building, I think. Are you sure it's open?" Uncle Mike protested.

"I have a reservation. I'd like to give out my gifts right now. I admit they're boring gift cards, but I was in a hurry...I love getting to see you all, and, well, Merry Christmas..."

"What about your presents?" Jenny wailed when Amy handed her the envelope with her name on it. "I wanted to watch you open yours. I got you something really special." She looked almost tearful.

"I'm really sorry. It's okay to leave them under the tree. If I can, I'll be back for Midnight Mass. But if I don't make it, I'll pick them up tomorrow when I say goodbye to Mom. It's just been a rough week, the trip was long, and I'm really tired."

Silence. Uncle Mike picked up his envelope, then put it down again. Jenny fiddled with the seal on hers, then laid it down and stared at her plate.

"Hey! It's okay, everyone," Mom trilled with false cheer, bursting into the room from the kitchen. "Amy, we're just so happy you could make it at all. If we're lucky, and you can get back here in a few hours, that'll be great."

More silence. Amy put on her coat, grabbed her purse, and was gone.

As the car warmed, she felt a jab of guilt, but shoved it away as she felt herself relax. Ah, solitude, and no more Twenty Questions.

Driving to the motel, she noted how little her old neighborhood had changed. But, as she neared the small business district, she saw that familiar clothing and book shops had been replaced with neon-lit nail spas and pizza joints. She had to look twice to be sure she was where she remembered the motel parking lot to be.

Wait, several more buildings should be beside the motel, as she recalled. Instead, now there were only dingy snow-covered vacant lots, each enclosed by saggy chain link fences. Yes, she was in the right place, and with the next-door buildings gone, she realized how close to the freeway the motel was. Few cars were parked in the motel lot. Maybe there was a parking garage out back.

Once in the foyer, she noted the decorated plastic tree and a lone woman behind the desk. The nearby bar was open with a man slouched on a tall stool, staring toward a muted TV overhead, while the bartender dried glasses. Gas logs burned in a small fireplace in the lounge, but nobody was soaking up the ambience. She wondered, If there's nobody to soak up ambience, is there ambience to begin with?

"Where is everyone?" Amy asked the attendant. "I assumed business would be booming this time of year."

"No, this is actually our slowest time of year. Most folks seem to prefer staying with family for the holidays. In fact, I can offer you an upgrade free of charge tonight."

"I'd never pass that up!"

The attendant apologized for having only first-floor vacancies. They were remodeling and Amy was forced to return outdoors to find her room. She passed an empty concrete outdoor pool standing cold and forlorn. Within just ten feet of her door, the rusted fence sulked, and the noisy freeway overpass loomed overhead. She shivered a bit and hurried to get the door unlocked.

Inside at last, Amy turned on the lights. Hmmm, vanilla pudding décor. Good, a desk and office-type chair. White sheets—she undid the corners of the bedding—good, no bedbugs. The bathroom had generic white towels, plastic glasses and bar soap. She hated bar soap. This is an upgrade? Not exactly paradise, but big on solitude. Just what she needed.

Traffic noise seemed magnified. Maybe she could tune it out or put in her earbuds. She peeked through the drawn curtains. Her view of the prison-like fence and empty pool was less than comforting though, and being that close to a large traffic artery made her feel vulnerable.

Feeling uneasy, she called the front desk to ask for a room change, maybe on the other side of the building. Amy recognized the voice of the attendant, who apologized again for the remodeling. No other rooms were available. She wondered, How could that be? I'm practically the only one here.

Miffed and still ill-at-ease, Amy decided a shower would help her mood, despite the bar soap. Snuggling in her jammies afterward, she set up her computer, hands poised over the keyboard, ready to work.

But the hurt in Jenny's eyes interrupted, refusing to go away. As she scrolled through office emails, her hands slowed on the keys. The frown on her mom's forehead and resignation in her voice chastised her, disrupting her ability to work.

Try as hard as she might, she could not squelch the internal monologue: I'm tired. I have a right to be here. I don't want to be there and have more questions about dear Kevin who dumped me. I don't want to stay there and be forced to ooh and aah as everyone opens inane gifts that are merely fodder for garage sales. And Midnight Mass! Good grief, Jenny wasn't the only one who would be yawning in ten minutes flat. C'mon brain! C'mon fingers! I've got work to do.

She typed some more, trying to find her work groove. But it kept fading as she recalled the lights at home, the mingling of voices, the tantalizing aromas—how unlike the empty and silent bar and sterile lounge downstairs. Oh, yeah, and what had the attendant said? "Most folks seem to prefer to stay with family for the holidays." She gave up, deciding to take a well-deserved nap.

Amy pulled back the covers, reassuring herself that at least this place was clean, comfortable, and so much better than having to participate in the ritualistic nonsense going on at home. She closed her eyes and relaxed, trying to ignore traffic noises. But after many long minutes, sleep continued to evade her. She got up, looked out the window. No change: emptiness and desolation. She turned on the TV. Every station played holiday music or was loaded with sappy Christmas scenes. With a heavy sigh, she flipped it off.

What a lousy idea this was. She sagged onto the bed, admitting at last—I'm not happy here; in fact, I'm miserable.

"Most folks seem to prefer to stay with family for the holidays." Well, she thought, I'm not most folks...or am I?

There was just no escaping that internal monologue. Why had she agreed to this visit in the first place? Certainly not to stay in this place. The image of an empty pool, empty lots, an empty lounge, an almost-empty motel. Tis the season to be jolly—here? Not.

Amy got up, pacing, her mind refusing to be still. She looked at the clock...10:30 pm. In less than an hour, her family would be going to Midnight Mass. Without her. Is that what she wanted?

Yes...or well, maybe. She couldn't sleep and couldn't work here, so why stay? It might not really be that awful to spend an hour or so in church with her family. In fact, they couldn't talk and gawk at her while they sat in the pews. And since she was in a church, she might even have a chance to pray, if she hadn't forgotten how. What a concept!

What to do? What to do? Still pacing, Amy chewed on her pinky fingernail, thoughts swirling. Finally, she threw up her hands, sighed deeply, and picked up her cell phone. She dialed the familiar number.

"Mom, if I'm still invited, I think I'd like to join you for Midnight Mass."

Judith K. Werner

Dr. Judith Werner taught English for a decade before becoming a board-certified family physician. After 8 years of medical training, Dr. Werner practiced for 24 years in the Metroplex. She was elected the first female medical staff president at Methodist Hospital System in 2000. In 2017, she published her first book, *ReMarkable: The Grit and Grace of Mark Clifton,* and is currently writing a second. A Cedar Hill resident, she and her dog Teddy are a therapy team.

Vanilla Mama
By Catie Riley Wright

"We'll be all right, Kit. Some way, somehow, we'll figure it out." Those were Daddy's words after Mama had passed.

Mama always said I had a knack for sniffing people out. She said I could look into their eyes and interpret their soul's whispers. Daddy's soul's whispers didn't match up very well with these words that slipped out of his mouth.

"What do you think it means to *die*, Daddy?"

"Well, I suppose it's when somebody's gone and ain't never coming back."

"Well, then Mama didn't *die,* Daddy."

I could tell he didn't like those words. I could tell by the way that one vein that runs across his forehead got a little bigger. I figured I should probably keep quiet for the time being.

* * * * *

Pickles is my best friend. She used to be called "Freckles," but some kids at school misunderstood and thought it was "Pickles" and the name just kind of stuck. Funny thing is, she hates pickles. Then again, she hates her freckles, too.

One day, I was over at Pickles' house. I had just told her about my "gift," I guess you could call it. I told her how, when I touch things that belong to other people, I just somehow know their story.

I looked it up, once. *Psychometry* is the important name for it. If I could choose a different "gift," then I probably would. But I guess I'm stuck with this one.

Pickles stuffed a necktie into my hand and told me to prove it. So, I started telling her about the man who showed up when I was holding it. She couldn't see him. I guess you could say the people and their stories show up in my imagination. Sometimes it feels like I'm just making stuff up.

Pickles' grandma came barging in. I guess she heard me telling Pickles stuff she didn't want me saying.

"Where'd you git that, child? And who told you that?" She snatched that necktie right out of my hand. The man disappeared. My tongue was real fat inside my mouth. I couldn't move it in the right way to explain.

Pickles answered for me. "Grandma, you gave me that necktie of Grandpa's after he died, remember? She wasn't doing nothing wrong, Grandma. Please don't be mad."

Before Pickles got that last part out, her grandma had already bust back out the door.

Pickles whispered to me, "How'd you know all that about my grandpa? Did somebody tell you all that?"

"Naw, Pickles. I'm telling you, sometimes when I hold stuff, I just *know* about the person who owned it."

"I believe you," she finally said.

* * * * *

At school one day that following week, Pickles whispered to me, "You can thank me later. Just do your thing."

"My thing?" I whispered back.

"Yeah. You know. Your psychotic thing. That thing you did with Grandpa's tie."

"Dang, Pickles, what did you get me into? I don't like surprises. And it's *psychometry*."

"Yeah, that."

By the time we got outside for recess, there was a line of kids holding things in their hands.

First up was Bobbie Rae. Pickles held her hand out and Bobbie Rae gave her a dollar.

"You're *charging* people?"

She winked.

I took the necklace from Bobbie Rae. When I told her that her aunt was glad that Bobbie Rae won the fight over the necklace, she snatched it back and ran off, bawling. I don't especially like being the reason for people being upset. I looked at Pickles, but she wouldn't meet my eyes.

Next in line was a kid named Charley. He gave Pickles a dollar and gave me a key. He bounced back and forth from one foot to the other as he told me how he found the key in his great-grandfather's house but didn't know what it went to. I could see in plain sight his great-grandfather using that key to open a safe that was tucked away behind some farm equipment in a barn. I told him what I thought it was to, handed the key back to him, and you'd have thought I handed him a coupon for a lifetime supply worth of candy or somethin'. I thought maybe Pickles' idea wasn't so bad, after all. If I can make people happy with my "gift," then why not?

Next up was Billy Gene Simmons. He should've been named Bully Gene instead of Billy Gene, if you ask me. One time, he took my ruler without me knowing it and wrote a bunch of our spelling words on it, then stuck it back inside my desk. He told the teacher I was using it to cheat on the test, and I lost recess that day *and* got a zero on the test. He was always doing mean stuff.

Bully Gene handed me a pair of gloves but refused to give Pickles a dollar.

"Let's see what she can do, and then we'll see about that dollar."

Pickles started to put him in his place, but I told her it was all right. If there's something to be told, it should be told, even if the person is a mean jerk-face.

I held the gloves, but nobody showed up. I took a deep breath and concentrated real hard. Nothing. I turned them over a couple times. I even put them on. Still, nothing.

"What's the matter, Kit? Can't find a fib fast enough?"

I'd had enough of Bully Gene. I stepped up to him and got in his face. My nose smashed against his. Pickles pulled me back and another kid stepped between us, and it's a right good thing, 'cause I could feel my fingernails digging into the palm of my hand, and I wasn't exactly sure what my fist had in mind.

"Come on, Kit, let's go. That was a dumb idea I had." She turned to the group of kids waiting in line. "Move along! Show's over."

Once they cleared, I said, "Ya gotta check with me before you do stuff like that, Pickles!"

"I'm sorry, Kit. I really am."

I didn't tell her at the time, but I did accept her apology.

And I didn't regret forgiving her, even when some other kids at school called me a liar and a phony.

I'll tell you what. I ain't no liar, and I ain't no phony.

* * * * *

Even after a month of Mama being gone, Daddy still hadn't said a word about her. He hadn't even moved any of her stuff. It was all just like she'd left it. Except it was dusty. Mama wouldn't like that.

"Daddy, what are we gonna do with Mama's stuff?"

"What do you mean what're we gonna do with it?"

"Well, I mean, ain't nobody using it. Maybe we could find somebody who could."

"Who could what?"

"Use it."

I saw that forehead vein get big and I saw him swipe his cheek, but he turned so quick, I wasn't sure if he was wiping off a tear or what. He walked out. I sat down in Mama's chair and picked up the book she had left on the end table. I kinda felt bad for her that that was the last book she'd chosen to read. She couldn't find nothin' better? I fell asleep in her chair, and

Vanilla Mama

when I woke up the next morning, I was in pretty much the same position.

"I'll be back later." Daddy's voice startled me.

"Where're you goin', Daddy?"

"I said, I'll be back later."

I heard his truck engine rumble and the tires slowly crunch the gravel as he pulled away. Usually he would ask if I wanna come along. This time, not only did he not invite me, but he was keeping it secret where he was going. *Since when does he keep secrets? Mama never kept secrets.*

I decided to follow him. I jumped on my bike and pedaled as fast as I could to keep him in sight. When I saw him park in front of the florist, I could hardly believe it. *Flowers! Mama ain't been gone six weeks and he's out buying flowers for some broad? Just wait until I find out who it is. No wonder he never talks about Mama! He's already off foolin' around with somebody else!*

To say I was angry would have been an understatement.

I hid around the corner and waited for him to come out, and when I heard him rev up his engine, I hopped back on my bike.

I followed him through town. By the time he came to a stop, my face felt chapped from the wind slapping my wet cheeks. I used the bottom of my shirt to blow my nose. I dropped my bike right there on the side of the road, and I was ready to tell him exactly what I thought of this sneaking-around business.

He rounded the corner and I ran to catch up, but just as I made the turn, I realized we were at the cemetery where they buried Mama. I saw him walking down a hill, toward her gravesite.

To say I felt guilty for thinking all those bad things about my daddy would have been an understatement.

What I didn't feel guilty about was hiding behind a bush and watching him. I guess he wasn't there just too long, but it seemed like he went through a lot of emotions in that short amount of time. I saw him smile. I saw him cry. I even heard him laugh. I wished I could hear what he was saying to her.

He dusted off her headstone and put the flowers in the vase, and once, he turned to look back. I stayed behind the bush as he passed. I waited until he turned the corner before I got up and dusted myself off.

I figured I might as well go say hello to Mama, too. I didn't have anything to bring except myself. Mama would be okay with that.

Once I reached her grave, I understood all those emotions that must have been going through Daddy, because the same thing happened to me. I smiled. I cried. And I even laughed. Something about being there brought the funniest memories of Mama to mind.

Before I got up to head back home, the neatest thing happened. A hummingbird flitted down to me and hovered right in front of my face, inches away. I could feel a soft breeze and there was a hum coming from its wings, and it just looked me in the eye for at least a full minute. Everything got real quiet. There was something magical about the way it looked at me. I felt like I knew what it was thinking: *Just be happy.*

Funny thing is, that's what my mama always used to say. She always said that the worst thing people can do is to take life too seriously. "Just be happy," she'd say.

I wondered if the hummingbird was passing on a message from Mama. I mean, why not? If I can read into people's stories by holding their stuff, then why couldn't an animal, like a hummingbird, serve as messenger?

The hummingbird swooped off, but the magical feeling remained.

I kissed my palm then rested it on top of Mama's headstone, then got up to leave, when somebody caught my eye. It was Bully Gene Simmons. I wasn't sure what to do, so I watched him from across the way. I looked around but didn't see anyone else in the cemetery. It was just us.

It seemed like ole Bully Gene experienced what Daddy and I both had experienced. But he was at someone else's gravesite. I wondered whose it was. And what was he was saying?

I saw him set something on top of the headstone. I couldn't tell what it was, so when he walked off, I went to investigate.

A dog collar? Who leaves a dog collar on top of someone's headstone?

I picked it up and the story flooded me. I saw Billy's dad, and I saw their dog. I could tell that they died on the same day. The dog was drowning, and his daddy went to save him, but the collar slipped, and he pulled that collar right off, and then both of them went under. That's when I saw my own daddy. He pulled their bodies out of the water. He pushed down real hard and fast onto Billy's daddy's chest. Daddy's eyes looked wild. He was scared.

Then I felt something shove me so hard I lost my footing and hit the ground. It was Billy. Before I knew it, he was calling me a grave robber, and we were tumbling around on the ground. We both got a couple good punches in before we were just plumb tuckered out. He had some blood on his lips and his arm was pretty scraped up. I wondered if I looked as messed-up as he did.

He hollered, "Why're you following me?" There he went, accusing me of stuff that ain't true, again.

"You think I don't have better things to do than follow you around? Get over yourself, Bully Gene!"

"Then why're you here?" He was still sucking wind. So was I.

I wasn't going to say anything, but since I finally knew his story, I couldn't really blame him for being so mean to everybody all the time. Mama once told me, "Hurt people hurt people." I guess that's pretty dead-on.

"I'm sorry about your daddy. And your dog."

He wouldn't look at me.

"I saw it, Billy. I saw it all. That collar you left behind said it all."

Billy scowled, then his face eased up a bit.

"It wasn't your fault," I told him.

His face started to scrunch up again.

"Billy. Listen."

He glared at me for a good, long while, without blinking.

"There wasn't nothin' you coulda done. There wasn't nothin' *anybody* coulda done. Not even my daddy."

His eyes met the ground. He put the back of his hand to his mouth then pulled it away and looked at the blood smear. Then he looked back at me.

Finally, he spoke. "I know your daddy tried to save 'em. I can't help being mad that you still got your daddy but I ain't got mine."

It was quiet a minute before he spoke again.

"I'm sorry I treated you the way I did. Those gloves...they've just been sitting in the garage, collecting dust. Nobody ever even used 'em. It made sense that you couldn't pull a story out of 'em 'cause they don't have a story to tell."

I shook my head and stood up. I think he knew what I meant: None of that mattered. I held out my hand to help him up. I was a little surprised he took it.

* * * * *

Christmas used to be my favorite holiday, but I think that was all because of Mama. Now, it was hard to see much of a reason to celebrate. I was surprised when I got home to see that Daddy had taken the tree and boxes of decorations down from the attic.

Vanilla Mama

I sat down, waiting for him to ask me where my cuts came from. We both sat there and just looked around at the boxes with Mama's handwriting on them: *Christmas wreaths. Christmas stockings and decor. Kitchen – Christmas.*

I peeled open one of the boxes, and the scent of vanilla came wafting out of it.

"I'll be right back," I said to him.

"Where're you goin'?"

"I said, I'll be right back."

I went to the kitchen, opened a cabinet, and got the vanilla extract.

Money was always a little tight at our house, so splurging on things like perfume was usually out of the question. So, Mama would dab a little vanilla behind her ears. Sometimes, she'd even dab some behind mine. We'd smell like cookies.

I dabbed some on my wrist and stood there for a bit, sniffing it in.

I went to Mama's closet and ran my hand across the garments until one thing in particular stood out to me. It was Mama's favorite scarf. There was a lot of love and happiness in that scarf. I put a little vanilla on it. And then I dribbled on a little more, "for good measure," as Mama would say.

I went back into the living room where Daddy was, and I wrapped the scarf around his neck. I half-expected that vein to pop out. But it didn't.

"I saw you at the cemetery today," I confessed.

"I saw you, too," he replied. "I thought I was going to have to step in, but you can hold your own, can't you?"

"Wait. What? You saw... Huh?"

"Feisty like your mama." He grinned.

And then, we laughed.

Big laughs. Like the kind of laughs where you struggle to get your breath back kind of laughs.

When we could finally catch our breath again, Daddy held the scarf to his face. "I was wondering what to keep and what to give away. I think this is the perfect thing to keep. It was her favorite. And it smells just like her."

I said, "No more secrets, ok, Daddy?"

"No more secrets. We'll figure all this out, Kit. We're gonna be all right."

Daddy's soul whispers seemed to match up pretty well with the words that slipped out of his mouth.

Catie Riley Wright

Catie is a writer and yoga and meditation teacher, Vice-President of DAWG, member of SCBWI and DFWWW, and partakes in a local critique group: KidLitTexas. Seeds of love for writing were planted, took root, and have been blooming since childhood. Catie voyages along the path of lifelong learning, frolicking in the foliage, delighting in the journey.

Made in the USA
Lexington, KY
21 December 2018